Thugs Cry 3
Respect My Gangsta

Ca$h

Lock Down Publications &
Ca$h Presents
Thugs Cry 3

.

Ca$h

Lock Down Publications
P.O. Box 1482
Pine Lake, Ga 30072-1482

Visit our website at **www.lockdownpublications.com**

Copyright 2017 Thugs Cry 3

First Edition June 2017
Printed in the United States of America
This is a work of fiction. Names, characters, places, and incidents either are products of the author's imagination or are used fictitiously. Any similarity to actual events or locales or persons, living or dead, is entirely coincidental.

Cover design and layout by: Dynasty's Cover Me
Book interior design by: Shawn Walker
Edited by: Shawn Walker

Stay Connected with Us!

Text **LOCKDOWN** to 22828 to stay up-to-date with new releases, sneak peaks, contests and more…

Thank you!

Submission Guideline.

Submit the first three chapters of your completed manuscript to ldpsubmissions@gmail.com, subject line: Your book's title. The manuscript must be in a .doc file and sent as an attachment. Document should be in Times New Roman, double spaced and in size 12 font. Also, provide your synopsis and full contact information. If sending multiple submissions, they must each be in a separate email.

Have a story but no way to send it electronically? You can still submit to LDP/Ca$h Presents. Send in the first three chapters, written or typed, of your completed manuscript to:

LDP: Submissions Dept
Po Box 1482
Pine Lake, Ga 30072

DO NOT send original manuscript. Must be a duplicate.

Provide your synopsis and a cover letter containing your full contact information.

Thanks for considering LDP and Ca$h Presents.

Dedications

This book is dedicated to LDP's COO, and my personal editor, **Shawn Walker**.

Queen, despite the personal issues you faced as we worked on this long-awaited project, your unmatched dedication to LDP and to myself supplied you with the energy and motivation to make sure we delivered this book to our readers, finally.

Thank you for everything.

I also dedicate this book to my son, **Cortez.**

Man, when they convicted you and gave you life, it broke my heart. And it underscored the title of this book, THUGS CRY.

I did just that! But I'll fight until there's not a drop of blood left in my body, and not a single coin left in my bank accounts, in an effort to bring you home one day. I love you, man. Stay strong. Your pops got you.

Ca$h

CHAPTER
1

"**I**'m here! Where you at, pussy boy?" CJ's voice echoed loudly and carried with it a tone of deadly drama.

His eyes bounced off of the many shades of discolored bricks around the infamous government housing projects known as Little Bricks. The boarded-up windows and condemned units, which once housed life, was now a portal for death. Today would give the city a chilling blast from the past, when gunplay and murder was an everyday occurrence.

There was no sight of his nemesis, Nard, but CJ could feel that bitch nigga'z presence in the air as surely as he felt death lurking around every corner.

This is what it had come down to. Under any other circumstances, CJ would have made them niggas come to him and then served them ice cold revenge. But Nard had forged the upper hand by snatching up CJ's brother from another, Raheem, and holding him captive.

CJ was desperate to reverse that shit.

Hot surges passed rapidly through his body as he thought of how somewhere, bound and gagged, Raheem was hostage to those grimy ass niggas and he knew they would surely kill him if he hadn't shown up.

It's do or die, CJ mumbled through clenched teeth. He took one last glance up toward Heaven where his girl, Tamika, rested in paradise, offering a few words. *See you in a minute, shorty.*

He lowered his gaze and then looked deep into the crevices of the buildings. "Where ya punk ass at? Show yo face, coward muhfucka," he called out again.

"I'm right here, bitch nigga. Look around, I'm not hard to find!" Nard stepped out of the apartment that he'd been hiding in.

He had Raheem in front of him like a human shield. One hand held Raheem by the back of the collar, while the other held a Glock Nine to the back of his head, locked and loaded. If CJ flinched, he was gonna put his man's noodles on the pavement.

CJ knew how Nard got down. His trigger finger itched to put something hot in his chest but there was no way to wet Nard without bodying Raheem, too. That was a risk he was unwilling to take because if it hadn't been for his mistakes, his man wouldn't be in that position.

Fuck! CJ snorted under his breath. He couldn't believe he had let a little young nigga, like Nard, gain the ups on him. Not after all the muhfuckaz he'd gone to war with and prevailed over on the road to riches and hood fame.

There has to be a way to flip the script and regain the upper hand, CJ thought.

Sensing that CJ was contemplating letting his gun roar, Nard tightened his grip on Raheem's collar and ducked further down behind him. A quick shift of his eyes confirmed his shooters were in place, and on point. He spotted them, clad in black, lined up in several doorways. If CJ tried anything, they were going to Swiss cheese his ass.

CJ had already surveyed the area. He saw gunners posted up in breezeways, behind partially cracked doors and on the rooftop of the building Nard had exited. None of that worried him, though. His only concern was Raheem.

He cursed himself for allowing his fam to get involved in the beef between him and Nard, as he faced what could be his final moments.

Raheem sat at the bar inside of CJ's crib out in New Haven, Connecticut. His elbows rested on the counter top with his hands steepled under his chin. Despite grieving the suicide of Sparkle, his only true love, Raheem was concerned about what CJ was going through.

Nard had murdered CJ's girl, Tamika, her mom and her cousin. He could see the pain in CJ's face, and he knew retaliation was a must. The way CJ was built there was no way he wouldn't avenge that shit.

And there was no way Raheem would let his mans go to war without him at his side.

"Just give me the game plan, my brotha. You know I'm gonna ride," he said.

"Nah, fam, I'ma handle it myself. The streets ain't your life anymore." Raheem was one of the few that had made it out of The Bricks and had done something legitimate with his life. "I'm not lettin' you return to the very shit you moved away to escape from," stated CJ, adamantly.

But Raheem was too loyal to be dissuaded. He looked his best friend in the eyes and replied, "CJ, this ain't about the game. This ain't about The Bricks either. You're my brotha from a different mother, and what hurts you, hurts me. When you bleed, I bleed."

"Fam, I can't let you do it." CJ stood firm.

"And you can't stop me either," he said with conviction that was unwavering.

In the end, CJ had relented and his dawg had rode shotgun, never voicing a regret. Not even when CJ's ego caused him to make a crucial mistake.

CJ replayed it all in his mind, in a nano-second, as he looked at Raheem with regret. Their bond was from the cradle to the grave, but Rah's life deserved a much better ending.

Over Raheem's shoulder, Nard flashed a gloating smile. CJ sneered at him and spat on the ground. Even from the distance of about twenty feet that separated them, CJ could see that his mans had been severely beaten. One of his eyes was swollen completely shut, blood covered his face and his body seemed limp.

An intense pang shot through CJ's heart and the blood in his veins boiled hotter than lava. "Let him go," he belted.

Surrounded by a small army, Nard felt invincible. "Let him go?" He laughed smugly. "Nah, it ain't gonna be that easy, blood. I'ma find out how low your nuts hang." He slid a gun from his waist and held it down at his side.

"They hang to the muhfuckin' ground, nigga! You see I'm here. I ain't scared to die," spat CJ.

"We'll see," said Nard.

"You'll see? Nigga, you can see right now." CJ ripped his shirt off and pounded his chest with a fist. "I'm the muhfuckin' best that ever did it!" he proclaimed with the defiant arrogance that had propelled him to the top of the drug game.

But Nard was just as egotistical. And fueled by a deep hatred of CJ, that had escalated the night CJ made Tamika clown him in front of a club full of people, he was determined to make CJ bow down. "You can't be the best when there's only one of me," he slung back.

"Young boy, you're a *Cam'ron* wannabe. Fuck you saying? How are you the best hiding behind the next nigga? Let him go and let's play with these tools," CJ challenged. "Just you and me. Show me how low your little ass nuts hang."

"This how low they hang, fuck nigga!" Nard barked. He placed the gun against Raheem's leg.

Boom!

***

Inside of a gutted-out unit, that had been 26-year old Shabazz' home for the past two weeks, he had heard the loud gunshot. He hopped up off of the floor and quickly stepped into his rundown Timbs. He walked past a milk crate, that served as his dining table, and hurried to the window to see what the fuck was going on.

His first thought was that those punk ass Newark cops were chasing squatters and dope fiends away, who took refuge inside of the dilapidated apartments to get away from the cold temperatures that had dropped into the low 40's as of last night.

But why would five-oh be busting shots at homeless people? he wondered.

As Shabazz made his way to the front window, he heard the unmistakable bark of street niggaz embroiled in a heated exchange, that increased by the second. He moved to the side to gain a better look through a space between the boards, that covered most of the window. From his shaded view, he scanned the area in an attempt to ID one of them.

"Fuck!" Shabazz said as he strained to get a better look.

He glanced over to his far right to see a sleek, black sports car parked haphazardly in the middle of the street, with the driver's door swung wide open.

Shabazz didn't have to guess who the expensive whip belonged to. He knew of only one person in the hood who drove a Maybach.

"CJ! What the fuck is going on?" Shabazz squinted.

When his sights set on Newark's most notorious drug dealer, Cam'ron Jeffries, standing bare-chested beside the Maybach, bouncing from foot to foot, boisterously, he knew, then, shit was about to be catastrophic.

Shabazz repositioned himself to see CJ yelling at Nard, the young hustler who was making a name for himself in The Bricks.

He didn't know Nard personally, but he had seen him around the city on many occasions. Secretly, he admired what he had been able to accomplish in the game at such a young age. But what Shabazz felt for CJ was beyond admiration, it bordered on idolization.

Shabazz wasn't a dick rider, but he had no problem saluting a man's accomplishments. He knew firsthand how hard it was to rise from the dirt up. CJ had done that and a whole lot more.

In The Bricks his name was legendary, and like most other kingpins that had come before him, it was inevitable that some young wolf would come for his crown.

Shabazz shook his head at the fatalistic results that we're about to be played out, right before his very eyes. Two beasts, both with indomitable wills, stood in the middle of the street, locked in a tangle with steel and bad intent. He was certain one or both of them would end up dead.

Pressing his unshaven face further against the window, he watched the deadly drama unfold.

***

CJ fought back the urge to raise his arm and let his tool spit. The level of testosterone that flowed through his body was barely containable. He felt in his heart that he could take on Nard and his punk ass crew and walk up out of Little Bricks with all of their blood on his hands. But Rah would certainly get caught in the crossfire, if Nard didn't kill him as soon as the first shot rang out from CJ's strap.

Fuck it! I'm not risking my peeps' life, CJ decided. He mean mugged Nard, who was still shielding himself with Raheem's body.

CJ let his finger ease off of the trigger. He spread his arms out wide and shouted, "Fuck you wanna do? Stand here all day tryna build up the courage to kill me? "

Nard smirked. "I'm not gon' kill you. I'ma make you murk ya'self. If you love your man and want me to let him go, eat your gun, bitch ass nigga. Take ya'self outta the game."

Fuck no! Shabazz said to himself as he watched on. He had no way of knowing how trill CJ and Rah's bond was, but he suspected Nard would kill CJ's boy regardless. *Might as well go out with your banger poppin'. Take a few niggaz to Hell wit'chu. Real shit.*

CJ unzipped his pants and pulled his wood out. "It's all dick over here." He took a piss in Nard's direction. "This is what I think of you and your bitch ass crew."

Behind the window, Shabazz covered his mouth with his hand to keep from cheering. "That nigga, CJ, hard as fuck!" he whispered.

Nard wasn't impressed. "You think I'm playin' with you?" he yelled. Then, to reinforce his cold bloodedness he shot Rah again.

"Ahhhh!" This time Rah cried out in excruciating pain as the hot, sizzling bullet tore through his insides. Blood ran from his body and into the freshly planted snow. He curled up within himself and groaned heavily as beads of sweat formed on his forehead, despite the chilling cold.

Nard smiled menacingly. "I'ma make him suffer," he taunted CJ.

Rah winced as the pain from the gunshot set his insides ablaze. Somehow he summoned up the strength to yell to CJ. "Kill this nigga, yo!"

CJ, who had murdered mercilessly over and over again, couldn't bare seeing his main mans suffer, but his nemesis showed no mercy.

Nard pressed his heat to the back of Raheem's head and sent a chilling stare back CJ's way. "It's either him or you. Eat that gun, nigga, before I release all your mans' brains over here."

For some unexplainable reason, witnessing this, Shabazz snatched his Nine off of his waist. Their beef had nothing at all to do with him, but he was ready to thrust himself dead in the middle of it. But a quick glance at all of the gunners, whom he had concluded must've been down with Nard, made Shabazz think better of it.

"Let him go, he served his purpose. This is between me and you," he heard CJ bellow.

"Do it! Pull the trigger and end yo' life, and I'll spare your mans'," said Nard.

Shabazz shook his head *no*, as if CJ could see him.

"Lil' punk muhfucka," he screamed at Nard. "You think you're saying something? Huh? Huh?"

In the middle of the snow covered street, CJ remained gangsta. He stood up on his toes and bounced from foot to foot, full of adrenaline. His tatted chest heaved up and down, and his arms flung out at his sides. Instead of cowering, he embraced the ultimatum like the real nigga he had always professed to be.

"Kill ya'self or I'm slaying ya mans, B. This is your last chance." Nard retorted.

"Nigga, fuck you. You ain't saying shit! I'm G'd up 'til my feet up. I'll die for my nigga. Can you say that, punk muthafucka?" CJ shoved his gun in his own mouth.

Shabazz' eyes grew big. This was like something he would see in a cinema, only it wasn't a movie. This was real life. "Nooo, son, don't do it," he mumbled.

Boom!

The single gunshot sounded like a loud clap of thunder. Shabazz stared in disbelief as CJ's head exploded in a spray of red and his body crumpled to the ground.

"Oh, fuck!" Shabazz' mouth was left wide open and his head shook from side to side.

He watched as Nard let CJ's boy fall to the ground. A second later, several of the men that had been posted up, watching Nard's back, appeared at his side. One by one, they walked over to where CJ's body lay sprawled out on the ground and pumped an exclamation shot in his corpse.

Shabazz didn't like that at all. *He's already dead. Why y'all gotta disrespect him like that? Regardless of y'all beef, that nigga was a street legend. You don't do him like that!* His brow knitted and his mouth was tight. His hand wrapped around his tool, but he wisely chose to stay put, even as he witnessed them pick CJ's body up and toss it in a dumpster like trash.

Shabazz could barely contain his fury. He bit down hard on his lip and took a deep breath, battling back and forth with the voice that calmed the beast resonating within.

Outside, Big Nasty lifted Nard's arm in victory. "It's over, dawg. You're the new king," he anointed.

Nard smiled. "We own The Bricks!" he boasted, and all of his minions applauded.

Y'all bitch niggaz don't own nothin! thought Shabazz. *You didn't murk CJ, he gave his life for his mans. That's real G shit.* He tapped his chest with his fist in salutation.

Beyond the window, Nard stood over the one who CJ had sacrificed his life for. His gun was aimed down at Rah. While his team urged him to empty his clip in him, Nard searched his mind for a way to put his signature on this particular kill because Rah had withstood all forms of torture in refusing to set CJ up.

Nard's brother, Man Dog, could see the wheels turning in his head. "Just do that nigga," he said.

But Nard was on a narcissistic high. "Nah, son, he thinks he's hard. I'ma leave him here to die in the same streets he couldn't leave alone. Or maybe he can crawl in the dumpster and die with his mans."

Man Dog laughed. "You a cold muthafucka."

"Let's go. Fuck 'em!" Nard waved his arm as he headed to the car.

"Yeah, fuck 'em!" They chanted in unison as they spat at Rah's blood soaked body.

With chuckles and banter of their success they all moved out, leaving Rah to die slowly. What they hadn't counted on was his impregnable will to live and extract revenge.

And that's gon' be their demise, thought Shabazz after he raced outside to find Rah still breathing.

CHAPTER
2
Eric

Shit had gotten real in the streets, but I was trained to go. My murder game was official and my attitude was straight gangsta. So, when those niggaz did the unthinkable to Rah, me and the entire crew was ready to send mad heat at 'em

Along the way, something my brother, CJ, once said would be reinforced in all of our minds, over and over again.

"The game is a cold-hearted bitch. It can take you to the highest heights and then sink you to the lowest depths, all in the same day. And no matter how hard a nigga is, if you fuck with the streets long enough, you'll eventually find out that thugs cry, too," he schooled.

Understanding that, we were determined to make sure that our enemies shed the last tears.

Down in the Iron Bound section of Newark, inside a warehouse that had become our headquarters, I knocked on the door to CJ's office but received no answer. At the moment, I had no reason to be concerned. I just figured my brother needed a little time alone.

Like the rest of us, he was real fucked up over Raheem's kidnapping. With each passing day, the stress lines in his face grew deeper. Lately, I could hear the tension in his voice when he spoke. And our failure to find out where Nard was holding Rah compounded all his worries.

The latest pics Nard sent confirmed what we all suspected: Rah was being tortured. But there was no doubt in our minds how Rah would rock. He would choose a bullet in the head over betrayal in the heart. That's just how real he was. Mad niggaz claimed to be about that life, but Raheem lived that shit, 24/7, 365.

On one hand, his unquestionable gangsta fortified us. We could plot our moves without having to worry that he would bitch up and flip. On the other hand, his thoroughness caused us to fear the inevitable—he would refuse to fold and Nard would murk him.

Just thinking about that shit caused me to shake my head in frustration. Rah wasn't family by blood but he was as much of a big brother to me as CJ. Throughout my life, I could count on him in times of need, so his predicament had me vexed.

I let out a long sigh and clenched my fingers tightly. *I need my nigga back.*

The pain in my chest was indescribable. That's how much love I had for Rah. When my brother made that call to Atlanta, asking him to come back to Newark to help us in a street war that had left CJ's girl, Tamika, and her family dead, fam didn't hesitate to gather up a few of his soldiers in the *'A'* and board that flight.

A few days later, with two ATL goons, DaQuan and Legend, accompanying him, Rah arrived in Newark with one thing on his mind—stacking bodies.

Together, we made many mothers mourn their sons.

Legend and DaQuan quickly proved their mettle and we became joined at the hip. But the other side didn't fold. They had managed to slump DaQuan, though, and now that they had Rah captive, all of us was desperate to get him back unharmed.

No one was saying it, but we all knew that the longer those niggas had him, the less likely we would ever see him alive again. We had already lost one real hitta, DaQuan, to their guns, losing Rah would crush us all.

The mere thought of that made my knees weaken. I placed my hands against the sides of the door frame to steady myself. After straightening my back and shaking that image from my mind, I turned from CJ's office and walked back into the main area of the warehouse. Legend was just returning from making a quick run to the store when I entered the room.

"Sup, my nigga, anything new?" he inquired as he sat large White Castles bags down on a work bench.

"Nah, son, ain't nothin' changed. Those bitch niggaz are still playing cat and mouse," I somberly reported.

"It's all good," Legend nodded his head up and down, "they're about to feel our wrath."

"Say that!" intoned Snoop, who was sitting on a crate cleaning his AK-47 assault rifle.

"Know that!" Premo co-signed our enemies' death warrants as he rose up off of the couch that sat in the middle of the spacious warehouse and walked over to see what Legend had brought back to eat.

Reaching inside the bags, Snoop pulled out burgers, fries and some other sandwiches and passed them around. I unwrapped my chicken sandwich and took a bite. I hadn't eaten in two days but I didn't have an appetite, so I sat the sandwich down on the bench and watched the others eat while my mind replayed everything that had happened since the beef with Nard popped off.

Over several months, both squads had taken losses. We left some of their crew with dirt faces, while they snatched the hearts out of our chests with DaQuan's murder. Nearly three months had passed since that unforgettable day. But when I closed my eyes at night, I still saw vivid images of my dude stretched out on the pavement.

"We gotta hurry up and find these niggas and kill 'em," I blurted out. "They gotta pay in the worst way!"

"Fa sho! I promised DaQuan's girl that I would bury every one of those bitch-made muthafuckas!" Pain resonated from Legend's voice as he slung his burger across the room. "I'm tired of sitting around waiting to hear from those pussies, I'm ready to wreak havoc around this bitch!" He snatched his machete off of a nearby table and held it down at his side.

"I'm wit'chu, Black." Snoop brows knitted as he chewed on his food.

"All of us are with it, but like CJ said, we gotta move cautiously until we get Rah back, then we can smash everything. No matter what, we can't do anything that might make them kill Rah," said Premo.

I nodded my head in agreement but Legend obviously felt differently. He let out an exasperated sigh. "Man, let's keep it one *hunnid* -- y'all really think Nard is gonna let Rah live, knowing how shorty get down for his?" He looked from Premo to me. "Be real, my nigga, what do you think?"

"I don't know, son. I'm just hoping..." I casted my eyes to the floor and let my voice trail off.

"I got that same hope but I'm also a realist, ain't no way they're letting homie go."

"Fuck is you saying, yo? You trying to say Rah is already dead." I reached out and shoved Legend. I was ready to fight but to his credit he recognized my aggression for what it was, hurt.

"E, ain't nan man in this room love Rah no more than I do. I'll lay my life down for homie. But we can't keep underestimating the opposition, those niggas are killaz too," he said.

"Fuck those pussies!" I spat, refusing to give them any props at all. If they were really about that murder shit, they wouldn't be hiding like a bunch of hoes.

"I feel you. But sitting around waiting for them to call our shots ain't getting Rah back. I say we hit the streets and let our tools spit. Put that bitch nigga, Nard, under so much pressure he'll have no other choice but to release Rah," said Legend.

"That shit sounds good, nah mean? The only problem with that is none of Nard's people are around for us to smash," I reminded him. Like a coward, Nard had ordered all of his drug houses to shut down, and he had pulled his people off of the streets.

"Ho-ass muthafuckaz," spat Legend, echoing my sentiments.

We all grew quiet as a feeling of helplessness washed over the room. I grabbed a few sandwiches off of the table. "I'ma go see if CJ wants something to eat." Feeling mentally weary, I made my way back to his office.

As I reached the door, I thought about what Legend had said. Maybe we did need to turn the heat up on Nard by crushing any and everybody associated with him, regardless to how loose their connection was. But who was I to question my brother's strategy?

CJ had proven, over and over again, that his gangsta was unmatched. His body count exceeded all of ours put together. And in spite of the current situation, he remained my hero.

The others on the team didn't agree with every decision CJ made, though. They felt some of the things he'd done was plain reckless. But that was part of what made him a beast. He was capable of killing on impulse and with no regard.

With his hands still wet with blood, he might hit the club and stunt on muthafuckaz. A body could be in the trunk of his whip and CJ would be in the club popping bottles like he didn't have a worry in the world. Niggaz respected him, but they feared him even more. In my eyes, absolutely no one measured up to him.

Rah was different, though. He was a thinker and much more humble than any of us. And when it came to warfare, son always anticipated the enemy's next move. That's why I had always felt that if anybody got caught slipping, it wasn't gon' be him.

Damn. How did they get you, fam? That was the burning question in my mind.

I stood there tryna fight back a tidal wave of guilt that surged through my heart. If I could turn back the hands of time, I would've never let him leave the club to take Kenisha home without me that night.

"Damn, son, I fucked up!" I leaned my head against the wall outside the door of CJ's office.

Though the guilt I felt was deep, there was no way it measured up to what I imagined my brother was feeling. Him and Rah came up together eating Ramen Noodles off the same fork. CJ had chosen the street life while Rah had made it out, only to be called back to bust his gun at our sides. Now his life was in the enemy's hands.

Deep down, we all knew what the outcome would be, but we weren't ready to accept it. Until Rah's body turned up, I was not gonna lose hope. Because if Allah truly protected the good, my nigga was gonna be a'ight.

Slightly comforted by that thought, I raised my head and knocked on the office door. "CJ you a'ight in there?" I waited for a response but got none.

I knocked again, harder this time, but he still didn't answer. "Bruh, I brought you something to eat," I called out.

When the only response I received was more silence, I turned and walked back up front. Legend and Snoop was huddled together talking in hushed tones. Premo was staring out of a window with his back to everyone. I walked over and placed a hand on his shoulder. I could feel the tenseness in his muscles.

"Anything moving out there?" I asked in a low voice.

Premo replied with a slow shake of his head, that instantly made my blood turn hot. "Nigga, why you acting defeated?" I questioned him in a harsh tone.

"Save that shit, yo! This ain't the right time," he said over his shoulder.

I took a deep breath and let it out slowly. As I contemplated our next move, my mind began to shift to Legend's way of thinking. Sitting back doing nothing was like defanging a wolf. Me and my niggas were killaz, it was time to do what killaz do.

I cleared my voice and looked Premo in the eyes. "You say nothin's moving out there, right?" My voice turned gravelly.

"Nah, son. Not shit," he restated.

"Well, we're about to make some shit move. C'mon, let's go holla at CJ and see if we can get him to take the clamps off of us. It's time to murder some muthafuckaz!" I dropped the food right there on the floor and turned to look at my other mans. What I saw in their eyes reconfirmed my trust in their gangsta.

Legend snatched his machete off of the table and gripped it with force. Earlier, he had used it to chop the hands off of a muthafucka that we suspected of having a role in Rah's kidnapping. He raised the bloody blade in the air and sliced it back and forth. "Fuck cutting off a bitch nigga'z hands, I'm 'bout to decapitate me a bitch!" he vowed.

"That's what the fuck I'm talm 'bout." Premo got crunk. "We gotta remind niggaz who the fuck we be, nah mean."

Snoop whipped out his tool and click-clacked a bullet in the chamber of his fo-five. "Muthafuckaz about to meet their Maker, son. Word!" he proclaimed.

I let a smile play across my face. Now my team was talking the type of shit I needed to hear. If Nard was gonna kill Rah, we had to show him we would retaliate with force.

With a plan formulating in my mind, I led the way to CJ's office to let him know that we wanted to unleash terror in The Bricks. No more waiting! Fuck that chill shit his police connects was talking 'bout. There wouldn't be peace in the streets until Nard and his whole team had tombstones with their names on them.

Knocking on the door again, I said, "Yo, Big Bruh, can we come in?"

This time, when he didn't answer, I stepped forward, turned the knob and pushed the door open. We entered one behind the other. The chair behind CJ's desk was unoccupied and turned backwards, as if he had gotten up in a hurry. My eyes surveyed the office suspiciously. CJ was nowhere in sight and the back door was wide open. The cold November wind whistled through it and rushed up on us in a chilly blast.

"What the fuck?" uttered Snoop.

Legend hurried to the door and peered out into the back lot. "You see his ride?" asked Premo.

"Negative, man, it's gone."

An ominous feeling came over me. I slammed my palms against the door frame and let out a pained cry. "Fuck! They got him! I can feel that shit in my heart, yo."

"Those bitch niggaz ain't got shit!" Snoop disagreed. "There's no fuckin' way they ran up in here and snatched him up without us hearing a sound."

"No muthafuckin' way! CJ would've went out in a blaze, and a coupla them would be laying on this floor beside him," said Legend.

Premo stepped back inside and pulled the door closed. "True story. He probably went looking for Rah on his own. That must be the reason he sent all of us out of his office earlier, so we couldn't stop him from going rogue," he surmised.

That made sense to me. I could picture CJ saying to himself, *Y'all niggaz ain't gotta look for me, I'ma look for you!*

But Nard and 'em couldn't be taken lightly. "We gotta find him, ASAP."

I whipped out my iPhone and made the call. After the phone rang three times, I was sent to voicemail. Panic filled my chest as I hung up and immediately pressed REDIAL. When I was sent to voicemail a second time, a feeling of dread coursed through my body and choked off my breath.

"What up, E?" I could barely make out Premo's voice as I staggered behind the desk and sat down heavily in his chair. I let my head rest on the desktop as tears forced their way into my eyes.

"He ain't answering, yo." I said in a tone muffled by despair.

"Shawdy, what the fuck?" Legend's voice boomed. "Show some faith in your brother's gangsta. You know CJ is about that gunplay as much as anybody. You know he can handle himself in any situation. Wherever he's at, you can bet it's on his own terms."

"I hear you talking." My response held little conviction because my heart told me that CJ was dead.

I lifted my head and wiped my eyes with the heel of my hands. The pain in my heart was indescribable but the thoroughness of my bloodline rose to the surface. I was my brother's keeper and, no matter what, I would not wilt.

"You a'ight, folks?" asked Legend.

"Nah, blood," I answered truthfully, "but it's way too soon to mourn." I stood up from the desk and took charge. "Lock up everything and let's roll out. Snoop, you and Premo ride together. I'ma ride with Legend. Search the whole muhfuckin' city until we find CJ. If my brother is dead, I'ma turn The Bricks blood red."

CHAPTER
3
Eric

After padlocking the back door, we hurried to our cars and went in search of CJ. As Legend drove through the city, keeping an anxious eye out for CJ's Maybach, I continuously called his phone. Each time, it rang a few times before going to voicemail. Finally, I decided to leave a message with extreme urgency in my tone.

"Yo, bruh, answer your phone. You got a nigga worried about you. Hit me back when you get this." I stared at the screen desperately trying to will it to light up with CJ's number, but no call back ever came.

We drove through our spots up and down Clinton Street, asking if any of our block boys had seen him. No one had heard from CJ or knew where he was at nor had they seen any of his whips passing through the hood. Every call we made brought the same response, and Snoop and Premo were encountering the same disheartening answers.

Talking to Premo on the phone, I said, "Y'all head out to East Orange and see if those niggaz out there have seen him. Me and Legend gon' try to find that lil' young broad, Kenisha, that he fuck with. Maybe he's chilling with her, just tryna clear his head."

"Say no more."

I let out a sigh of frustration as I ended the call. I didn't know where Kenisha lived and I doubted CJ would be laid up in some pussy at a time like this, but I had to turn over every stone. "Yo, you know where lil' mama live?" I asked Legend.

"Nah. I just know her pops is an Islamic minister or some shit like that." He stopped at a traffic light at the intersection of Central Avenue and Grove Street.

I leaned my head against the dashboard. "This shit is fucked up!"

"Don't panic, fam. We gon' find him," Legend attempted to reassure me but his confidence did nothing to allay my fear.

I sat up in my seat and I tried calling my brother once more. The phone rang twice and then, finally, someone answered.

"Hello." The voice didn't belong to CJ, though.

I glanced down at the screen to make sure I hadn't dialed the wrong number. When I saw that I hadn't, I got pissed the fuck off! "Who the fuck is this?" I gritted.

Legend's head snapped in my direction. "Is that CJ?" His voice was filled with hope.

I shook my head *no*. On the other end, the man said, "My name is Shabazz. Are you CJ and Rah's people?"

"Fuck is it to you, nigga? Put CJ on the phone," I snapped.

"Blood, if you're his peeps, I got some bad news."

"I'm his people. What bad news you got?" My body slumped down in the seat as I anticipated the worst.

"CJ is dead, man, and Rah is fucked up real bad. I don't think he gon' make it, yo."

"Fuck is you saying, nigga?" I cried as pain and anger gripped me like nothing I had ever felt before. "Play with this shit if you want to and end up in a goddam casket. Put my brother on the phone right muthafuckin' now!" I didn't wanna believe my ears.

The light turned green but Legend didn't move. Horns honked and drivers behind us hurled insults that under any other circumstances, would've got them wet the fuck up. But me and Legend was oblivious to everything outside of the vehicle.

"Bruh, you got five seconds to put CJ on the phone!" I threatened.

"B, you not listening to me, yo. CJ is dead!" Shabazz' voice sounded like it was about to break. "He's dead, man. Those niggaz did him dirty."

"Blood, don't tell me no shit like dat!" I exploded.

"Son, you don't know how bad I wish I didn't have to."

Legend reached over and took the phone from me. "Yo, talk to me, my nigga. What the fuck is going on?" He pulled off and turned into a lot and parked.

"Put that nigga on speaker." I ran a hand down my face to wipe the flood of hot tears that poured from my eyes.

Legend took the phone away from his ear and put it on speaker. Shabazz said, "Yo, son, I don't know you but since y'all calling CJ's phone, I guess you're who you say you are. Like I said, CJ is dead, and ol' boy did him real foul. Your mans, Rah, is barely alive. They fucked him up real bad, yo. That's all I'ma say on the phone. Just meet me at University. The ambulance is rushing Rah there now. Hurry up!"

The line went dead. Legend just let the phone fall from his hand. He dropped his head against the steering wheel and mumbled incoherently as we both tried to process the man's words.

"Ain't no way in hell my brother is dead. *Not CJ.* I refuse to believe that!"

"Damn, my nigga, this some bullshit." Legend slowly raised his head and looked at me. Unspilled tears brimmed his eyes. "I can't even think," he said, barely above a whisper.

I couldn't think clearly, either. The news had shattered my world but until I saw proof that my brother was dead, I refused to accept it. "Fam, we gotta go to the hospital to see if what he was saying is true," I spoke in a broken tone.

As Legend drove to University, we both held on to hope that my brother wasn't dead. "That was some bullshit, shawdy. Them niggaz ain't done killed CJ. This is some type of set up. But if they think we ain't gon' show up, they got the game fucked up," he spewed.

My head was all fucked up and I couldn't stop the tears from falling from eyes. Somehow, I managed to call Premo. As soon as he answered, I told him the business.

"How the fuck could that happen?" He was bewildered. But the fact that Shabazz answered CJ's phone led him to believe it had to be true. "And if it was a setup, they wouldn't want us to meet them at the hospital. They would know that Hot Top be all around that bitch," he said, meaning the police.

"Yeah, you're right," I agreed. "I'm still not believing that shit until I see it with my own eyes. Meet us at the hospital. Man, I'm telling you if this shit is true I'm going on a muthafuckin' rampage!"

"Me too." Like mine, his voice was strained with emotion.

I hung up the phone and glanced at Legend through my tears. His jaw was set and his eyes burned fiery. But when he glanced back at me and spoke, his country voice was calm. "Shawdy, we don't know nothin' yet. Whatever the outcome, though, we not gon' fold. You understand me?" he said with conviction.

I just nodded my head. For a long moment, we rode in complete silence. As we got closer to the hospital, reality punched me in the chest. Who the fuck was we trying to fool other than ourselves? "He's gone, yo. Them bitch ass niggaz killed my brother. I can feel it in my soul."

I silently prayed that I was wrong. But in my heart of hearts, I knew that I wasn't. All I could do was hope that Rah wasn't dead, too.

CHAPTER
4
Eric

As soon we pulled into the hospital's parking lot, Legend hopped out of the car and raced inside. I pulled into a vacant parking space, closed both of our doors and hurried inside behind him.

A nigga'z heart was pounding hard as hell as I walked through the Emergency Room doors. Inside it was mad pandemonium. Tragedy or some form of worry was etched on every face I looked into.

"Noooo, not my baby!" screamed a heavy-set, black woman with a dirty scarf tied around her head. A doctor in a white lab coat tried to comfort her, but she started fighting him. "You let my baby die!" she cried.

The word *die* rung in my ears on repeat. Was my brother really dead? I wanted to close my eyes, blink twice, and wake up from this nightmare. But the fact of the matter was this was not a dream. Those were real tears pouring down my face, and real worry sizzling through my body as I pushed passed a horde of people in a desperate rush to reach the front desk and get some answers.

Legend was a few steps in front of me, slinging muthafuckaz out of our way. As we emerged from the crowd of people in the ER, I noticed a familiar face. It was Paris, a homegirl from Little Bricks, who worked at the hospital. A few years ago, she had been one of my brother's side chicks.

Our eyes met and I hurried up to her. "What's up, ma? Tell me what's going on. Did they bring CJ here?" I asked in a harried tone.

"No, but they brought Raheem in."

Legend leaned in from behind me. "Is he gonna make it?" he asked.

"I don't know. I heard one of the other nurses talking and she sounded doubtful." Paris choked up.

Legend's head dropped to his chest, and my knees buckled. *No, not Rah.* This shit was bad. I titled my head to the sky and silently sent a prayer up for my nigga, hoping he would pull through.

Finding the strength to stand up straight and face the truth, however painful it might be, I steadied my legs and asked Paris, "What about my brother?"

She looked at me for a second, and then she lowered her eyes to the floor. Angrily, I reached up, grabbed her by the face with both hands and forced eye contact. Tears trailed down her face and she fell into my arms sobbing. That's when I knew for sure that CJ was gone. I just wanted confirmation.

"Paris!" I held her away from me and shook her violently. "Stop crying and answer my question!" But no matter how hard I shook her, she just couldn't force the words out of her mouth.

Legend stepped up and barked in her face. "Answer him! Is CJ dead?"

Before she could pull herself together and stamp our fears true, I felt a hand on my shoulder. I released Paris and spun around quickly. Standing there was a dark-skinned dude who was rocking a light, scraggly beard, a gray coat and a black hoodie. I knew who he was before he identified himself.

"I'm Shabazz, yo. You're Eric, CJ's little brother, right?" He held his hand out for some dap, but until I knew for sure he was official, I was treating him with suspicion, so I left his fist hanging.

"Yeah, I'm his brother. How do you know me?"

"I used to trap on Hawthorne before I went away on a lil' bid. You and CJ used to come through there sometime."

I studied his face for a minute and suddenly I recalled seeing him around our spot he had mentioned. My suspicions eased up a little but this wasn't a reunion. I needed to know what had happened to my brother.

"Give it to me raw, yo. Is my brother dead?" I asked.

Shabazz slowly nodded his head up and down. "Yeah, fam. I'm sorry to have to tell you that. But if it's any consolation, he went out real gangsta."

He kept on talking but I barely heard another word. My body slumped as I tried to envision living on without my heart. My brother was everything to me, and know they were telling me he's gone. "Are you sure?" I asked again.

Shabazz nodded *yes* a second time, and then Paris removed all doubt. Sniffling back more tears, she said, "The paramedics that brought Rah in said it was bad. I didn't see CJ's body because they took him straight to the coroner's. But I knew it had to be him because they described CJ's Maybach..."

I put my hand up to cut her off. I didn't want to hear nothing else until I gathered myself. Legend threw an arm around my shoulders and gave me a brotherly hug.

"It's gon' be a'ight," he consoled.

"No, it's not. But it's damn sure about to get ugly," I replied bitterly.

"I'm wit' dat." His tone mirrored mine.

When I looked up, I saw Premo and Snoop coming through the door, followed by a half dozen or so of our foot soldiers. I could tell from their aggressive postures that each one of them was strapped and ready to bang on an opponent. Cops were all around the place, and their eyes followed Snoop 'nem all the way over to us.

I G-hugged Premo first, then Snoop.

"What's the business?" Snoop asked, looking at me with sad eyes.

I knew what he was asking, and my answer came out tinged with the pain that was in my heart. "He's gone, bruh. Those bitch ass niggaz killed him." I reached up and caught a falling tear with the back of my hand.

"It's killing season!" Snoop gritted.

"Shh!" Legend quickly put his finger up to his lips, urging us to tone down. "Fam, the po's are all over this bitch and they're sweating us hard. "Let's step outside."

We all looked up and saw Newark's Finest eyes beamed in on us. As we turned and headed outside, I said to Shabazz, "You come, too." I wanted the rest of the crew to hear, first-hand, the story he had to tell.

Outside, we stood in a circle with the wind whistling around us as Shabazz replayed what had happened, blow by blow. Each word that left his mouth brought a tear from my eyes. In my mind, I drew a vivid picture of the events as he detailed them. Everything he recounted personified the bond CJ and Rah shared, and although I was hurting bad inside, my chest swelled with pride knowing that my brother had given his life for his partner. I couldn't be mad at him for that because I had no doubt Rah would've done the same for him.

What made my blood boil was when Shabazz told us how Nard had thrown CJ's body in a dumpster and proclaimed himself to be the new king of Newark.

I clenched my fist and gnawed my teeth in anger. "There will never be another CJ! What my brother did in this muthafuckin' city can't be duplicated. I promise y'all, before it's all said and done, I'ma do that bitch nigga, Nard, a thousand times worse than anyone can imagine."

"Death to his bitch ass!" said Premo. He held out his fist and I bumped it with mine. Snoop, Legend and the others followed suit.

I dried my eyes and looked around at the others. The pain that showed on their faces was as real as mine. CJ was like God in our eyes. Many people outside of our crew disliked him, but to those of us that he had love for, there wasn't a better nigga.

"Let's go in here and check on Rah, then we'll go to morgue to identify CJ's body," I said. I dreaded having to do that but it was inescapable.

We began to head back inside, moving as a unit. Suddenly, Snoop grabbed Shabazz by the collar and mugged him hard. "Hold up! How the fuck we know you're not down with the other side?" he questioned.

"I understand how you're feeling, yo. But you ain't gotta come at me like that. I didn't do nothin' to your mans, blood. If I could've helped them, I would've. But Nard and 'em were deep. They had choppaz and that pussy ass nigga, Nard, was using Rah as a shield. If I had clapped at him, I might've shot Rah by mistake. Even CJ couldn't do nothin'. He went out like a gangsta tho'. Wasn't no ho' in his blood. I'll forever remember that," said Shabazz.

"I hear you. But you haven't convinced me that you're not the enemy," spat Snoop. He eased his toolie out.

"Bruh, if it was like that Rah would've never made it out of there alive. They left him for dead. I'm the nigga that held his head in my lap so he wouldn't choke to death on his own blood.

"I didn't leave his side until I saw the flashing red and blues turn into the corner. And the only reason I left then was because I didn't want them jakes taking me down to the precinct and questioning me. I'm a street nigga. I don't talk to cops." His mouth was tight, as if he was insulted that his sincerity was being questioned.

I reached out and grabbed Snoop by the elbow, and led him a few feet away from the others, but he kept his stare fixed on Shabazz. His apprehension told me he was ready to murk dude.

"Fam, I think he's telling the truth. I see it in his eyes, and I can hear it in his voice," I said.

"Fuck that nigga, yo! I wanna nod him!"

I knew where my nigga was coming from, his grief over CJ's death made him want to clap *whoever*. I felt the same way but I was trying hard to keep my head. I placed my hand on his shoulder. "Stand down, my G. We're gonna make those niggaz pay. Shabazz ain't one of them though."

"You trust son, yo?"

"I don't trust no man that ain't broke bread or shed blood with me, but I believe what he told us. I've seen him around and from what I recall he don't rock with those niggaz. If I'm wrong, we'll bury him beside them."

Snoop nodded his head in agreement. He shoved his hands in his pockets and took a deep breath, letting it out slowly. "*Damn!* I can't believe this shit. CJ dead? Son, my head is all fucked up." Tears streaked down his face in the form of two rivers.

I gave him a long G-hug. "We're about to wipe out Nard's entire bloodline. That's on everything I love," I vowed.

"I'm ready to ride on him right now."

"I feel you, but let's go check on Rah first. Then we gotta handle things with CJ. After that, we gon' crush everybody connected to Nard."

"Real shit," he said with conviction.

We walked back over to where the others stood. "What's the verdict?" asked Premo.

I looked from him to Shabazz, whose eyes held no fear. "Homie good," I announced, dapping him up.

Shabazz' shoulders relaxed. "I appreciate that, son. You'll see, I'm official."

"You better be," I warned. I gave him a cold stare, exclamating my seriousness, and then we all walked back inside.

Ca$h

CHAPTER
5
Eric

Rah was in surgery and the doctors gave him a 50/50 chance of surviving. I was concerned, but it was hard to show it because my brother was lying on a cold, steel table somewhere.

I had already lost my Mom Dukes and my little sister—now this.

CJ wasn't only my big brother, he was my idol. He had taught me everything I knew, from hustlin' to women. I had no idea what I would do without him. Though death was as much a part of the game as stacking money and shining, I had never expected my brother to be the one to get killed.

They didn't have to throw his body in the garbage can, though. That was some real foul shit. I wouldn't sleep peacefully until we had avenged him in blood.

Still reeling from the news, I sat down on one of those hard, plastic chairs in the waiting area of the Emergency Room, while Legend and 'nem tried to get a minute by minute update on Rah. I lowered my head into my hands and said a quick prayer that he would pull through, and then images of what had happened to CJ flashed in my mind. A loud, angry scream escaped from my mouth. I pounded my fist in my hand and cussed God for letting those niggaz do that shit to my brother.

When I looked up, all eyes were on me. I pounced up out of my seat breathing flames. "Fuck is y'all looking at, yo? Y'all ain't never seen a thug cry?" I belted as I looked from one face to the next.

No one met my stare but the cops that were present. In my state of mind, I wanted to whip out and fill their asses with something hot just for refusing to turn their heads.

Premo must've read my mind. He stood up and whispered in my ear, "Don't do it, E. Hold it in and unleash it on the muhfuckaz that did this shit."

"You're right, yo," I said, sniffling.

We sat back down, and I wiped the tears from my eyes. But nothing could wipe away the intense pain that ran through my heart.

"Rah is gonna be in surgery for hours. Let's go see about your brother," said Legend, who was seated between us.

"Somebody gotta stay here with Rah," I said.

"I'll stay," Snoop volunteered.

"If y'all don't mind, I wanna stay too. I'm not trying to get all up in your mix but I wanna know that Rah pulled through, nah mean," said Shabazz.

I could tell from the look in Snoop's eyes that he was about to reject the offer. I silenced him with a low gaze. "Let him stay. If it wasn't for him, Rah would be dead in the streets." I turned to a couple of our foot soldiers that stood at my side and told them to make some calls and gather up all available Intel on Shabazz.

"You better turn out to be exactly who you claim to be," Snoop threatened him.

Shabazz didn't blink, which was another sign that he was official.

I dapped Snoop. "If Rah comes out of surgery before we get back, hit me up."

"Copy."

Me, Legend and Premo left the hospital to make a trip that neither of us looked forward to. Not a single word was spoken between us on the drive to the coroner's. When we arrived there and walked inside of the building, to my surprise the detective named Cujo, who was CJ's connect, was waiting in the lobby. He walked up to me and greeted me in a somber tone.

I returned his greeting with a simple head nod.

"Do you know what happened?" he asked.

"Nah!" I kept my reply short to hide my intentions. Cujo would want peace but I planned to bring murder.

As if he could see right through the maze, he said, "We'll talk later. Right now, we need an official identification and you have to be the one to do it. But it's definitely him, and it's bad. I mean *baddd!*"

I swallowed hard, and then forced the words out of my throat, where they'd been lodged. "I'm ready."

As we proceeded to a room in the basement of the building, I tried to prepare myself for what I would see. Shabazz had told us CJ had stuck the gun in his mouth and pulled the trigger, so I expected it to be an ugly sight.

I had blown dudes faces off and blasted a few dead in the chest with a pump shotgun, so I had seen the gruesome aftermath, up close and personal.

Considering I was no stranger to death, I thought that would have prepared me for what I was about to see, but it hadn't. And from the solemn looks on the other's faces, they weren't either.

When the coroner pulled back the white sheet, I looked down at CJ's body and literally gasped. His chest was full of bullet wounds. The whole top of my nigga'z head was gone. His left eye was blown completely out of the socket. And his mouth was twisted grotesquely.

"Look at what they did to my brother," I cried, as I sunk to my knees. Tears blinded me and I sobbed so loud, my voice echoed off of the walls. "I'ma kill every one of those muthafuckaz! I'ma make 'em die slow and painful! Every single one of them!"

My chest heaved up and down with each sob that erupted from deep in my soul. They didn't just kill my brother, they annihilated him. What they did to him was overkill, and it was flat out disrespectful to the boss nigga that he had been in life. To see his head and body tattered from their bullets and their ruthlessness hurt me to the core.

Legend reached down and helped me to my feet. His face was wet with tears and, like mine, his eyes bore fire. "Do you see how those bitch muthafuckaz don't him?" My voice cracked as I pointed to the remnants of my brother that was on the table.

"I see." Legend shook his head from side to side in despair.

The corner, an older black man, asked in an officious tone, "Can you confirm the identity of the deceased?"

"Yes, he's my brother, Cam'ron Jeffries," I regretfully replied.

When the man reached down to pull the sheet back over CJ, Legend grabbed his wrist forcefully. "Not yet, give us a moment."

The coroner looked up at Cujo, as if seeking his permission. "It's alright, Bill, let's give them a moment a privacy."

I looked at the rogue cop and nodded my head in appreciation.

As soon as Cujo and the coroner left out of the room, I summoned each one of my niggaz closer to the table and made them take a good look at what Nard and them had done to CJ.

"Y'all see this?" I pointed to CJ's half gone head, and then to his bullet-riddled torso. "Burn this image in your minds so you'll never forget what we owe the enemy. We can't stop until we've done each and every one of them as cold as they did my brother."

Legend looked down at CJ and closed his eyes. Tears spilled from the corner and ran down his face. "We're gonna avenge you, dawg," he said on pained breath.

Premo stroked CJ's blood-stained face with the back of his fingers. "Bruh, you were the spoon that fed me; the shield that protected me, and the force that drove me. I promise you, those niggaz are gonna die a horrendous death."

Premo didn't cry but the anger that flashed in his eyes conveyed the feelings that was in his heart. Without uttering another word, he turned and walked out of the room.

Legend looked at me then back down at CJ. "I understand why you did what you did, my nigga. Even in death, I salute you." He put his heels together, placed his right hand to the side of his face like a soldier and brought it down in a sharp arc. "Salute to one of the realest to ever walk the streets," he said in a voice that shook with emotion.

He patted me on the shoulder, consolingly, and then left me alone with my brother. As soon as the door shut, I broke down. Tears dropped from my eyes and onto CJ's face. I reached down and gently wiped them away.

How did I let this happen to you, big bruh? I was never supposed to leave your side, not for one second! Man, I let you down. I just wish you would've told me you were going to meet those niggaz. I would've died by your side ...

The pain in my heart choked off my words. I laid my head on my brother's chest and wept like a baby. CJ had taught me everything I needed to know to make it in this cold, hard world without being anybody's puppet. He had given me all of the mental jewels to rule the streets, and I admired him for that. But there was nothing I had learned, during my tutelage at his side, that prepared me to live without him.

Ca$h

I didn't know if I could go on forever without CJ, but I knew one thing for sure and two things for certain: Newark, New Jersey was about to become the murder capital of the country.

CHAPTER
6
Nard

A couple of hours after slaying CJ and leaving Rah to meet his homie in hell, I was at home and in the shower, washing those bitch niggaz' blood off of me before some of it seeped into my pores and diluted my thoroughness.

As the water ran over my lean but chiseled frame, I felt like I was on top of the world. I had dethroned the king of Brick City, a nigga who no one thought I could conquer.

Every other crew that had gone up against CJ was no longer around to tell the story, but I was on a whole 'notha level.

"I'm a muthafuckin' beast!" I gloated.

Just thinking about how strong my reputation in the streets was about to become had my chest on swole. Every nigga in the city would bow at my feet now, and ho's would be on my dick like crazy. That was a gift and a curse, though, because the last thing a nigga needed was the wrong bitch on his team. I had learned that the hard way fuckin' with Tamika's disloyal ass. Just thinking about that ho put a frown on my face.

Yeah, ma, you thought that nigga was a better man than me, huh? Well, I just sent him to join your punk ass. Now y'all can be together forever since that's what you wanted.

I let out a small chuckle as I turned the water off, stepped out of the shower and toweled myself dry.

A few seconds later, a fresh bolt of anger shot through my body, hardening the face that I stared at in the mirror as her biggest act of betrayal pounded heavy in my mind.

That punk ho killed my baby for that nigga!

I didn't think I would ever get over that. But now that they both were dead, I had gotten justice for my seed, nah mean? Yet and still, I couldn't even force a smile on my face.

It was all to the good, though. CJ was gone and I was the last man standing. Hands down, I was *that nigga* now. Somebody should've told CJ not to come for me! And they should've warned his mans, Rah, to stay in his lane instead of involving himself in a war that ran deeper than he could've ever imagined.

Nigga. should've stayed in his lane! I said to myself as I pulled on a fresh pair of jeans and stepped into a new pair of Timbs. I had achieved what every block boy dreams of accomplishing, but I knew that I couldn't afford to let my guards down if I wanted to remain on top. *Heavy is the head that wears the crown.*

Tempering my excitement, I made my way downstairs, where I found my crew celebrating. A slight frown etched itself on my face as I stopped in the doorway of the large living room and watched them turn up.

Quent grabbed a bottle of Ciroc out of the ice bucket on the portable bar, that sat against the wall. He popped the top and walked to the center of the room. His adrenaline seemed to be pumping stupid hard. He bounced up and down on his toes, and his voice overflowed with mad confidence, as he addressed the others.

"Who owns The Bricks now?"

"We muhfuckin' do!" shouted my brother Man Dog. He pulled Lemora onto his lap and tongued her down.

"Say that shit with your chest, boo," she egged him on.

"We own this *bee-yatch*!" he belted louder.

"Yes, y'all do, papi." She laughed as she began pouring champagne in his mouth, straight out of the bottle. After he guzzled down a mouth full, Lemora leaned down and kissed him deeply.

Quent raised the bottle high above my head in salutation. "To the victors goes the spoils. Money, power and respect."

My mans hooted and hollered in celebration.

Standing there quietly, I looked around the room at the top echelon of my team. Besides Man Dog, there was my main goon, Big Nasty, Quent and Zakee. Together, we had grinded hard. All of us were determined to get rich or die trying. Right now, we were winning. But I was under no false illusion. The game wasn't over. In fact, it had just begun. Remaining on top would be twice as hard as the climb to get there. But, obviously, my team didn't realize that yet.

"Y'all my Day 1 niggaz. I fuck wit' y'all the long way," I watched Man Dog stand up and announce.

Leaned against a wall, Quent tapped his chest with a fist. "One love, fam."

"'Til the grave," said Zakee.

Big Nasty, a huge muhfucka and a man of few words, put his fist in the air in a show of solidarity. His loyalty could never be questioned. He had put in major work for the team. In fact, it was his penchant for torture and murder that was most responsible for our reputation on the streets. Niggaz knew all of us was about that gun smoke, but they straight up feared Big Nasty, who had been bodying muthafuckaz since I was a lil' snot nose admiring him from our sixth-floor window in The Bricks. I used to marvel at the way he stepped out on the block and put fear in even the baddest cats. Back then, I had no way of knowing he would one day become my chief enforcer.

Quickly, my mind drifted from Big Nasty to two of our comrades that were no longer with us. I squeezed my eyes closed, tightly, to fight back the tears that tried to slip out.

Show and Talib—we lost y'all along the way, but today we avenged your deaths. Rest in peace, yo. I miss the fuck out of y'all, son. Word.

When I opened my eyes, I saw everyone looking toward the doorway, staring at me.

"You a'ight, B?" asked Quent.

"More or less." I walked over and sat down at the end of the sofa.

Silence filled the room. Everyone seemed to be waiting to judge my mood before continuing. After a minute or two, Man Dog picked back up where he'd left off.

"Today, we settled all scores. From now on, the streets are gonna bow down," he exclaimed. "Every one of you in this room went hard. You proved to me that our team can't be touched." he locked eyes with his girl. "You, too, Lemora," he added.

Though she didn't really hustle with us, she was always around. And when we murked the nigga who had abandoned Show, leaving him to get ambushed by CJ and 'em, Lemora had pumped some lead in that coward's ass right along with us. So, I had no problem with him acknowledging her role in our takeover.

"Thanks, papi." She smiled from ear to ear.

Man Dog smiled back, wider than a muhfucka and then he turned to me and winked his eye. I suspected he was about to say some off the wall, crazy shit, but I was in no way prepared for what was to come. None of us were.

Smiling arrogantly, he said, "Yo, last but not least, we gotta congratulate the real gangsta up in this piece." He strolled across the room to where Big Nasty's pit bull, Lil' Nasty, laid quietly at his owner's feet. Man Dog bent down and rubbed the dog's huge head. "You'sa muthafuckin' G, too. You straight maimed Rah. Bit that nigga all in the face and gnawed on his leg like it was a doggie bone. For that, I got a nice reward for you, boy."

As if he could truly understand what Man Dog had said, Lil' Nasty licked his hand excitedly and wagged his tail.

Man Dog then nodded his head at Zakee, who immediately got up and went outside. I looked at my brother questioningly, wondering what he was up to, but I remained silent. The sly grin on his face hinted at something wicked.

A minute or so later, Zakee returned with a red nose female pit. The bitch was muzzled, but she still pulled at her leash. Lil' Nasty pounced up on his feet, growled and barred his sharp teeth.

"Calm down, boy, you about to get ya dick wet." Man Dog laughed. "The bitch is in heat, go ahead and tear that shit up."

We all watched Lil' Nasty approach the other dog, snarling. As he got close to her, the scent of her hot pussy must've drew his ass in. He stopped growling and started sniffing her. My mans cracked up when Lil' Nasty's dick popped out, pink and harder than a mofo. In the next instance, he mounted the bitch and went to work.

"Yeah, fuck that bitch!" railed Quent.

"Smash that ho!" intoned Man Dog, drawing Lemora's ire. She mushed his head.

"Eww, bae, y'all some nasty ass niggaz." She covered her eyes with both hands.

"That's how I'ma rip into your ass tonight," said Man Dog, laughing harder.

Lil' Nasty had a hump in his back. He was balls deep up in that pussy. Everybody was wildin' out but I was not amused. In fact, their raucous behavior had me incensed. *We still got work to do! Fuck is we celebrating, yo?*

I pounced up from the sofa and snatched somebody's gun off of the table nearby. In three long, purposeful, strides I was standing over both dogs. Gritting my teeth, I aimed the toolie down at the female pitbull's head and squeezed the trigger three times, rapidly.

Boom! Boom! Boom!

The dog's head exploded in a burst of skull and blood, and her body flopped to the floor. Lil' Nasty started barking loudly and gnashing his teeth at me. For a second or two, I thought I was gonna have to lay his ass to rest, too. I pointed the gun at him and kept my finger poised inside the trigger guard.

"Grrrrrrrr!" He bared his teeth.

I bared mine, too. I was a split second away from turning that muhfucka into a throw rug when Big Nasty's voice boomed from across the room.

"Sit, boy! Sit!"

Lil' Nasty obeyed him instantly. But he kept his eyes trained on me and he continued growling under his breath. His chest heaved up and down.

I looked that killer canine in the eye and spoke to him like he was a human being. "I ain't your next meal, yo. But if you leap, I'ma damn sure make you mine."

"Lil Nasty, c'mere!" commanded Big Nasty.

The dog pounced on all fours and went and sat at his master's feet. I let the banger fall to my side. As I lifted my gaze, my eyes met Big Nasty's. From the look on his face, I could tell he was relieved that he hadn't had to scrape his dog up off of the floor and then decide if it was worth catching beef with me about it.

From less than six feet away, my face remained hard as granite. Big Nasty was my *peeps,* and I knew he loved that dog more than anything in this world, but I would bury both of them if push came to shove.

My look must've conveyed my thoughts because Big Nasty nodded his head up and down. "What's understood don't need to be said," he spoke in a tone of respect.

"Facts." I dismissed any tension I might've expected him to retain and then I looked around the room at my peoples. When my eyes settled on my brother, the orchestrator of this clown ass shit, I erupted. "You think it's a time to play, yo? You think this shit is fun and muhfuckin' games?"

"Yo, calm the fuck down! Why you buggin'? CJ and Rah is dead. Those other niggaz ain't shit to worry about." Man Dog picked up a bottle of Patron, put it to his mouth and turned it up. When he let it down, he wiped his mouth with the back of his hand and loudly proclaimed, "Fuck those bitch ass niggaz. Let's turn up!"

Scowling, I took four long strides over to him and slapped the bottle out of his hand. "Get back on point! What the fuck is your problem?"

"Nah, what's yo' problem, B?" He reached out and shoved me. I stumbled back and fell over the table behind me.

When I hopped to my feet, I was breathing flames. "Everybody leave! Right now!" I pointed toward the door.

There was no protest. One behind the other, they filed out. Big Nasty was the last to leave. With a firm grip on Lil Nasty's collar, he walked up to me and threw his free arm around my shoulders. "One love, nephew. To the grave. Nothing and no one will ever come between us. No matter what."

"One." I echoed him.

He let his arm fall from around my shoulder and turned from me to Man Dog. He looked at him and he just shook his head.

"It's whatever, yo!" Man Dog snarled.

Big Nasty let the snide remark bounce off of his massive chest. "Y'all work it out. Blood is thicker than anything," he said before walking out of the door.

As soon as I heard the front door close, I stepped up in my brother's grill. Before I could check his ass, I caught a glimpse of his bitch posted up on the couch as if my orders didn't apply to her.

"Yo, ma, you hard of hearing?" I spat.

"No, I'm not. And I mean no disrespect, Nard, but I move on my man's command. No one else's." Lemora got up, walked over to Man Dog and wrapped her arm around his waist.

Her loyalty was admirable, but she had the game fucked up. And I was about to teach her a lesson about defying the *true* Boss.

Still gripping the gun, I raised my arm and pointed the banger at her head. "When I say bounce, you muhfuckin' bounce!"

"Lil' bruh, hold the fuck up!" Man Dog hopped in front of her, shielding her from the heat I was about to send her way.

"That bitch better step then or I'ma fuck up that weave she rocking."

"Why I gotta be a bitch?" Lemora bucked up.

"Would you rather be a *dead* bitch?" I spat.

"Yo, ma, c'mere!" Man Dog cut back in. He grabbed his girl by the arm before she could say something that would get her wig split, and pulled her toward the door. "Go home! I'll fall through there later." I heard him say as he let her out.

Lemora uttered something unintelligible and then I heard the door slam loudly behind her.

Yeah, bitch, be gone!

Now it was time to put my brother back in place. *Fuckin' trying me!* I bristled inside as I felt the four-pound weight of the Nine still in my hand.

Ca$h

CHAPTER
7
Nard

Man Dog came storming back in the room like he was ready to punch me in my shit or something. He stepped over the dead pit bull and got all up in my piece.

"Nigga, have you lost your goddam mind?" he steamed.

"Nah, big bruh." I shook my head from side to side and kept my voice even keeled. "But apparently, you have."

"Fuck is you talking about?" His tone was mad confrontational and I wasn't feeling that shit at all. Yeah, he was the oldest but I was the shot-caller. I shouldn't have had to remind him of that but I didn't hesitate to.

With the gun still down at my side, in a non-threatening manner, I deepened my voice to convey the seriousness of my statement. "Man, you know what the fuck I'm talking about. You challenged my authority in front of others. And you put your muhfuckin' hands on me! Don't ever do that shit again."

"What? You think you're talking to Quent and 'em or one of our workers?"

"Not our workers, bruh. *My workers*. Don't get it fucked up."

"Nah, son, you got things fucked up. You didn't build this shit on your own," he contested.

"Nigga, I'm not trying to hear all that noise. You heard what the fuck I said. Do that shit again and I'm going to treat you like we didn't come out of the same womb." I pointed my finger in his face.

Man Dog slapped my hand down. "Lil' ass nigga, I practically raised your ass! Don't get power struck. I'll whoop your ass like you're still that punk ass lil' boy I had to protect when muhfuckaz used you take your candy."

"Ha! Ain't a nigga alive ever took a goddam thing from me." His memory must've been skewed from too much Patron and weed. Growing up, I had never needed his protection and I didn't need it now. "I came out mama's womb a beast. So, you can dead that lame shit you're talking. Fall your ass back in line or get cut the fuck off."

Whop!

In a flash, Man Dog's fist collided with my jaw. "You're a beast, huh? Bring that ass then, nigga. Show me you're a beast."

I staggered back a step and tasted the blood that ran into my mouth from my busted lip. Without even giving it a second thought, I raised my arm a few inches, aimed the ratchet at my brother's leg and squeezed the trigger.

Boom!

The sudden impact of the bullet knocked him off of his feet.

"Aww shit!" Man Dog grabbed his leg and winced in pain.

"If I bleed, you bleed." I looked down at him with regret but with no remorse. "Test me again and the next bullet is going up top."

"Fuck you, Nard!" he spat.

"I'ma pretend I didn't hear that. Because if I thought you meant it, I would have to do something that would really hurt mama. I love you, bruh, but you better get your mind right. And while you're at it, train your bitch or I'll train her for you."

He looked up at me with cold eyes. "Fuck you! I'm going to make you pay for this!"

Had Man Dog been anyone else but blood those threats would've gotten him fitted for a coffin. But I knew he was talking out of anger and hurt. I was hurt, too, because things never should've came to this.

Deep down I wanted to apologize but I refused to show weakness, even to my own flesh and blood.

"I warned you not to test me again." I shoved the banger down in my waistband, took my shirt off and tied it around his leg to staunch the bleeding. "Come on, man, let me help you up and take you to the ER."

"Get the fuck off of me! Nigga, let me bleed to death. Ain't no love!"

His words caused a bolt of pain to shoot through my heart. We hadn't even been on top 24 hours yet, and the infighting that usually brought down a squad had already begun. It was not what I envisioned the day being like.

I closed my eyes and let out a long, hard sigh. When I opened them, Big Nasty was standing in the doorway of the room with his gun out.

"Something told me to come back and make sure everything was a'ight, boss man. I heard a gun clap, and that's why I ran in here without ringing the doorbell," he explained as he walked over to us.

"It's all good." My voice was strained with pent up emotion. I had clapped my own fam. *You see what the game does to muhfuckaz?* The little bit of conscience I had tugged at me.

Big Nasty tucked his gun and then he spoke with a gentleness that told me he understood the conflict I felt over what I had done.

"Boss man, call somebody to clean up around here. I'm going to take Man Dog to the hospital. Luckily, it don't look too bad." He had squatted down to examine my brother's wound.

"Okay. And hit me up as soon as they tell you something."

"I will." He easily picked Man Dog up.

My brother glared at me with tears in his eyes. I didn't know what to say, so I just placed a hand on his shoulder.

He looked down at my hand like it belonged to Lucifer. And when he looked up and our eyes met, I prayed to God that what I saw in my brother's eyes would lessen with time.

The last thing I wanted was to make our mother have to bury one of us and then have to forgive the other one.

CHAPTER
8
Nard

I walked behind Big Nasty as he carried Man Dog outside and laid him in the backseat of his truck. On the inside, I was a ball of emotions but I didn't shed a tear.

"No matter what you think, I love you, my nigga," I said to Man Dog before Big Nasty closed the car door.

It crushed my heart when Man Dog turned his head away from me.

Seeing the hurt on my face. Big Nasty said, "He'll get over it. Just give it time."

"I hope you're right." We dapped each other and then I watched him climb behind the wheel of his Durango. In the front passenger seat sat Lil' Nasty. He leaned over and licked Big Nasty's face.

That's the type of loyalty I'm going to need all of my people to have. No exceptions. But after what had just happened between me and Man Dog, *would he ever have undying love for me again?* I wondered.

Blood is thicker than water. My top goon's words reverberated in my mind. I couldn't bank on that, though. I had been hearing that all of my life, and yet, I knew boo coo muhfuckaz who had crossed a family member in the most treacherous ways.

As I stood there with my hands shoved down in my pockets, and my shoulders slumped, watching Big Nasty back out of my driveway and drive off, I promised myself I would do everything in my power to repair my relationship with my brother.

Don't let the money and power change you. I wouldn't. I just hoped for their sake, my mans didn't let it change them either.

When the Durango turned the corner and disappeared from sight, I headed back inside. The short walk up to my door felt like a million-mile walk. Stepping back into my living room, I stopped and stared down at the dead pit bull and the blood that soaked my hardwood floor. All of a sudden, my anger resurfaced.

I trekked up to my bedroom and grabbed my cell phone from the table by the bed. As I dialed Quent number and waited for him to answer, I managed to calm myself down. *A boss is never a slave to his emotions.*

"Whud up, fam?" Quent answered.

"Where you at?" I asked calmly

"On my way back to The Bricks?"

"What about Zakee?"

"He right here rolling with me. Why? You need us to handle something?"

"Yeah, come back to the house."

"Copy that."

"A'ight. One."

I hung up and peeled off my blood smeared clothes. After my second shower of the day, I felt more relaxed and my mind was clearer. Man Dog would be alright and things would quickly get back to how they had been before today. I had to believe that.

Twenty minutes after I changed into some fresh gear, Quent and Zakee arrived. I instructed them to clean my living room and to get rid of the dead dog.

"I need the floor to be spotless," I said.

"We got you, fam," promised Zakee.

"Cool. Make sure y'all lock up when you leave."

I went outside and hopped in one of my whips, headed to my plug's house. Man Dog was still on my mind and turning on music didn't do much to change that. Rick Ross was rapping about the some of the same shit we was living. His lyrics rang hollow to me, though. Because if he was living it, he wouldn't put it on wax.

Fronting ass muhfucka. I changed the music to R&B and let it take my mind off of the streets until I pulled into my connect's driveway and killed the engine.

As I stepped out of my ride, I glanced up at the graying sky. Soon, evening would surrender to nightfall. I wondered how long it would be before CJ's and Rah's bodies were discovered. By morning, probably, and the streets would know whose hands they had been killed by.

I smiled wide as I ducked my head against the cold, brisk wind and walked up on the porch and rang the doorbell. David X hadn't been expecting me because I rarely went to his house. So, when he opened the door, a look of puzzlement was written across his face.

"Is everything okay?" he asked in a whisper.

"Things are better than okay." I smiled triumphantly.

He stepped to the side and invited me in. "Keep your voice down, my daughter is in the bedroom resting," he said in a hushed tone as he led me into the study and closed the door behind us.

I removed my hoodie from over my head and took a seat on a large leather couch that faced the door. Staring at me was a framed photo of David X posed with several civic leaders and other influential Blacks. I leaned back with my arms thrown across the top of the sofa and studied the various Islamic artifacts on the walls. A large picture of David X speaking at a conference sat on the corner of his desk.

Little did his constituents know, The Good Minister was knee deep in the game. In the public's eye, he fed the poor free meals but behind the scenes, he helped serve them crack. I didn't have a problem with him, though, because he was helping to make me rich.

He took a seat behind the large mahogany desk and steepled his hands under his chin. "So, tell me, what's so urgent that you have to come to my home uninvited? I thought we had an…"

"Never mind all of that," I cut him off. "I took care of our problem. Both of them. And I didn't want to deliver that news to you over the phone."

David X lifted an eyebrow. "Both of them?" he asked.

"Yeah, Rah *and* CJ. They're both dead. Deceased."

"You're bullshittin' me." He unsteepled his hands and leaned forward on his elbows. "How did you get to CJ?"

"I used his weakness against him." I smiled cleverly.

Grinning, David X leaned back in his chair. "Give me details."

I stood up and re-enacted everything that happened. I was real animated as I described CJ blowing his own brains out.

David X listened without comment until I was finished. "That was a boss move. Any fool with a weapon can murder a man, but to make him commit suicide—that's deep, my brother," he complimented.

"I told you *you* could believe in me." I stopped pacing back and forth.

David X nodded his head in acknowledgement of my gangsta.

However, when I described what we did to Rah, he seemed a bit conflicted. I knew it was because, like himself, Rah was Muslim. But David X had to have known we was gonna kill

Rah when he set him up for us to kidnap him. "We couldn't let him live," I said.

"Yeah, I know. You did what you had to do." He took a deep breath and then let it out slowly.

"Ain't no mercy in this shit. You know that. But look at it this way, we're about to get stupid rich. With CJ out of the way, we'll have The Bricks on lock. This is what you wanted," I reminded him. "We've been preparing for this day ever since you started fucking with me. CJ just gave me a reason to murk his ass sooner rather than later, nah mean."

"Yeah, I know what you mean."

"Remember when we first hooked up a year ago, you told me if I was going to be in the game, go for it all. *'Go hard and you won't have to do it for long,'* that's what you told me, right?"

"True indeed, black man," he reflected.

"Well, did I go hard enough for you?"

"You did," he acknowledged with pride. "But what about his remaining crew?"

I weighed his question for a minute before answering. With their *daddy* and his right-hand man gone, the others lacked the sophistication to rebuild their empire. But that would not stop them from busting their guns at us in retaliation. So, I was not going to underestimate them by expecting them to just fade to black.

"A living enemy is still a dangerous one, no matter how wounded they may be. I won't sleep good at night until every last one of CJ's crew is dead," I said after thinking it over.

"Indeed, my young brother. No wiser words have ever been spoken."

Just then, there was a light knock on the door followed by a very soft voice. "Daddy, are you in there?" Before he could reply, the door swung open and a little, cute, sexy babe stepped into the room wearing an air of innocence that piqued my interest. After the shit Tamika pulled, I was through fuckin' with hood bitches.

The next woman I claim as mine will have to be different. I had promised myself. Well, on first impression this cutie definitely fit the bill.

Me and baby girl's eyes met and I felt an instant attraction between us. After soaking in her downstated beauty, I respectfully lowered my gaze. I didn't want my plug to think I was lusting over his daughter. But for some reason I couldn't resist looking up at her and staring.

"Kenisha, I have a visitor. Please give me a moment, Princess." His transformation was instant.

"Oh, I'm sorry," Kenisha apologized. She must've felt my eyes on her because she turned her head and stared at me.

I nodded my head as a way of speaking.

"Hello," she said politely but her gaze seemed to carry a bit of suspicion.

She looked at me like she had seen me before. Shorty was vaguely familiar to me, but I couldn't place her face.

I tried not to stare at her plump little ass as she turned and left out of the room, closing the door quietly behind her. The instant she was gone, David X came from behind his desk and put an arm around my shoulder. "I want you to relax for a few days and let's see how much heat is on the streets. I'm going to triple up on the shipment. Everything is aligned for you to be the new King of Newark. Let's not blow it."

"Never that." I assured him.

"And don't come to my house again unless I summon you here. We don't want to be seen in each other's company."

"Understood."

As I left out of David X's crib, I could've sworn I saw shorty peeking out of the curtains of one of the bedroom windows.

I'm sure we'll meet again somewhere, baby girl, I thought as I climbed in my whip and mashed out.

Ca$h

CHAPTER
9
Kenisha

I didn't let the blinds close until his taillights faded out of sight. *Hmm. I know I've seen him somewhere before.* I jogged my memory for a clue as to where that could've possibly been, but nothing came to mind. I knew for sure that a nigga with the aura I'd felt coming off of him wasn't a part of my usual circle. *Nope, can't be. I probably met him while hanging out with Jada*, I guessed.

My cousin knew all the big ballers and lil' daddy definitely had the air of a nigga that got major cake in the streets. The feeling that came over me when our eyes met was the same breathless feeling I got the first time I met CJ. I was stuck on stupid over his trifling, cold-hearted ass before he spat the first syllable at me.

But why would a street dude be here talking to Daddy? I wondered. My father was many years removed from that lifestyle. The only explanation I could come up with was that Daddy must've been trying to introduce Islam to him to get him out of the streets.

"Good luck with that," I said out loud and with sarcasm. In the short time I had been around CJ, I had concluded that men like them were married to the streets and nothing short of a fatality could get them to walk away.

Several of CJ's boys had been killed since we hooked up. Yet the rest of them, including CJ, was still out there living reckless. *Who was I to judge them, though?* Shit, I was super attracted to those thuggish muthafuckaz. I just regretted getting pregnant by the most heartless one of them all.

Sighing over my predicament, I stepped away from the window and laid back on the bed. My mind flashed back to several nights ago when I had ran into CJ and his bitch at the club. Full of liquor, I confronted that black fucka only to get treated like I was just a basic bitch, and not the sweet young girl who had given him my precious virginity.

"Why the fuck you here?" he snapped.

"Why you not answering my calls?" Water formed in the corners of my eyes.

"Look, you know what it is!" His tone was dismissive.

"No, I don't. Why don't you tell me?" I snarled.

"I'm chillin' with my girl and my fam." He looked over at the ho like she was better than me. "I'll call you when I have time," he continued without even turning back to look me in the face. And then he hurled one final insult. "Now take your ass home."

That shit crushed my heart and I lost all control. Tears poured down my cheeks and my body shook with anger. I raised my drink and tossed it in his smug ass face. "You heartless muthafucka!" I hissed. "I hope you die in the streets."

I tried to hurt him like he was hurting me. But CJ's heart was made of ice. He just looked at me and chuckled and then coolly wiped the drink off of his face with his hand. Beside him, his bird ass bitch went slap off.

"Oh, no the fuck you didn't!" She jumped in my face and got popped right in her goddam mouth. And before long we were tearing each other to pieces.

CJ's boy, Raheeem, finally pulled me and the bitch apart and convinced me to let him take me home.

"Shorty, this isn't a good look. You can't let no man get you all twisted like this," he said as he listened to my cry in the passenger seat.

I told him that it was deeper than he knew. But when he asked me to explain, I just kept quiet. No one besides myself knew that I was pregnant with CJ's child.

After that night, slowly the pain I felt and the tears that stained my pillow, turned into hate. I laid in bed thinking of ways to make CJ suffer for discarding me like I was nothing.

I hate you! I hate you! I hate you! I screamed silently as I found myself crying now.

I didn't want Daddy to hear me so I turned onto my stomach and pressed my face down into the pillow. I thought about the baby growing inside of me. It would be a constant reminder of my heartbreak but I would love it with all of my heart. And in turn, the baby would love me. Much more than its daddy ever had.

With so many thoughts, fears and regrets running through my head, I drifted off to sleep.

Sometime later, I was awakened by my cousin Jada's ringtone.

I let the first, second and third calls from her go to voicemail. But when she called back a forth time, I reached over on the table, picked up my phone and answered. "Jada, what is it?" My aggravation was thick.

"Gurl, have you heard?"

"Heard what?"

"About CJ," she replied.

"Fuck CJ! Whatever it is, I don't even care. I'm going back to sleep. Goodbye."

"No wait! Bitch, you're not understanding me. They found that nigga dead with his whole head blown off! And Rah is barely alive."

I gasped. "Jada, are you sure? CJ is dead?"

"Yep. It's been all over the news."

"Oh, my God!" The phone slipped from my hand and fell to the floor.

I hope you die in the streets. Those were my last words to him. And now they had come true. A tidal wave of guilt and regret washed up on me in a *whoosh*. I felt a sharp pain in my belly. CJ's child must've been wailing inside of me; crying for the father they would never get to know.

Suddenly, my breath felt restricted in my chest. I rolled onto my side and brought my knees up to my chest as I clutched my stomach with both hands. I remained in the fetal position until the pain subsided and my breathing returned to relative normal.

Somehow, I found the strength to pull myself up on my feet. I didn't even know that I was crying until I looked around the bedroom for the television remote and had to look through blurred vision.

I wiped the tears with both hands and finally located the remote on the floor next to my phone. When I bent done to retrieve it, I heard Jada's raised voice belting through the phone.

"Cuz, are you okay over there? Say something! Girl, let me know you're okay!"

I ignored her and turned on the TV. As soon as it came into focus, I went straight to the local news. I sat there staring at the screen, and shaking, for what seemed like a long time. And then, CJ's and Raheem's pictures came on the screen.

In a solemn voice, the newscaster reported on the incident. My heart beat at a rapid pace, as I listened to his every word. Rah's picture faded from the frame that was to the left of the reporter, leaving only the image of CJ. It looked like an old police mugshot and his eyes seemed to be staring at me.

The next words out of the newsman's mouth weakened my knees. "Cam'ron Jefferies was pronounced dead on the scene," he confirmed.

"Noooo!" I fainted.

***

"Baby, wake up!" Daddy's voice caused my eyes to flutter open. He held a wet face cloth pressed against my forehead and his strong arms cradled me like they did when I was a child. "What happened, Kenisha? I heard a loud noise and when I ran in here you were passed out on the floor. Are you okay?"

"No, Daddy, he's dead — he's really dead. I told him I hoped he die in the streets, and now it's come true. Oh, God!" I reached up and wrapped my arms around his neck, and cried against his chest.

My father just held me and let my cry until my deep sobs became sniffles. "Kenisha, who's dead?" He asked softly as he lifted me up and gently laid me on the bed.

I wanted to just blurt out, *The father of the child I'm carrying,* but I didn't want to cause Daddy to have a sudden heart attack. So, I began at the beginning when I first met CJ at the mall that day.

Daddy listened without interruption. When I was finished telling my story, including the news that I was pregnant, I could hardly look him in the face. I was so ashamed of myself for falling for a nigga who never gave a fuck about me. I was more ashamed that I had gotten pregnant and now this baby would be a statistic — another fatherless child.

"Daddy, are you mad at me?" I stared at the floor.

"No, princess. I'm not mad but I am disappointed." He sighed heavily as he ran a weary hand down his face.

"I'm sorry." I broke down in sobs again.

"It's okay, Kenisha. But you haven't told me who this dude is or how he got killed."

"His name is Cam'ron but they called him CJ. He was from The Bricks. The guy, Raheem, who brought me home the other night is his best friend. On the news, they said CJ was pronounced dead on the scene and Raheem is in the hospital, barely clinging on to life."

I was expecting a response from my father but all I got was silence. When I looked up his face was ashen. *All of this must be too much for him.* I thought. I was his little, innocent princess. His heart had to be shattered to pieces.

"Daddy, I'm sorry." My voice cracked.

After another long moment of silence and several deep, deep breaths, he said, "It's okay, Kenisha. Lay down and get some rest. We'll talk more later." I had never heard him sound so hurt.

He walked out of my bedroom and pulled the door up behind him. I stared up at the ceiling and tears began pouring down the sides of my face. I knew I had let him down, and that bothered me. But Jada's description of what happened to CJ bothered me even more.

They found that nigga dead with his whole head blown off!

I had loved him and I had hated him, but he didn't deserve that.

I hope whoever did that to him die a death a thousand times worse, I said to myself.

And poor, poor Rah. He was so sweet and kind. *Lord, please, don't let him die, too,* I prayed.

I laid there a bit longer, crying, grieving and feeling awful for what I had wished upon CJ. The tears seemed to flow forever. Finally, I climbed out of bed and went to the bathroom to wash my face. Afterwards, I went to find Daddy to apologize to him again.

When I reached his study room, I heard him talking to someone in a raised tone. He looked up and saw me standing there through the cracked door. He sat the phone down in a hurry and stood up from his desk.

I pushed the door open wider and went inside. That's when I saw a half empty bottle of Jim Beam in front of him. Drinking was something I hadn't seen him do in more than ten years. It went against his Islamic faith, and I wondered why he even had liquor in the house.

Now probably wasn't the best time to bring up the subject but I wanted to let him know that, in spite of everything, I wasn't going to throw my life away. I would still make him proud of me. But when I opened my mouth to speak, he put up his hand and silenced me.

"Not now, princess. Please, sweetheart, let's talk later."

"Okay." I turned around and hurried out of the room before he saw me break down in tears again.

I was halfway back to my room when I decided to go back in there and insist that he allow me to tell him my plans moving forward. I needed to talk to him about it now to ease his mind from the stress I was causing him.

As I approached the study the second time, I heard Daddy bark angrily, "I want that shit handled ASAP! You fucked up now finish it!"

Ca$h

CHAPTER
10
Rah

I could hear faint voices all around me, but I couldn't make out who they belonged to. The last thing I recalled was hearing the wail of an ambulance and then being lifted off of the ground and placed on a stretcher. I would never forget the muthafuckaz who had done this to me. Nard and them was gonna pay in the most gruesome way.

Anger surged from the top of my head to the bottom of my feet. Leaving me alive was gonna cost every one of them their life. And for what they did to CJ...

I couldn't even complete my thought. It felt like all of the oxygen left my lungs. When I tried to gulp in some air, my chest burned. I breathed in the unmistakable smell of a hospital and heard the soft beep of what I guessed was a heart machine.

Slowly, I strained to open my eyes, but my left eye felt swollen shut and I was too weak to open the right one. I wanted to believe I was dreaming because the memory that played in my mind hurt much more than the pain that was wrecking my entire body. But I knew it wasn't a dream. My homie, my A1, was gone.

I felt a tear trickle from the corner of my eye and slide down my face. It was followed by another and then another. I tried to reach up and wipe them away as the scene of CJ putting the gun in his mouth and pulling the trigger flashed in my mind, but I couldn't lift my arms. I tasted salty tears in my mouth and felt the immense pain in my heart.

Without CJ, nothing would ever be the same. From kindergarten 'til the very end, I had been my brother's keeper and he had been mine. No matter what bullshit tried to come between us we brushed it off and remained Aces through it all. Loyal to one another 'til the end. *Not even death would break our bond,* I vowed to myself.

"I love you, my brother. You gave your life for me and I'ma do the same for you. Whether it's life in the pen or lying face up in a box. But before I go, I'ma settle all scores. Every one of your enemies are gonna die by my hands. Every muthafuckin' one of them, son! Word!"

Tears burned my eyes before they slid down my cheeks. I turned my head a fraction of an inch to the side and a sharp pain shot straight to my brain. My face and lips felt swollen and my neck ached terribly. But I could feel myself coming out of the groggy haze I was in. The voices in the room became clearer and I strained my ears to listen.

"The bullets went straight through his legs without hitting any bones. However, one of the gunshots did strike an artery in his left leg causing a severe loss of blood. As a result, we had to give him an emergency blood transfusion. Besides that, he has suffered other injuries, none of which are life threatening by themselves, but together they are cause for concern. His condition is still critical but stable. I'll allow you to visit with him for a very brief while, but he'll need his rest."

"Okay, Doc."

Recognizing Eric's voice, I tried to open my eyes and sit up. But again, my body would not cooperate. I felt him place his hand on my shoulder. "Yo, son, I'm right here," he said.

I managed to part my lips but nothing would come out.

"Don't try to talk, B. What's understood don't need to be said. We're about to wild out, yo." His voice was low but strong.

"*CJ?*" The question was in my mind and heart, but I couldn't tell if it was audible.

"Rest, fam. We'll talk 'bout dat."

"CJ!" I demanded to know what I already knew. I just needed to hear it confirmed.

Eric let out a deep sigh that answered my question without him having to utter the words. Tears began to pour from my eyes and I let out a pained cry.

"Sir, I'm going to have to ask you to leave now. You're upsetting the patient and that is not good for him." The nurse's tone was stern, but not as firm as Eric's.

"Don't touch me! This is my people and I would never hurt him. I'll leave in a second and let him rest, but don't you ever put your hands on me again," he warned.

The nurse gasped and then she walked off. "Rest up, my nigga, and get well. All our mans and nem are right outside praying for you, son. Trust, we're gonna hold things down until you recover. I love you, Rah. No homo." He squeezed my arm gently.

I heard the soft patter of his footsteps fade as he left the room. Knowing my peeps like I did, I knew somebody was going to feel their rage.

"Sir, I'm going to give you something for the pain." The voice that temporarily interrupted my thoughts was kind and gentle, and her touch was even softer.

Every inch of my body ached. But it was my heart that was most crushed. Nothing would ever be the same without CJ. And Newark would not be the same once I recovered from my injuries. Muthafuckaz had ripped my heart out of my chest. So, now they were about to feel the wrath of a good nigga gone bad.

I tried to walk straight and show respect to every man's hustle. But I guess y'all mistook my humility for weakness. I guess y'all pussy ass niggaz don't realize what happens when you fuck with a silent killa! Is this really what the fuck y'all want?

I'm taking my kufi off and I'm going against everything that Islam stands for besides a Jahid! Y'all are about to get a war that The Bricks won't ever forget! When you killed my nigga, you killed the old me! Say goodbye to the nice guy!

Now anybody can get it! Any fuckin' body! By the time I sit my banger down, the bodies are gonna be stacked so high they're gonna have to declare a state of emergency around this bitch!

David X, I want your head muthafucka! You're not no minister. You're not a Muslim. You're a bitch ass, snake bastard, hiding behind Islam. You ride with Nard and them? Okay! Okay, Ock! Now you're going to die with them. My thoughts were straight sinister.

I felt my face tightening into a scowl as the events of the night I took Kenisha home came back to me in perfect clarity. I had tried to protect her, and her pops ended up selling me out. And all the while Nard held me hostage, I kept playing that shit over and over in my mind until it became clear to me.

When David X went back into the bedroom, that's when he made the call. And he kept me talking long enough for Nard to get there.

The blood of a Muslim was said to be sacred. But mine had mattered none to him. So, now it was an eye for an eye.

Minister David X, I'm going to murder you like the dog muthafucka you are, yo!

As the Demoral flowed from the IV down into my veins, numbing my pain and making me drowsy, I plotted the most vicious murders imaginable. I didn't give a fuck who got caught up in the cross fire. If they weren't with me, they were against me. My mind was made up—no mercy!

Now I'ma show the world why they call this place Dirty Jersey.

CHAPTER
11
Eric

"They tortured Rah, yo. Fucked him up bad. Son's eye is blue/black and his head is mad swole. But we gotta thank The Most High for wrapping His arms around a thug." Standing in the center of the small circle formed by my mans, I pointed my finger toward the sky.

"What the doctors saying?" asked Snoop.

"He's in critical condition. Bruh lost a lot of blood. They shot him several times and he has some other injuries. The doctors give him a 50/50 chance, but you know Rah is cut from a different cloth. He was tryna talk so I know son gon' make it," I said.

"And if he knows what happened to CJ..." Premo didn't finish his sentence. He lowered his head as if the words were too painful to speak.

"Rah knows." Shabazz cut in. Hours had passed since we first met up with him, but I allowed him to remain around since he had practically saved Rah's life, and he appeared sincere about helping us get revenge.

I nodded in agreement. "That's why I feel my nigga gonna pull through. He loved CJ like a blood brother. There's no way he's gonna close his eyes for good without making this whole city shudder, nah mean. And that's the mission we should all be on," I said as we huddled together outside of the ICU.

"I'm ready, yo," said Snoop.

"You already know my get down," added Premo.

We kept our voices low so that our conversation wasn't overheard. I looked at Legend whose eyes were in the shape of slits. There was no need to say anything to him, murder was always foremost on his mind.

After giving it a moment of thought, I turned to Shabazz. "Blood, this ain't your war, so you don't have to get involved. We appreciate what you did. I can give you some guap and…"

"Save dat, son," he cut me off. "I'ma ride because I always admired your brother. Just put me on when all of this is over."

"The ride might get bumpy, my nigga. We got guns, they got guns. Are you built for that?" I questioned.

Shabazz looked at me as if the question was an insult. "I'ma let my actions speak for me," he replied with a face of stone.

I nodded my head in respect. So far, I liked what I had seen in him. If he could live up to what he was saying, he would be a real asset. It was about to become beast season and there was no place for fake niggaz on the team.

Glancing over Shabazz' shoulders, I saw the two toy cops the hospital had patrolling the floor. There was no way I was gonna count on those clowns to protect Rah. "Yo, Premo, you stay here and guard the room in case those niggaz try some cruddy shit. You never know, muhfuckaz will sell out their own mama for a grip."

"Fuck that, yo! I wanna be on the front line," he protested. "Let Legend stay here and we'll handle the streets. He's not from The Bricks no way."

"Fuck that mean? Shawdy, you questioning my gangsta?" Legend stepped in his face. "You better watch what the fuck come out of your mouth. I lost my personal homie up here," he reminded us, referring to DaQuan. "And I might not have known CJ as long as you, but that was my nigga, too. Not to mention, what those niggaz did to Rah. I'ma make 'em pay for that with their lives."

"I feel you, fam," Premo conceded. "Fuck it, y'all pull up on those bitch made niggaz and lay them on their backs. I'll stay here with Rah. I wish a fuck nigga would run up in here on some dumb shit!"

Just like that, the disagreement between them was diffused. I was glad to see that because the last thing we needed was to start beefing with each other.

"So, it's settled. We're gonna roll out. Premo, you stay back and hold things down," I said. Him and Legend dapped each other up.

"Hold it down, bruh. Don't let nothin' else happen to my G. If he wakes up, let him know we're riding for him. And if any nigga tries to pull a stunt, you light this muhfucka up." Legend held his stare.

"Son, you already know," replied Premo.

"Let's bounce." I headed off and my niggaz followed.

Inside the elevator, me, Snoop, Legend and Shabazz remained quiet as the car descended to the bottom floor. I didn't know what thoughts consumed their minds, but the only thing on mine was bloodshed. Nard had to pay, and he had to pay tonight!

As luck would have it, I encountered Cujo out in the parking lot. He cut me off on the way to my ride and guided me away from the rest of the crew.

As soon as he opened his mouth to speak, I cut him off. "I'm not trying to hear nothing about peace. So, if you're about to tell me to chill, you can miss me with that shit."

"I'm not about to tell you to chill. I'm about to tell you where Nard's father and stepmother lives."

Instantly, the scowl left my face. I leaned in and listened attentively as he gave me every little detail. When he was finished, I asked, "Can we touch them tonight?"

He answered by nodding his head up and down. "I'll make sure that there's no squad cars in the area. Whatever mess you leave behind, my boys will clean it up. We'll put word out to the news agencies that the old man was involved with drugs and so forth."

"A'ight." I turned to go and rejoin my mans.

"Eric!" Cujo called out before I walked away.

"Yeah?" I stepped back over to where he stood.

He looked me dead in the eye and said, "Don't ever bite the hand that feeds you."

"And you said that to say what?" I held his stare for a few seconds and then I turned and walked off. Whatever it was he was trying to convey to me didn't mean shit at the moment. The only thing on my mind was slaying Nard's pop and 'em, and making him feel my pain.

***

Hours later, we were parked outside of a white and brown two-story house that sat on the far end of a corner street. Their truck in the driveway matched the description that Cujo had provided.

The lights inside the house were already out and the street was quiet and poorly lit. The moon casted a faint light over the area but not enough to deter us from our mission.

As we got ready to exit the vehicle, I passed Shabazz one of the extra ratchets I had brought along. He accepted it and immediately checked the clip to make sure it was loaded.

"You sure you wanna rock with this? Because once we go up in this house and do what we're about to do, there's no turning back." I studied his face for the slightest sign of hesitancy, but I saw none.

"You don't have to worry, yo. With me it's blood in and blood out," he said with conviction.

I watched him slam the clip back in to the Glock like a pro. That made me know that he had handled a tool before, and it gave me a measure of confidence that he wouldn't wig out when we started dome calling those inside of the house.

If I'm wrong, I'ma leave him slumped right beside them, I told myself as the four of us exited the vehicle.

Snoop slid up on me before we reached the house. "Son, you sure we can trust this nigga?" he whispered.

"If we can't, his mama will have to bury him." I said in a normal tone. It didn't matter if Shabazz overheard me because I meant that shit. As long as he was official, he didn't have nothing to worry about. "You and Legend go to the back. Me and Shabazz going in through the front," I directed Snoop. "When you hear us kick in the door, you do the same."

"Copy."

I allowed them time to get in place. When I figured they were at the back door, I slipped my banger off of my waist and gripped it with both hands. "At the count of three," I said, lifting one of my Timbs off of the ground.

"Let's do it." Shabazz raised his foot too.

"One. Two. Three."

Wham! The door slammed inward. I paused to see if an alarm would go off. When there was no sound, I entered with a single purpose—find and murk everything inside.

The downstairs was dark and quiet. Being that it was close to midnight, I expected the couple to be upstairs in bed, but it surprised me that no one had come running down to investigate the loud noise. Seconds later, I heard the backdoor come crashing in. In the blink of an eye, Snoop and Legend was at our sides.

I led the way as we found the stairs and hurried up them. When we reached the top, I saw a soft beam of light coming from the first bedroom on our left. I nodded for Shabazz to follow me inside. Snoop and Legend went to check the other rooms.

With Shabazz closely behind me, I eased the bedroom door open and stepped inside. As I walked softly toward the bed, I saw a man and a woman cuddled together in sleep. Several empty bottles of wine sat on the nightstand, which explained why the hadn't heard the noise.

I hoped their drunk asses had fucked good before they fell asleep because they wouldn't get the chance to ever do it again.

Whap!

I slapped the man across the head with my Nine. "Wake your muthafuckin' ass up!"

"Ahh! What the fuck!" He yelped as he awakened to a nightmare.

His wife eyes blinked open and she screamed. Shabazz cracked open her head with his tool. "Bitch, make another sound and I'll silence you forever." His tone was no longer mild. He grabbed a handful of her hair and shoved his gun in her mouth. "Test me!"

She sniffled back tears and looked over at me with pleading eyes that had zero effect on me. If she feared Shabazz, in just a minute, my actions would make his seem meek.

"Why are you here?" asked Nard's father.

"Your sons killed my brother. So, I'm killing everybody related to them, starting with you and your family."

His eyes grew big, as if my statement caught him by surprise. Cujo had told me he wasn't involved with Nard's street business but that wouldn't spare him my wrath.

"Now, wait one goddam minute! We don't have shit to do with what those boys do. Both of them are grown men and she's just their stepmother." He looked over at the woman apologetically.

"Tell that shit to God!" I spat as I tightened my grip on my heat, ready to cook her shit.

Before I could squeeze the trigger Snoop and Legend came in the room with a small boy in tow. He looked to be four or five years old.

Looking down into the little boy's face, I saw he had a slight resemblance to Nard and Man Dog, which had to be the by-product of all three of them having the same father.

I smiled demonically as a plan of brutal revenge popped in my mind. Nard had taken my brother from me and I would do the same to him. *An eye for an eye.* It didn't matter that the little nigga standing before me, shivering, was barely old enough to pee straight. His brothers' actions had sentenced him to a horrible death.

I looked back at the father. His eyes pleaded for mercy that my soul did not contain.

"You love your son, don't you?" My tone was purposely antagonizing.

He nodded his head up and down vigorously. Beside him, the boy's mother's face flooded with tears.

"Bitch, don't cry!" I snapped.

"Face your son's death like my brother faced his." I knew she wasn't Nard and Man Dog's mother but she was now married to their daddy, and the son she had with him shared half of their bloodline. A bloodline I was hell bent on eradicating.

In a low-pitched voice, filled with grief, I recanted CJ's encounter with Nard as Man Dog and the others held Rah hostage. I carefully repeated every single word and reaction Shabazz had described, down to when CJ pulled the trigger and blew his own brains out.

The step-mother dropped her head and muffled cries managed to escape from beneath the strip of tape over her mouth.

Whatever she was feeling in no way could compare to the pain I felt when I pulled back that white sheet at the morgue and saw what remained of CJ.

Fresh hot tears burned my face as the image lingered in my mind.

"You muthafuckas are about to feel what I'm feeling!" I said angrily.

I grabbed their young son by the collar of his pajamas shirt and shoved my banger in his mouth, forcing it to the roof. He gagged on the cold metal and tried to step back but I yanked his little ass forward.

"Do that lil' nigga!" urged Snoop.

"For CJ," added Legend.

That's all I needed to hear to let go of whatever tiny bit of mercy that may have crept in my chest.

"Revenge is a merciless bitch!" I said as I squeezed the trigger and blew out the top of lil' man's head.

He was so light in weight that I was able to hold his collar and keep his body from falling to the floor, despite the fact that a lifeless body was heavy as fuck.

With his blood all over him, I drug him over to that bed, hoisted him up and dropped him on his terrified daddy's lap.

"His blood is on Nard's hands, be sure to tell him that when you see his bitch ass in hell."

The man squirmed back and forth trying desperately to free himself from the tight restraint but his effort was useless. I aimed my gun down at his lap and fired shots into his son's torso.

Boc! Boc! Boc! Boc! Boc!

Cujo had the block secured so I was unconcerned with the noise. I just let my heat spit.

The mother's stifled cries were louder now. "Noooo! Oh God!" Her head lashed from side to side in what appeared to be a futile attempt to shake the gruesome sight of her son being killed from her mind. Tears streamed from her eyes and her breathing was labored, and heavy with pain, as she mumbled, tearfully, "Oh God! Not my baby! Oh, my Lord!"

"It's too late to call on Him, right now you're in the hands of the muthafuckin' devil, yo." My words were so cold they chapped my lips, but CJ's death had turned me heartless.

I looked to the right and saw a nigga who was more merciless than me.

Reading my wet eyes, he said, "Let me do the bitch and let that nigga watch the same way Rah had to watch someone he loved die." Legend offered.

I didn't even have to think about it.

"Do what you do, G." Before I could step aside, Legend was already pullin' his machete out of his backpack.

A minute later, I stood transfixed in that one spot as I watched him hack the woman's head off. It rolled off of the bed and thudded down to the floor. But son wasn't done yet.

"This what the fuck happens when your peoples fuck with mine!" Legend breathed heavily.

He hacked her left arm off at the shoulder and then her right one off at the elbow. By the time he moved down to her legs, her blood was everywhere. It was on the ceiling, the headboard and all over the walls. The bed was soaked in blood and her husband was drenched in it.

The horror taking place right beside him must've been too much for him to bear; he groaned loudly, his eyes widened in horror, and his entire body trembled before he suddenly passed out, with his body and his head slumped half way off of the bed.

"Snoop, sit that nigga up and slap his ass back awake. He's going to witness every second of this shit." I was emphatic about that.

Snoop followed my command. The tears Nard's father had shed must've loosened the tape over his mouth, because I clearly heard him cry. I snatched that shit off of his mouth and gritted, "Fuck is you crying for? Man up, like my brother did!"

He didn't boss up, though. Instead, he whimpered. "Lord, have mercy!" His shoulders shook as sobs escaped from his quivering lips. "What kind of animals are y'all?"

"The kind that vengeance bred!" I replied, then I turned around and looked at Shabazz.

I could tell he wasn't used to the type of bloody carnage that he was witnessing because he looked like he had seen a ghost. His face was ashen and his mouth was agape.

Behind me, Legend's machete had to be going dull. I heard numerous *thwacks* as he struggled to sever the woman's last limb. But my concern was Shabazz. He had pleaded to be down with us, but now that he had a front row seat to our vicious get down, *was he really built for this shit?* I wondered.

If he wasn't, even with Cujo's protection, he could become our downfall. He wouldn't be the first nigga whose conscious drove them to the prosecutor's office unpressured.

Bust him and leave him dead right here, yo. If you don't, you'll live to regret it, my subconscious reasoned.

My inner voice was stronger than it had ever been. I was seconds away from popping a couple of slugs in Shabazz' head when he said the one thing that saved his life.

"Yo, son, let me murk that nigga. Ain't no mercy around this bitch." Sincerity flashed in his eyes, causing me to ease my finger off of the trigger.

"Handle your business." Somewhat reluctantly, I moved aside and allowed Shabazz to prove his get down.

As Shabazz methodically approached him, the man shivered and shook, and his eyes were bulged out in terror.

"Son, please don't kill me! Have mercy on me. I'm begging you!" he sobbed pitifully. "Please! I don't wanna die!"

I was disgusted by his cowardice. If a muhfucka had just murked my peoples, I wouldn't be begging the niggaz for mercy. I would be trying to break free and take one or two of them to the grave with me. *Bitch ass nigga! Crying like a ho!*

His tears were wasted, though. Shabazz ignored all of that shit. He took three steps forward and placed the tip of his gun directly against the father's left brow.

"An eye for an eye!" he bristled.

Boom!

The man's head snapped back and then bounced forward.

Boom! Boom!

The .44 Magnum roared in Shabazz' grip, obliterating Nard's daddy's entire forehead. But Shabazz wasn't done with that nigga. It was as if he instinctively knew I was doubting his viciousness. He stared over the body and fired shot after shot into the dead man's chest. He looked zoned out. He didn't let up on the trigger until the clip was empty.

Click. Click. Click.

"It's over yo." Snoop put his hand on Shabazz' shoulder, snapping him out of that crazed zone he had slipped into.

When our eyes made contact, I saw in his that he official. I didn't utter a word. I just nodded my head at him, approvingly. One killa to another.

Ca$h

CHAPTER
12
Nard

As soon as I got word that Man Dog was going to be okay, I felt better. Big Nasty said the bullet had gone straight through without hitting any bones. *Good.* That meant he would be back on his feet soon. I knew we would need to talk and squash the bullshit that happened between us before we could move forward. He would be mad, but at the end of the day, blood was thicker than bullshit. So, I expected everything to be good with us.

Besides, there was no time to waste beefing with each other. Rah was still alive, which meant all of our attention needed to be focused on him because there was no doubt in my mind if he recovered from his injuries he was going to come at us with everything he got.

I wasn't shaking in my boots, though. Shid, his blood was no more sacred than the next nigga'z. I had fucked up by not making sure he was dead when we shot him up and let him die slowly. I blamed my swelling arrogance for that, it was something that I had to keep in check. Otherwise I was destined to fall.

With those thoughts in mind I pulled up on one of my little mans who put in work for me, from time to time.

Recognizing my whip, he came right over and leaned his head in the car.

"Sup, kid" I greeted him with some dap.

"It's your world," he said.

"Hop in, yo, I need to holla at you."

Chip walked around to the passenger side and climbed in. "Just tell me who and as long as it's not family, they can get dealt with."

"They're not family but this job won't be easy. You'll have to get up in University Hospital and finish this nigga off. He's probably in ICU."

Chip let out a low whistle. We both knew that there were metal detectors he would have to get past, but there were other ways to kill than by gun.

"You're talking about Rah?" he guessed correctly.

I nodded my head once.

"Yeah, I figured that. You know how the streets talk. When they found CJ slumped, I remembered hearing that y'all were beefing. So, I figured that was your work. Salute. I never would've thought you could outlast him."

"Who says it was me that done him in?" I smirked

"I feel you, my nigga," he chuckled.

Chip was solid. He had smoked two niggas over in Irvington for me last year. But what was already understood didn't have to be said.

"Sup, yo? You want the hit or not?" I asked.

"How much are you paying?"

"Twenty-five bands."

"Double it up and I'll shake something."

"Bet."

We shook on it before he slid out of my whip and went to rejoin his homies on the porch of their trap house. I honked my horn as I drove off, and all of them niggas threw up the peace sign.

Stress had a nigga hungry and tired as I drove back to my house. Luckily, there was some left-over pizza in the fridge. I popped it in the microwave and then fucked it up.

Later, I managed to get a few winks of sleep in on the couch. Quent and 'em had cleaned up the area where I killed the dog. Staring at the spot, I started thinking about Man Dog again.

He should've known I wouldn't approve of the way he chose to celebrate, and then he made matters worse by openly challenging me in front of the crew. Brother or not, I couldn't overlook that. Had I allowed him to test me without paying a price, the seeds for one of the other to revolt would have been planted. Still I regretted having to shoot him. Our pops had always taught us to ride for and with each other—but never against.

If one of you get into a fight, the other one better jump in or I'ma whoop his ass when he come home. I recalled him telling us when we were young. And when we fought one another, he would beat us fiercely.

Ma Duke couldn't stand to watch pops beat us but as I grew older, I understood he was teaching us to have love for each other that could not be compromised.

I knew it was just a matter of time before he found out what happened. Pops would summon me over to his house and give me a lecture. Afterwards, we would probably smoke a blunt together and then I would end up playing the Xbox with my little brother Day Day, while my stepmother fried us some fish, that would make the visit all good.

As I thought about the venom my pops would spew, I realized that it had been several months since I had seen the old man. The streets and all of its demands had monopolized my time. I made a mental note to fall through my pops crib soon. In spite of the distance that life had forged between us, I still loved my old dude.

With him and Man Dog it was different. My brother didn't fuck with Pop because he shitted on our mother. But I understood, their relationship didn't reflect what the old man felt for me. I hadn't been able to get Man Dog to see it like that, though.

If that nigga don't fuck with Mama, I don't fuck with him. Real shit! He always said.

It had been 10 years since Pop left our Mom Dukes for Angela, and neither Mama or Man Dog had gotten over it.

I thought about calling Pop up and telling him the business myself, but I decided to cross that bridge when I got to it.

I got up and moved around the house. My mind wouldn't let me chill. Every noise sounded like the patter of feet or the rustle of bodies moving. I went upstairs and loaded up my AK-47 and my AR-15 and I stood in the window all night. Because if CJ's crew knew where to find me, I was going to send their assess to the same place the nigga they looked up to was.

***

Daylight found me still posted up in my bedroom window over-watching the front. However, the persistent ringing of my phone forced me to walk over to the table by the bed.

"Sup, yo?" I answered.

"I need a favor," said David X.

"Whatever I can do, just ask."

"I'm going out of town for a week or two, and I don't feel safe leaving my daughter here. Remember, Raheem can connect me to you. I don't know if he's able to talk yet, but if he is, we have to assume that he'll send his goons to my house. I don't want Kenisha to be here when they come." He explained.

"That's no problem. You want me to come through and take her to her mom's?" I guessed.

"No! They probably know where she stays too. I got a place in Harlem, no one knows about it. Take her there, and Nard, keep an eye on my daughter. Don't let anything happen to her. She is my world."

"I got you. Give me an hour or so?" I said, checking the time on my screen.

"A'ight, any news on Raheem?"

"Not yet, but I got somebody on it."

"Okay, if you need some help let me know. I'm sure I can get one of my FOI brothers in there to see him." Said Minister David X.

"No need to do that. I'ma handle it. It's personal." I stated.

"A'ight." He understood. "One."

"One."

I hung up and took a quick shower. After getting dressed, I hurried over to David X's house to do what he wanted me to do for his daughter.

Ca$h

CHAPTER
13
Kenisha

I couldn't stop crying. Although I hated CJ for the way he did me, the truth was I loved him, too. The pain in my heart was so intense I could hardly breathe. Nothing I've ever experienced hurt so bad. The greatest loss I'd suffered, up until this, was when my dog got hit by a car and died. That was ten years ago, and occasionally I would still cry over it. Only God knew how long I could grieve over CJ.

"My child's father," I whispered to myself as I placed both of my hands on my belly.

A hard knock on my bedroom door caused me to sit up. I knew that I was too weak to stand, so I called out, "Yes, Daddy?"

"Honey, come to the living room I need to talk to you."

"Okay, I'll be right out." I tried to make my voice sound as normal as possible, but obviously, I had failed.

Daddy let himself in my bedroom.

"Kenisha, are you okay?" he asked as he approached the bed.

"Yes, I just broke up with my boyfriend, I'll be fine." The lie tasted like acid on my tongue, but the truth would have rocked Daddy's world.

"His loss." He bent down and kissed my forehead. "I'll be waiting in the living room."

As soon as he left out, I ran into the bathroom and hugged the commode. Vomit spewed from my mouth as a fresh wave of tears poured from my eyes. The news reporter's voice drummed in my head, over and over again.

Still, I couldn't believe CJ was dead. Yes, I hated him for doing me so dirty, but a part of me loved him. Lord knows I didn't really mean what I had said to him, but I would never get to take back my hateful words.

Another gush until my inside were empty and all I could do was dry heave. Knowing Daddy was waiting for me, I summoned up the strength to pull myself to my feet and clean up the mess I had made. I washed my face and hands, brushed my teeth and rinsed my mouth. I checked my reflection in the mirror. My eyes were red and puffy from crying and my hair was all over my head.

Tears continued to pour from my eyes as I tied my hair back in a ponytail and wiped my tears with the back of my hands. Just when I thought my tears had stopped the flood gate reopened as I recalled giving CJ my virginity. He had been so gentle with me that day, but in the end, I had been nothing but another piece of pussy to him. Suddenly, anger replaced my grief. I wiped away the last tear I planned to shed for that muthafucka.

Once I got myself together, I found my dad in the living room pacing the floor. Worry lines creased his face making him look twenty years older than he was.

"Kenisha, have a seat," he said in a dour tone that frightened me because the only other time he had sounded like this was years ago, when my mother had been in a near fatal accident and he had picked me up from school and delivered the news.

"Daddy, has something happened to Mom?" My heart beat rapidly as I remained standing.

"No, honey, it's nothing like that. What I want to talk to you about has to do with things going on at the Temple." He continued to pace back and forth.

I let out a huge sigh of relief. As long as Mommie was okay I could handle any other news.

"Dad, what's going on?" I sat down on the sofa with my hands folded in my lap.

Daddy finally stopped pacing. He sat down beside me and explained his predicament. He told me there was dissention at the Temple where he ministered. It had reached such a level that it was no longer safe for me to remain in Newark.

"But, Daddy, why would someone from the Islamic community want to harm me?" I was totally confused.

"Baby, they'll hurt you to get at me." He went on to tell me a story about a clique of young radical Muslims who were moving against the old guard. "Things have gotten violent and I don't want to risk you getting caught in the fray. These young boys are out of control. They'll kill anyone to establish their idea of Islam, and since I'm vehemently opposed to that, I can't be sure they won't come after you," he said.

"Okay, so you want me to go back to Mom's?" I asked

"No, honey, that might not be safe either. Someone I trust is on their way to pick you up. They'll take you some place secure. You are to stay there until I tell you it's safe to come back to Newark. Do you understand?"

"No, I don't and you're scaring me. What about Mommie, will she be in any danger?" I questioned him.

"No!" he replied without further explanation. "Just trust me, Kenisha. Now hurry, go pack your things."

I did what he asked because I trusted him. But I still couldn't comprehend his logic. However, the graveness in his voice confirmed how serious it was to him. Therefore, I had no choice but to be as concerned for my safety as he was. Besides, the thought of disobeying him never crossed my mind.

"So, am I allowed to call Mommie and Jada while I'm out there?" I wanted to know.

"Yes, but tell no one where you are. No one." He emphasized.

"How long will I have to stay there?" I sighed.

Daddy creased his brow. "I'm not certain how long you'll have to stay but hopefully it won't be very long. Now go get ready." His stern gaze warned me not to debate with him.

I stood up on unsteady legs and returned to my bedroom. So much was coming at me so fast, I felt dizzy. It felt like I was trapped in a bad movie, in which I didn't belong in. When I finished packing, I took a shower and threw on a pair of stretch jeans, a sweatshirt and some lip gloss. I had just finished getting ready when Daddy called out for me.

"Kenisha, your ride is here!" he bellowed.

When I walked into the living room and saw who it was standing there to take me away, I had a slight smile plastered on my face, in spite of the circumstances.

Daddy made the introductions.

"Benard, this is my daughter Kenisha. Kenisha, this is Benard."

"As Sailum Alaikum," I greeted him, assuming he was Muslim. His reply caught me off guard.

"Sup, yo? You can call me Nard."

"Uh—okay," I stumbled over my words.

"Nice to meet you, Nard." I looked from him to Daddy and raised a questioning eyebrow. The look on my face said, *Dad, this nigga is a straight street thug.*

My father nodded his understanding.

"You can trust Nard one hundred percent," he said.

Trusting Nard wasn't the problem, I wasn't sure I could trust myself. Because baby boy exuded all of the things that made me fall for CJ. And the look in his eyes told me that he found me attractive, too.

CHAPTER
14
Nard

I was leaned against the kitchen counter watching *ma* put away the groceries we had stopped and bought. Her little apple bottom had a nigga lusting, but I kept reminding myself that she was my plug's daughter, and therefore off limits. But I couldn't deny that my attraction to her was mad strong. She was cute as a muthafucka with a tight little jogger's body, and just enough ass and titties to fill up a nugga'z hands.

Beyond the physical assets she possessed, I could sense in her an innocence that stirred my desire. After fuckin' with nothing but hood bitches all my life, shorty would've been a welcome reprieve from those types of nothing ass hoes.

Kenisha hadn't said much on the ride out here. She had mostly spent her time texting back and forth with someone. Occasionally, she had wiped away tears. I had pretended to not notice that she was crying but I remained curious.

"Did your boyfriend break your heart?" The question on my mind rolled off of my tongue on its own.

"It's more than that. But if you don't mind, I don't care to talk about it."

"It's all good, shorty."

Her head snapped around and she gave me an ice-cold stare.

"Do not call me, shorty!"

"Word. But you need to check your tone. I'm looking out for you as a favor to your pops but don't get shit twisted—I'm not his *do boy*. This shit right here is boss." I pounded my chest hard with my fist and then I walked out of the kitchen with a serious unit on my face.

Twenty minutes later, Kenisha came into the living room where I was sitting. She placed a tray of sandwiches and chips on the table as she sat down in front of me.

"A little peace offering." She pointed to the food and added a smile to her offer.

"We're good." I said but my face still wore a frown. She had spoken to a boss like she was talking to a peon. That shit had me sizzling hot.

"Nard, I apologize if my tone offended you." She correctly interpreted my mood. "It's just that...." He words trailed off and her eyes watered.

"It's just what, ma? Talk to me." I placed her hand in mine. She didn't pull it back but she lowered her eyes to the floor.

"Someone I'm trying hard to forget used to call me shorty. Please don't call me that." She sniffled back tears.

"Alright, I can respect that." I couldn't help wondering if the person she was speaking of wasn't Raheem. After all, it had to be more than coincidence that *that* nigga had ended up at her father's house the night we snatched him up.

"What's dude's name? Maybe I know him. If so I can have a little talk with the nigga about making you cry." I reached up and caught a tear that trickled down her face.

"His name isn't important and, anyway, he got killed. I'm sure you didn't know him, though. He lived in North Philly." Her response settled my mind. At least she wasn't talking about Rah. But I was still curious to know how she knew him.

Before I could ask, I noticed her staring at the strap I had placed on the table. She looked from it to me and asked, "Nard, you're not NOI?"

"Nah, ma, I just fucks with your pops."

"You fuck with him how?" she delved.

Like the smooth criminal I had become, I lied easily.

"Your father is tryna pull me out the streets and bring me into the culture."

"Well, is it working?" She seemed astonished.

"Nah, not one bit." We both burst out laughing.

Kenisha grabbed a sandwich off of the tray and bit into it. "It's delicious, aren't you going to eat?"

I grabbed one of the turkey subs and a handful of chips.

"I see you're working with a little something." I complimented her and chewed at the same time.

"Oh, wait I forgot the pickles and the fruit punch." She bounced off with exuberance and headed back into the kitchen.

As I watched the sexy shape of her small but enticing hips, and jiggle of her little booty, I knew that my resistance wouldn't last forever. It's was like cupid's punk ass had shot a cold-blooded street nigga in the center of his heart.

***

Kenisha

I could feel Nard's eyes glued to my ass as I left the room. Normally, that wouldn't have excited me but my confidence had taken a serious blow after dealing with CJ, and I welcomed the attention.

Of course, it was much too soon for me to even think about hooking up with someone. Although I was doing a decent job of hiding it, I was traumatized by CJ's death. His body wasn't even in the ground yet, and I was wavering back and forth on my decision to have the baby. The last thing I needed in my life was another man. Especially a thug.

That didn't stop me from throwing my hips extra hard, though, because I knew Nard was watching and there had to be an underlying reason I had lied when he asked about a boyfriend. I wasn't trying to be a deceitful bitch, I just hadn't wanted to admit the truth. I was so ashamed of my predicament and I didn't want to be judged.

***

Nard

The vibration of my cell phone interrupted my thoughts about Kenisha. I fished my iPhone out of my pocket and answered the call without identifying the caller.

"Sup wit' it?"

Chip's frantic voice nearly busted my ear drums.

"I went there to handle that. They had mad security around his room but I played my way past it. I got all the way up to his room, yo. I had the pillow over his head, smothering him, when a nurse walked in and started screaming."

"Fuck outta here," I said in disbelief.

"Real spit, fam. I had to run that bitch over just to get away because that ho tried to block the door."

"Is your face on camera?"

"Maybe, but I wore a hoodie and some shades."

"That's what's up. Just lay low. I'll pull up on you, yo."

"Alright, I'm just letting you know security is about to be stupid tight around there after this," said Chip.

"A'ight, son, good looking out." I disconnected the call and slammed my phone on the table.

"Fuck!"

When I looked up Kenisha was staring directly in my mouth. "Is everything okay?" she asked.

"Not really, baby girl. But I got this." I picked my phone back up and walked out on the balcony. As I dialed Kenisha father's number and waited for him to answer, I thought about Rah's luck.

That nigga got more lives than a cat, I said to myself.

Ca$h

CHAPTER
15
Rah

The last nigga that tried to take me out didn't do anything but strengthen my will to live and extract revenge on our enemies. I knew Nard had sent whomever it was that tried to smother me, but again, I had survived and now I was getting stronger.

After yesterday's attempt on my life, two-armed policeman were stationed outside of my room, around the clock. The only visitor that was allowed in my room was Eric. That was cool because there was no better person than him to give me an update on what was going on in the streets.

In a hushed tone, leaning down inches from my ear, he described a vivid detail of what they had done to Nard's pops and his family.

"Legend is a beast, yo. I'm glad he's on our side. That kid is sick with that machete," Eric whispered.

I couldn't help feeling pangs of remorse for what was done to the woman and the kid, but I blocked that shit out. The other side had no mercy, and now neither did I. Nah mean?

When Eric told me the bodies hadn't been found yet, I concluded that winter's chill had kept them from stinking. But whenever the bodies were discovered to brutal dismemberment of a whole family was sure to bring mad heat. It would also send shivers throughout Nard's crew.

The next day, I woke up to find Big Ma at my beside. One of her longtime friends from The Bricks had called her after hearing about what happened to me and CJ.

Big Ma was all tears and nerves. She begged me to come back to Atlanta with her whenever I was released from the hospital.

"Please, Raheem," she cried.

Her tears penetrated my heart, but they couldn't alter the mission I was on. Only death could stop me from putting Nard and 'em in the dirt. I looked into my grandma's aging face and saw the worry in her eyes. But I refused to lie to her.

"Big Ma, you know how much CJ meant to me and you know if the shoe was on the other foot, CJ would stop to no limit to get at those who killed me. So, with all due respect to how you raised me, I'm gonna avenge my brother."

"What exactly are you going to do, Raheem?" she demanded to know, but I left her question unanswered because my intentions were darker than anything Big Ma could imagine.

I saw her heart break right before tears streamed down her face and pain strummed in my heart. It saddened me terribly to make her cry, but the Raheem Big Ma knew died when CJ took his final breath.

***

A week later, after finding out the hospital wouldn't release me to attend CJ's funeral, I signed myself out against medical advice and hired a private doctor and a private nurse to accompany me at the service.

The church was packed and hundreds of people stood outside in the cold listening to the service as it boomed from the large speakers that had been strategically placed around the church's grounds. The Bricks showed mad love to the street legend CJ was. Newark's finest were out in full force patrolling the area, making sure nothing popped off.

The atmosphere inside of the huge church was tearful and sad. The minister reminded us all that just a few years ago, he had stood in the same pulpit and presided over CJ's mothers and his baby sister's funeral.

"Now the son has been lost to this insidious violence that plagues the black community. When is enough going to be enough, black people?"

When Nard, Man Dog, and everyone they love is dead, I thought as the minister implored the mourners not to seek revenge. His pleas fell on deaf ears amongst me and my comrades.

Just the other day, the mutilated bodies of Nard's father, his wife and their young son had been discovered. It gave me a measure of solace to know we were not the only ones mourning today.

But Big Ma was right, nothing could bring my nigga back, but I would be a bitch in a skirt if I didn't send a bunch of muhfuckaz to join him.

As Legend pushed me in my wheelchair up to the stage where CJ's body lay in a splendid gold casket, I caught a glimpse of many faces etched in sorrow. No matter what anyone had *had* to say about CJ, it was evident that the streets loved him. He lived for that, and I was glad to see he had obtained it.

When I finally looked in the casket, I didn't know what to expect. The self-inflicted gunshot had blown half of his head away, which was why I was surprised he wasn't having a closed casket funeral.

My mouth spread into a smile when I saw the great job the hired mortician had done to reconstruct my nigga'z face. CJ looked like he had smoked a fat blunt of ganja and fell asleep. He had a slight smirk on his face as if he was saying, *Tell that bitch ass nigga, Nard, to suck my dick.*

I chuckled inside.

"Only you, nigga."

He was dressed in jeans and a Polo shirt, and he rocked a crisp pair of construction Timbs. His favorite platinum chain, with the diamond encrusted medallion of Tamika's face hung down to the center of his chest. His hands were folded just below. Ice blinged from his fingers and wrists.

Even in death, son was stuntin' hard.

I placed my hand on his heart and my mind went all the way back to our sandbox days. A loud pained cry bellowed from deep in my soul and I cried out.

"Man, I'm gonna miss you so much. Hold it down in Paradise until I join you."

I lifted myself up by the arms of the wheelchair and I leaned over into the casket and kissed my nigga'z cheek. It was as ice cold as the diamonds he rocked and that was the first time I think I truly accepted that CJ was dead.

A pain like nothing I had ever known surged through my body and grabbed a hold of my tongue.

"Nard!" I heard myself scream. "The world ain't big enough for you to hide!"

CHAPTER
16
Nard

Them niggas hit back hard, yo. Pops, Angela, Day Day. I counted the losses, and today, Papaya. I had just received a call telling me how she was gunned down.

I hadn't loved lil' mama, but her murder was another affront to me. Those niggaz were coming at me hard, disrespecting my gangsta, and fuckin' with my family.

The image of what they did to pops and nem was scorched in my mind. I had found the front door unlocked when I went by there to talk to my old dude.

The minute I stepped inside and saw bloody shoe prints on the floor, a feeling of dread came over me. I raced upstairs, calling Pop's name and hoping to find him injured but okay. But what I found was a massacre that had kept me up ever since I discovered it.

No one had to tell me who was responsible for the pure evil that was done to my peoples. I could even imagine what their last minutes had been like. And what they did to little Day Day damn near dropped me to my knees.

"Lil' bruh, I'm sorry, man. Damn, man, I'm sorry!" I said, close to tears when I saw his small body riddled with bullets and covered in blood.

"They didn't have to do that baby like that," Mama said when she learned of the details. "Y'all better make every one of those bastard suffer."

Mom Duke was gangsta. She knew I was cold when it came to that murder shit, and she knew Man Dog was about that life, too.

"Nard, all of this is behind that trifling bitch. I tried to tell you she wasn't shit."

Mama could go on and on for hours about Tamika even though the trifling ho was dead.

I never tried to stop her rants because she was right. Over and over again, she had told me to leave that bitch alone and send her back to CJ.

I should've listened but this war was inevitable because The Bricks never would have been big enough for the both of us. There could only be one King.

I stood amongst my mans and Lemoras, who was seated next to Man Dog on the couch in the living room. I reminded everyone, "The last time we were here there was a slight dissention in the ranks. But that's all behind us now." I walked over to my brother and we hugged.

I looked around the room as I resumed speaking.

"Y'all see what's happening, so everyone of us should be on point. Those niggas are on some cruddy shit, yo. Ain't no lines being drawed. You see what they did to Papaya, and all she ever did was give me some head."

"What did they do to her?" asked Quent. He had just returned from D.C. making a drop.

'They killed her in the parking lot of Short Hills Mall." Said Zakee.

"Shot that poor girl 23 times," added Lemora. She hadn't been a fan of Papaya's but the sorrow in her voice was genuine.

"Them niggaz gotta go. They're running around this bitch feelin' themselves." said Quent.

"Yo, and that foul shit they did to your pops and 'em. Son, we gotta blaze those
muhfuckas." Zakee became animated.

"Blood, you already know. We're gonna give my father and 'em a small, quiet funeral and then we're gonna act a fool. Nah mean?" I laid out the plan.

"Bruh, let's knock off that cracker, Cujo. He's the real power behind those bitch niggaz. Without his protection, they wouldn't be shit but some small-time block boys," suggested Man Dog.

I weighed the good and the bad of us murking a cop. If we did that, Hot Top would put The Bricks under siege. Every block would have to close down until the killer was caught.

"What do you think about that?" I posed the question to Big Nasty.

"You now it's whatever with me. But if you want the truth, that would be a reckless move. When a cop gets whacked, everything shuts down. They start snatching niggaz up and mufuckas you thought was official start singing. We won't come out on top like that. But it's your call," he said with mad respect.

The expression on the other faces told me that they weren't feeling what Big Nasty said. They were ready to go all out—fuck consequences.

I assured each of them that I felt the same way. "But we can't act on emotions or we'll hand those niggaz a victory without them having to shed more blood. They would love for us to do some retarded shit that'll get all of us booked. We'll end up in Rahway State Prison while those bitch niggaz will still be out on the streets running up a cheque," I calmly explained why killing Cujo wouldn't be a wise move.

I heard a lot of grunts around the room. No one challenged my wisdom, although it was clear they were frustrated.

"I understand how everyone is feeling, yo." I continued. "And I'm just as blood thirsty as anyone in this room. Me and Man Dog lost our pops and our little brother, but we gotta move smart," I cautioned.

"And quick. While Rah is still laid up in the hospital. Without him, who's over there calling the shots. Eric? Snoop or Premo? Those clowns can't match wits with us." Man Dog intoned.

"Niggaz don't have to be smart to kill. All they gotta do is squeeze the trigger. But I feel you, fam. Let's hit the streets tonight and fuck some shit up."

Man Dog was in no condition to ride out, but he gave Quent his strap to buss a nigga with.

***

By the time I made it back to Harlem the next day, we had left Eric and 'em two more fallen soldiers to bury and their spot in the Stratford Apartments had been turned into a crime scene.

When I entered the sixth-floor apartment, I found Kenisha, lying on the sofa staring up at the ceiling. She was motionless. Had her chest not been moving up and down I may have thought she was dead.

"I brought you some White Castle." I sat the bag down on the table.

"Thanks, but I don't have an appetite."

Looking down at her, I could tell she had been crying again. Without giving it a second thought, I bent down and kissed her on the corner of the mouth.

"One day it's not gonna hurt anymore, lil' mama."

"When?" she asked as fresh tears rolled down her cheeks.

"When you decide to be happy again." I stroked her hair and she reached up and rubbed the back of my hand before bursting out in sobs.

I gathered her in my arms and just held her and rubbed her back until her sobs quieted down. I didn't know what it was about Kenisha that made me want to love her and protect her from further heartache. We hadn't really talked much beyond surface things. And when I asked about her ex the other day, she went into a shell. I wanted to ask her about him again so I would have a better understanding of her pain, but she was too distraught for us to have that conversation right now.

"Shh! Don't cry, ma, it's gonna be okay."

I leaned in and pressed my lips to hers. Our mouths parted and our tongues locked. I tasted her salty tears as we kissed but they took nothing away from the sweetness of her tongue. As we embraced, her nipples caressed my chest through her t-shirt and I instantly hardened. But I didn't act on my strong sexual desire because I didn't want to fuck baby girl, I wanted much more.

I was surprised by my own feelings. Just a week ago, I had sworn off loving any bitch. And being in the middle of a deadly war was hardly the right time to catch feelings.

I pulled back and turned my head away from her. "We can't even do this, baby girl." I mumbled

"I know." She dropped her head.

The heat between us was scorching. Her body was calling me and mine wanted to answer, but my big head over ruled the smaller one. I got up and sat in the chair across from her. Neither of us said anything for a while and then her sweet innocent voice pierced the silence.

"Thank you," she said, barely above a hum.

"For the kiss?"

"Yes. And for not taking it any further." She lifted her eyes and looked into mine.

"I wanted to, but not like this. Not when you're vulnerable."

"Thank you," she said again.

"You're welcome. Now try to eat something." I encouraged.

Kenisha flashed a brave little smile, then she dug down into the bag of White Castle. Once she started eating, she didn't stop until she had smashed 4 burgers, 2 large order of fries and a chicken sandwich. I sat back with a smile on my face, watching lil' mama go in.

She looked up and smiled beautifully. "What are you laughing at Denard?"

"Nothing, ma. Gon' finish doing your thing." I chuckled as she licked the ketchup off of her fingers. "Real talk, though, I don't see where all of that goes."

She was as petite as a ballet dancer.

"To my head. Don't even try to spare my feelings, we both know I got a big jug." She clowned on herself.

I couldn't do nothing but laugh. Of course, baby girl was on that bullshit. Her head wasn't big at all.

'You're funny, yo." I shook my head and fired up a blunt.

Kenisha fanned the smoke from in front of her face. I offered to step out on the balcony to finish blazing, but she waved me off.

"It's okay," she said in a sugary tone.

"You sure, Big Head?" I busted a little smile.

"Yes. And your head isn't little," she teased back.

We joked back and forth for a while, then her face turned serious.

"Nard, if I ask you a question about your past will you be honest?"

"Yeah." I braced myself for her interrogation. But her question was mild compared to what I had expected.

"Have you ever loved and hated someone at the same time?" she wanted to know.

The question brought me face to face with my feelings for Tamika. Until this very moment, my anger over the way she played me only allowed me to hate that bitch. But as I pondered Kenisha's question, I realized how thin the line between love and hate really was. And for the first time since I shot Tamika in the head and took her life, I regretted pulling the trigger.

My eyelids lowered and my face sagged as happy memories of Tamika forced me to recall the good times. The way she made a nigga feel ten feet tall when she expressed her belief in my ability to rule The Bricks. The way a nigga'z world lit up when she came around.

"Tamika, why you make me do that shit to you?" I raged inside. "We would've been the King and Queen of The Bricks but you didn't keep it 100."

I couldn't keep the hurt and anger from showing on my face. Suddenly, I felt weight on my lap. Soft arms wrapped around my neck and then I tasted her lips again. And when her hands slid under my shirt, I knew that this time we wouldn't stop nor did I want to.

Ca$h

CHAPTER
17
Kenisha

I could feel his pain evaporating as my inexperienced hands caressed his chest with indescribable hunger. I could sense that he needed to heal his wounded heart, and I desperately needed him to heal mine.

When he cupped my breast, fire exploded inside of my body and my delicate flower moistened. I pulled back from our passionate kiss and buried my head in the nook between his shoulder and neck.

"Please make love to me." I cried literally.

He stood up with me still in his arms. I wrapped my legs around his waist and sought his lips again as he carried me into the bedroom. He used his foot to push open the door, laying me down on the bed and undressing me. We were both panting with pinned up need and desire.

I waited nervously as he undressed and then laid on top of me.

"You're beautiful, ma," he said, looking deep into my eyes. I pulled his head down to my breast so he could massage the ache in my nipple with his tongue. He did so expertly and I moaned his name.

"Nard please don't stop."

He sucked one nipple then he other. Back and forth until my legs trembled, then I felt his hardness pushing at my wet opening. I wanted to ask him to put on a condom, but I couldn't speak. I gritted my teeth an squeezed my eyes tightly as he pushed forward with his hips, and I felt the head of his dick dip inside my honey pot.

"Fuck you're tight, ma," he said.

I bit down on my bottom lip and spread my legs wider, hoping to ease the pain. My breath got caught in my chest when I felt him slide deeper inside of me. He wasn't as big as CJ but he was just as thick. He stroked in and out of my pussy a few times and then suddenly he stopped.

I opened my eyes and looked up at him. "What's wrong?"

"You're crying," he said gently

That came as a surprise to me until a tear trickled down into my mouth.

"Love my hurt away." I whispered as my hips began to move on their own.

"Let me do that for you, baby." The realness in his voice relaxed me.

"I can love your pain away, too, if you let me." I said with guiltless confidence.

This time, it was Nard whom closed his eyes. It was if he was trying to shut out her image.

Whoever she was had broken his heart. I could feel every ounce of his agony because my own was as fresh as an opened wound.

CJ had fucked me up. His callous rejection had made me magnify my every flaw. I was skinny with little ass. I didn't know how to give head. I was too young, too green. And most of all, I didn't know how to play my position.

I would never forget how he hurled insults at me with no filter. Or how he drove me to the point of contemplating suicide. Yes, I hated him but I loved the part of him that was left growing inside of me.

I willed my mind off of CJ and allowed myself to enjoy Nard's slow, passionate love-making. Our bodies were in tune from the start. He didn't have to tell me he loved me, because I felt it.

Even before today, we hadn't known each other more than a week but I knew in my heart we would be together until our dying days.

"Damn, ma, you feel so good," he moaned in my ear.

"You feel good, too, baby. Sssss!" He was deep inside of my existence.

I bit into his shoulder and hugged him tighter and he began to stroke harder, deeper, faster.

"I want you to be mine, ma."

"I wanna be yours."

"Say it to me, then." He gripped my ass and fed my pussy every inch of his dick.

"I'm yours, Nard." I cried out and my juices gushed down.

"And I'm yours, baby girl." He growled as he pinned my arms above my head and satisfied me for the second time.

A moment after I coated his shaft with my pleasure, Nard pulled out of me and covered my belly with his thick, hot seeds.

Ca$h

CHAPTER
18
Nard

I held baby girl until her eyes fluttered open and then I welcomed her awake with a kiss.

"Mmm," she licked her lips.

I stroked her eyebrow with my finger and stole another sweet kiss.

"I could hold you in my arms forever, ma."

"Until the streets start calling," she said.

"Even then, I wouldn't stay away long."

"You promise?" She played with the hair on my chest.

"Yeah, baby girl, I promise." Shorty had a nigga on some stupid soft shit. I wasn't buggin' over it, though. She was the perfect counter-balance to the savage I would have to be to finish annihilating the remainder of CJ's crew, especially Rah.

"Nard, I don't want to share you with no other bitch. I've been there and done that. If you can't help being a man whore, let's just forget about what just happened."

"Nah, we're good. I'm not even that type of nigga, yo. Just keeping it gangsta, I've been waiting for a woman like you to come into my life, but what's your daddy gonna say? You know we can't hide it from him. I don't rock like that."

"I don't know what he's going to say. I'm sure he thinks highly of you since he trusted you to be here with me."

Kenisha didn't know the half, and I wasn't about to inform her about her father's secret life. On the other hand, I didn't want David X to feel like I had betrayed his trust.

"He'll have no choice but to respect it if we got married. We could drive to AC," I said, meaning Atlantic City, "and do it the same day."

"Are you serious?"

"Dead ass."

Her eyes revealed she was down with the move, but all of a sudden, she became quiet.

"What's wrong, are you scared? You know, sometimes you just gotta move with the wind. I know we don't know each other like that, but it feels right to me." I spoke from the heart.

I knew things were moving dumb fast but I didn't give a fuck. I was gonna wife shorty if she agreed to rock my last name.

"Sup, ma? You down or not?"

The smile on her face slid off and hit the floor. Baby girl got teary-eyed again.

"Nard, I have to tell you something. After you hear what I have to say if you still want to marry me, my answer is *yes*."

"Talk to me, ma, tell me what's up, yo." I propped my elbow on the bed and rested my head on my hand.

"I'm pregnant and I'm going to keep the baby." She blurted it right out. "And before you go thinking I'm some kind of hoe, I'ma need you to understand that you're only the second man I've ever slept with."

There was no deceit in her voice, so I accepted her statement on face value.

"Where's the baby's daddy?" I asked.

"I told you, he got killed."

When I got quiet, Kenisha got out of bed, went into the bathroom and closed the door.

Moments later, I heard her in there crying. I wasn't a sucka for tears, so I let her cry while I weighed the bomb shorty had just dropped on me. My first thought was abortion. I quickly dismissed that. How could I ask her to do the same foul shit Tamika had done to my seed?

A petty nigga would've distanced himself from her situation, but I was on my grown man shit, nah mean? And baby girl was a jewel. So, I decided to rock with her for better or for worse.

I went and knocked on the bathroom door until it opened. Kenisha stood there with her head down and her shoulders slumped.

"Just tell me you don't want me now," she said.

"No, baby, that's not what I came to tell you." I wrapped my arms around her and pulled her against my chest. Stroking her hair, I said, "I'ma rock with you, ma. Because I believe you're worth it. I'm good with your situation, and I'm down with being a father to your child."

Her eyes lifted up slowly. "Nard, are you sure?" she asked timidly.

"Yeah, I got you, baby. Don't worry."

Kenisha reached up and wrapped her arms around my neck. Crying softly, she vowed, "You won't regret loving me. I promise you that."

"And you want regret being my wife," I said.

A week later, we got married at the Taj Mahal. We spent three lovely days shopping and gambling at the casinos. On the fourth night of our hastily arranged honeymoon, I received a call from Man Dog.

"Sup, bruh?" I answered as my new bride fed me grapes in bed.

"Rah just got released from the hospital," he reported.

"A'ight. You know what time it is." My heart beat hard on my chest. Shit *is real now!*

"Say no more," he replied, knowing what I meant. *Murder, murder, murder.*

I hung up the phone and told Kenisha in an excited tone. "Baby, I gotta go back to Newark, ASAP!"

Ca$h

CHAPTER
19
Rah
A month later

I had come home from the hospital weeks ago, I wasn't fully healed yet, but I was up on my feet and moving around with the help of a cane.

Shit had quieted down in the streets, but we were under no false illusions—the war was still as grimy as ever. Too much blood had been spilled and too many loved ones had been lost on both sides for there ever to be peace. Until one side or the other was completely wiped out, Newark's murder rate would continue to reach a record high. I figured, like us, Nard was holed up somewhere plotting.

While hunting down niggaz, we still had to conduct business because my people still had to eat. Besides that, with respect to CJ's legacy, I refused to let a muthafucka shut us down. I placed more gunners outside of our spots and supplied them with lethal weapons and ammunition.

Now that our trap houses had been refortified with additional killers, I sat down at a face to face meeting with Cujo. Eric flanked my side. A brotha who was introduced to us as Tim sat on the side of the table with Cujo. We were at the warehouse out in East Orange that had always served as headquarters for CJ.

I had never liked the cracker across from me. This reptilian looking muthafucka was getting fat off of black folk's misery, and that shit vexed the fuck out of me, yo. But I wore a hellava poker face.

"Raheem, I'm glad to be able to count you amongst the living," Cujo said. "From everything I've heard about you, you seem to be a reasonable man. And that's important because the young man sitting next to you isn't reasonable at all."

"Fuck you," spat Eric.

"See what I'm saying? He's a hot head just like his brother was."

Eric sprung out of his chair and lunged across the table, attacking Cujo. I didn't blame him. His comment rubbed me wrong, too.

Tim got up and pried Eric's hands from around Cujo's throat. When Eric's lock was broken, Cujo leaned over with his head on the table and started coughing and then gasping for air. His neck was red and his face had turned a dark pink. But Eric didn't seem to give a fuck.

"If you ever talk down on my brother again, I'ma crush your punk ass!" he fumed.

I allowed him to cool down on his own, a little, before I placed a brotherly hand on his elbow and guided him back down in his seat. If Cujo expected me to reprimand Eric, he sorely misunderstood my loyalty. 'Cause it wasn't to him.

A minute later Cujo caught his breath, and straightened himself up in his seat. Looking at me, he sighed heavily. "You see what I've had to deal with?" He threw his hands up in frustration.

"If you show respect, it will likely be returned. You can't talk to a man like he's a boy and expect him to bow at your feet. Ain't no pussy on this side of the table, yo," I said on even tone. I then looked up at Tim who was still standing.

"Yo, big boy, have a seat. You're making my finger itch."

Tim must've known about my rep or either he sensed that my warning was a one-time thing, because his big ass found a seat.

I looked from him back to Cujo and folded my hands on top of the table. "Gentlemen, let's talk business. At the end of the day, all the other shit is asinine."

"I agree," said Cujo. He let out another sigh and then he locked eyes with me and began explaining his position.

I sat and listened as he spoke about the savage murders Eric and 'em committed while I was in the hospital. "Shit like that make national headlines and then those Fed boys come rolling in."

"Don't you have one of those Fed boys you're talking about on your team?" I asked, referring to Federal Agent Michael Solaski, Cujo's link into an unlimited drug supply.

I had met the big headed white boy once when CJ and them had a meeting at this very spot.

"Yeah, but it gets bigger than him when entire families end up diced like a fuckin' carrot, my friend."

"Duly noted," I replied.

"Anyways, it took a lot but we were able to quiet the story in the news after a couple of days. We pinned the murders on some Rasta who has been robbing and butchering drug dealers up and down the East Coast."

I propped him with a head nod.

"Raheem, that can't happen like that again." He warned.

"I'ma get at my peeps."

"Thank you. Now, on to business."

I folded my hands on top of the table and listened intently as Cujo explained the agreement him and CJ had. When he finished talking, I spoke my piece, and then we concluded the meeting with a handshake.

"It's business as usual," he remarked.

"Indeed," I replied.

Cujo and Tim stood to leave. Eric was mugging both of them but no words were passed.

When they were gone, I threw an arm around Eric's shoulder. "Before it's all said and done, they'll respect your position," I promised him.

"Or get crushed," he said.

"It won't come down to that."

Cujo wasn't a fool. He needed us just as much as we needed him.

***

Nothing changed from the arrangement Cujo had with CJ. Although everything would go through me now, I made it clear to that cracker that Eric was to be shown the same respect shown to me. Because whenever we put Nard in the ground, I was walking away from this shit and turning the reigns back over to Eric, the rightful heir.

Within days of our meeting with Cujo, a shipment of 100 kilos of coke, 25 bricks of heroin and 100 pounds of sour was delivered to me. We distributed it to our spots on Avon Ave, 11th and Clinton, Branch Brook Park, the Spis and every other location we controlled. After that, we hit niggaz off who had their own blocks.

With business up and running again, I focused my attention on two things: finding David X and knocking the sauce out his head and locating Lakeesha so I could get her ass away from The Bricks before Nard found her first.

CHAPTER
20
Eric

We got word that Rah's sister was stripping at Jersey Girls out in Elizabeth. Fam took the news hard to the chest and really so did I. I had always had a thing for La, but she looked at me like a little brother, even when I got my weight up and rolled with the big dawgs.

It twisted my mouth when she had baby after baby by three different clowns. But I never spoke on it. The streets had taught me to let a ho be a ho. And since La was determined to lay on her back for those worthless niggaz, I just fell back. This time it was different, though. We was tryna save her stupid ass from getting splattered on the ground.

"Yo, B, go to the club and bring Lakeesha to me. And if she don't come on her own free will, y'all have my permission to drag her up out of there." Rah gave the order to Premo and Snoop, but I volunteered my gangsta.

"I'ma rock with 'em." I grabbed my jacket and my strap.

"That's peace, bruh. But you don't have to ride. Premo and Snoop can handle it," said Rah from the foyer of the joint he'd recently rented.

"You saying anything, yo." I shot back. I understood he was going out his way not to make me feel stepped on, but that wasn't even on my mental. I had relinquished my position to him without bitterness because he was mentally better equipped to lead us. And with CJ gone, there was no one I trusted more than him.

"I'm volunteering out of love, not duty, yo." I clarified my position.

"Overstood." His response hinted at how vexed he was over his sister's choices. Being around him on the daily, I had picked up on the fact that when something was really stressing him, he responded to questions in monotone.

"Don't worry, fam, I'ma bring her back," I assured him.

Because I planned to walk up in the strip club on some straight bullshit. I called two of our souljahs to meet us there. I had chosen not to bring Legend along with us because son was certifiable. Wherever we took him muhfuckas ended up headless and shit, and things didn't call for that this time.

An hour later, when we reached Jersey Girls, my nigga Malik and Young Stunna was already parked in the lot waiting for us. We got out of our whips, dapped each other up, and I gave them the game plan, as far as how I planned to handle things once we got inside.

"Bet that," agreed Malik.

"You know it's whatever with me, yo," said Young Stunna, who feared nothing.

I acknowledged his gangsta with a nod of my head, and then we mobbed up to the entrance of the club. Snoop and the owner, who was standing at the door, knew each other on first name basis. That got us inside without having to be searched, and it probably saved the bouncer a trip to the ER because I was taking my strap wherever I went. And any stupid muhfucka that tried to stop me was gonna get his melon crushed.

We were in the club only ten minutes when I saw Lakeesha come on stage. She wore a fire red wig, pasties over her titties, a thong that might as well have been dental floss and a pair of red stilettos. I grimaced as I watched her pop her pussy like she had been fucking since Pre-K.

When she spun around and made her ass bounce, niggaz made it pour dead faces all over the stage. La dropped her ass to the floor and then shimmied back up. Some clown muhfucka walked up to the stage with a bottle in his hand and stopped in front of her. In his other hand was a thick roll of Feddi. La's eyes seemed to light up when he held the money above his head for her to see.

"Bring that pussy to daddy," he said over the Nicky Minaj track.

Without hesitation, La squatted down until her pussy was level with his eyes. She gapped her knees open wide and then she pulled her thong aside showing him her bald mound.

I couldn't take another second of that shit! I stormed to the stage, grabbed son by the back of his collar and slung him the fuck out of my way. He bucked up until he saw my niggaz walk up, gritting their teeth and easing their hands under their shirts where heat rested.

"Y'all got that." He backed down.

"You better know it!" I watched him walk away.

I spun around and found La still in the same position. Frowning, I grabbed her by the ankle. Once my fingers encircled it, I locked onto that muhfucka like a vise.

"Get your trifling ass down from there!" I snatched her so hard her back smacked the stage.

"Fuck is your problem, yo!" spit flew from my mouth.

Two gigantic bouncers came flying toward me, but when those bangers came off of my dawgs' waists, everything stopped, including the music.

"Eric, what the fuck?" cried Lakeesha.

"What the fuck?" I slung her words back at her. "Why the fuck is you up here like some ho! Do you know who your brother is, yo?" I didn't give her time to respond. "Get your ass up and go put on some clothes before I punch you in your shit!" I let go of her leg like it was infected with the claps.

"Who do you think you are?" she screamed.

"A nigga that will knock your teeth out!"

"I wish the fuck you…"

That's all she got out before my hand shot up and wrapped around her throat.

"Fuck you talking to, yo? You in here showing random niggaz your shit like you're a nothing ass bitch. That's how you wanna be treated, yo?" I slung her back and forth tryna shake some sense into her dumb ass. And if I failed at that I was gonna shake that ho shit *out* of her ratchet ass.

She was clawing at my fingers and gagging for air. I let go of her and she fell to the floor, crying and gulping for oxygen.

My niggaz was lined up on both sides of me daring a nigga to invade our space.

I spotted another stripper close by. I pulled a stack out of my front pocket and tossed it in her face. "Go get her shit! Every last stitch. And don't make me have to send for you. Real shit, ma!"

***

When shorty returned with La's clothes, I had to drag her out the club, kicking, cussing and screaming.

"Keep wildin' and I'ma put your ass in the trunk," I threatened, but I was dead ass.

"I hate you!" she screamed as I shoved her into the backseat of my Lexus.

I tossed the keys to Snoop. "You drive, B. I'ma sit back here with this ignorant ass girl."

"Your mama ignorant!" she spat.

I reached inside of the car and slapped sparks out of her face. My Mom Dukes was dead and she knew that. She also knew I didn't play that shit. La was Rah's sister, but her breezy mouth was gonna get her fucked up.

I gave Malice and Young Stunna both a pound and a chest bump before they rolled out. Premo climbed in the front seat with Snoop while I got in the back with La. She scooted all the way against the door, as far away from me possible. I didn't say shit. I just sparked a blunt and got nice.

As we hit the familiar streets of Newark, I looked over to La. She had her back to me looking out of the window, but I could hear her sniffling back tears.

"You wasn't crying when you was bussin' it open on stage," I reminded her.

"Suck my dick!" Her lips were curled down and her eyes was hot with fire.

"When you get home, I'ma wash your mouth out with soap."

"Hmpf!" She scoffed, and tightened her mouth into an angry, straight line.

"Anyways, where ya kids at, yo?" When she didn't answer, I said, "You ought to be ashamed of yourself."

"Look who's talking." She breathed hard through her nose, and her tone was granite. "What makes you better than me? Because you run around killing people, you think your shit don't stink? Boy, boom!"

"It beats selling pussy, I tell you dat." I chuckled.

"Nigga, I don't sell pussy, I sell dreams," she retorted.

"More like nightmares." I laughed

"Fuck you, Eric."

"Nah, ma, I'm good."

She stared bullets at me before jerking her head in the other direction and looking out of the window. I wasn't tripping, I was done talking to her stupid ass.

We rode in silence after all that. At least, until we pulled into Rah's driveway.

I brought the car to a stop and slammed the gear shift into park. "Get out," I said.

"Where are you taking me?" she asked.

"Don't worry, you're about to find out."

"Ughhh!"

I ignored her little smart aleck expression. There was no need to check her any further. In just a minute, she was going to get put in her fuckin' place.

I could hardly keep the corners of my mouth from turning up into a smile.

This shit is about to be good! I said to myself as I led her slick mouth ass inside to face her brother's wrath.

CHAPTER
21
Rah

I looked at my sister with shame. She had to feel the same thing because she wouldn't lift her head and meet my stare.

"Come here," I said gruffly. It was the deepest my voice had ever gotten since I got shot in the throat years ago,

She stood plastered to her spot for a monument or two, and then her feet shuffled until she stood before me like a wayward child. Her arms were wrapped around her shoulders and her head remained down. I could hear her sniffling back tears.

Snoop and Premo excused themselves into another part of the house. Eric chose a front row seat in the leather recliner just a foot away from where we stood in the spacious den. Son's presence wasn't intrusive, E was family.

"La, what are you doing, yo?" My arms flailed up demonstratively. "Fuck is your goddam problem? Didn't I teach you better than that?" I looked her over from head to toe. The red wig by itself was bad enough because it didn't fit the image I had of my little sister. Then when I used a finger to lift her chin, I saw that her face was so heavily made up, she looked like a 40-year-old street walker, instead of like the 22-year-old queen I had schooled her to be. I could only imagine the things she had been out there doing. I shook my head from side to side and my face hardened.

"What?" she asked.

"Sis, do you even gotta ask that question, yo?" My chest heaved up and down as I fought a losing battle to keep myself calm.

"A bitch had to eat," she said, like the shit she had been doing wasn't a big deal.

Her words made me stumble back a few steps. After I balanced myself, I sent enough heat her way to burn a hole through her head. *A bitch had to eat.* Those were the precise words that had come out of my baby sister's mouth. I was appalled.

"Is that how you see yourself now? You're a bitch, huh? My baby sister!" I clenched my fist at my sides.

"Rah, you know what I mean." Her response came out so casual and matter of fact, it sent my blood pressure to the fuckin' sky.

"Nah, I don't know shit, La!" I exploded. "I just know what the fuck I'm seeing, yo. I just know what just came out of your mouth, and I just know that my little sister has been dancing at a fuckin' strip club!"

"What's wrong with that?" she sounded unperturbed.

"You don't see shit wrong with showing your muthafuckin body to different men? For real? You'll stand there and pop that lame ass shit to me!" I almost wanted to knock some sense into her head.

"Newsflash." She made quotation marks above her head. "Lakeesha has three kids so like it or not, big brother, niggaz have seen my body before!"

"That's not the same." I grilled her.

"You should be glad it's not the same. *Tuh!* Rah, I've been fucking since I was 13 years old. I.."

"Shut the fuck up!" I stepped forward and tried to cover her mouth with my hand, but she jerked away from me and kept on spitting truth that I was not prepared to hear.

As she went on, tears fell from her eyes and the heat on her words were just as scorching as the heat coming off of my brow. "Rah, I got three kids by niggaz that ain't ever gave me shit but a wet ass. At least at the club a nigga has to dig in his pockets to see pussy. So, fuck what you're talking about!" She reached up and wiped at her tears.

"I told you to shut up!" I reached out to grab her but she managed to step away, only losing her wig. I slung that shit to the floor as the anger inside of me made my chest swell enormously.

"Rah, I'm not a baby and you're not my fuckin' daddy, yo! Yeah, I pop pussy, so muthafuckin' what! Do you want to know what else I pop? I pop mollies, too, and when I'm on those muthafuckaz, I can suck the skin off a dick!"

I lunged at her with both hands. Pain shot though my body like a live bolt of electricity. I howled in pain but I held my grip on La's throat. I would kill her before I let her become a pill head or just another ratchet female.

The vein on the side of my temple pulsed with anger. "You wanna be a ho? Not my little sister! I would rather see you *dead*!" I squeezed harder.

"Fam! Fam! Let her go, son." Premo reached in to try to pry my fingers from around La's throat.

"Fuck dat!" I snorted.

"Rah, let her go." Eric grabbed me from behind, but my grip couldn't be broken.

"C'mon, my dude, you're going to kill her. Let her go, yo!" barked Snoop.

The boom of Eric's, Premo's and Snoop's pleas together brought me out of my rage. I let go of my sister's neck and she fell straight back into Eric's arms. I took a deep breath and let it out slowly. Lakeesha was looking up at me with eyes wide with shock.

"Somebody better get her away from me!" I huffed.

La looked at me like I had turned into a stranger, or worse, a monster. She had never seen this side of me but she would see even worse if she didn't get her shit together. Fuck her feelings, I was trying to save her life.

As I shifted my weight, pain shot up from my legs causing me to wince. Premo rushed over to me and guided me over to the couch.

"Dawg, you need to get off of your feet. You're not well yet."

I wiped at the beads of sweat that had formed across my forehead as I lowered my body down on the sofa. A few feet away, La was sobbing uncontrollably. Eric lifted her up into his arms like she was a baby.

He made eye contact with me and said, "I got her, fam."

After Eric carried her upstairs, I sat there quietly contemplating the event that led up to this. Things were supposed to have been much different for us than how they had turned out. But there was no time for me to harbor regrets.

Nah, no time for that, yo. It's time to kill.

I sat there for a half an hour plotting death and destruction while Eric attended to La.

Finally, he came back downstairs and announced, "She's gonna be okay. She cried herself to sleep. When she wakes up she'll love you again."

I had no doubt about that. But at the moment, I had to focus my attention on vengeance.

An hour later, my focus was intact. We headed out of the house intent on bringing our enemies to their knees, one painful tragedy at a time.

***

We knew David X had gone into hiding. My people had his house and Temple 7 in Harlem, where he ministered, under heavy surveillance and he had not been spotted for weeks.

"I'ma flush him out sooner or later," I said with supreme confidence right before I watched Premo and Snoop climb out of the car and launch two Molotov Cocktails through the front window of David's X house.

In the darkness of the moonless night, the inside of the brick house lit up the street as flames leaped from the windows and licked at the sky. That was my first message to David X, letting him know that there was hell to be paid for the foul shit he did.

I was looking out for your daughter, nigga, and you set me up for those niggaz? Before it's all over, you're gonna die with 'em!

He was exactly what I called him in my mind—a nigga—because no minister would've done what he did.

I didn't need proof that he was somehow tied in with Nard, because I didn't believe in coincidences. His was guilty and he was gonna pay.

As we drove away from the bristling fire, I gave directions to our next destination. This time, when we left the scene, my message was gonna ring louder than Congo drums, and I knew that a part of me would be lost forever.

But I hadn't started this war and I hadn't set the rules— the other side had. They had killed indiscriminately and without mercy. Tamika, her Mom Dukes, Danyelle, Daquan, My A-1, CJ, most of all. And I could add Shy, Nee Nee and others to that list. Because even though they hadn't died by Nard's guns, their blood was on the young boy's hands.

David X had conspired to add me to the list of bodies Nard had stacked. And for that he deserved no mercy, I told myself.

They started this! They're the ones who turned this shit savage. He's the one who violated what he was supposed to stand on as a Muslim. He welcomed me into his home only to plot my death. I tried to be righteous but those muhfuckas wouldn't let me stay on my deen.

"So, now I'ma give them what they want!" I said as we pulled up to the quiet house that sat in the middle of the block.

I knew Kenisha wasn't inside because we had a couple of our young goons watching the house night and day. They blinked their head lights on and off, acknowledging my arrival. I had been tryna reach Kenisha for weeks, but she seemed to have disappeared with her fraudulent ass daddy.

It's all good, yo!

I winced in pain as I extracted myself from the car. The walk to the front door seemed to take me forever, but I was locked in. I held a firm grip on my cane, limping forward with purpose. Winter was fading fast but the night wind was crucial as a mug. I ignored its vicious bite as I struggled my way up on the porch and rang the doorbell.

Moments later, she came to the door.

"Yes, who is it?" she sounded like I had awakened her out of her sleep.

"Ma'am, your daughter, Kenisha, has been in a real bad accident."

"Oh, my God," she cried.

I heard the dead bolt being slid back at the same time I snatched my strap off of my waist and flicked the safety latch off. When the door came open, the mother of David X's only child was looking at a good nigga turned bad.

She saw me raise my gun, and she opened her mouth to scream, but it never came out. My nine clapped and her head jerked back.

Boc! Boc!

I blasted her in the chest.

When her back slapped the floor, I stepped just inside the door and stood there over her. My intentions were to empty the clip in her head, but I guess I wasn't that cold, yet.

Turning to walk back to the car, I felt a stream of tears wet my face. It was the very first time I had murdered a woman. I had done what I had to do but, still, inside it tormented me. Women and children should be untouchable. But I couldn't play by those rules while Nard honored nothing.

I had to show him that I could be just as heartless as he was. Still, I hurt inside over what I had just done. The tears on my face proved what CJ had always told me. *Thugs Cry, too.*

Ca$h

CHAPTER
22
Nard

Baby girl was inconsolable. She didn't understand why her mother had been killed, and I couldn't tell her the truth. David X said it was best if we let her continue to believe the story he'd told her about the young upstarts who was tryna take over his ministry. Given the fact that his house was fire-bombed on the same night Kenisha's mother was shot dead, the story seemed creditable to my boo. But me and her pops knew the real deal.

Two weeks had passed since we buried Kenisha's mother, and hadn't a night gone by that I didn't have to hold her in my arms while she cried herself to sleep. I felt bad about the big secret I was keeping from her. I dreaded the day the truth came out, and to prolong that from happening, I kept her away from The Bricks and all the rumors that were in the air. I also blocked her communication with her peoples, Jada. That bitch was a problem I didn't need it want. She would likely know somebody, who knew somebody, who might spill the truth about why Kenisha's mother was killed.

Kenisha knew that I fucked with the streets hard, but ma didn't know about my beef with Rah. And she most def didn't have a clue that her pops was my plug and that he was heavy in the game. The last thing in this world he would want was for his baby to find out that his hands were dirty. And he definitely didn't want her anywhere close to the streets.

It was no secret David X had preferred that Kenisha not fuck with a nigga like me. But once we laid eyes on each other, nothing could've stood in the way of us getting together. Me and baby girl were drawn to each other like two magnets.

Our sudden marriage had both surprised him and caused him to spazz out. For a minute, I thought he was gonna have me killed. But after a few days, he cooled off and accepted what couldn't be undone. His remaining concern was that I keep that street shit far away from where me and his daughter rested. I promised to do everything in my power to honor that command.

"But the best insurance against any harm coming to my daughter is for you to kill Raheem. That brotha is a problem." He sounded worried.

"Eric too." We couldn't forget about CJ's little brother. His level of vengeance outweighed Rah's!

As spring established itself with temperatures that made it feel like summer, The Bricks seemed like Baghdad. We were crushin' a different one of those niggaz every week, but they were hitting us back just as hard. Hot Top patrolled the streets aggressively because of it. Every day, it seemed, road blocks were set up and muhfuckaz' shit was being searched with no probable cause. A few of my runners got knocked, and *those boys* raided several of my drug houses and arrested almost a dozen of my workers.

That shit was starting to hurt my pockets. But what infuriated me even more than the lost guap was the fact that none of Rah's location had been fucked with. We all knew that cracker, Cujo, was protecting him and that gave them a huge advantage.

"Yo, it's time for us to sit down and re-strategize. We just lost two birds and over $50,000 when they ran up in our joint on Clinton. We can't make a dime in Lil City because every time we reopen that location, somebody gets murked. If I do a body count, those niggaz are winning 10 to 6. Shit gotta change, yo! And it has to change fast," I railed, as I paced the floor of my den with my cell phone pressed against the side of my face.

"You're right, but don't worry, I got a few tricks up my sleeve," David X assured me but his words didn't put out the raging fire in my belly.

"Whatever you got planned, it better happen real soon or I'ma start being on some Taliban shit, yo! I refuse to let those clown ass niggaz win! That cracker is their power. If we knock his head off, it's a wrap for them. You know the saying: cut of the head and the body will so die."

"Just be patient and be safe, youngin'! I've been around since the 80's, this is not the first challenge I've faced. As long as we keep our heads, we'll prevail in the end. Nobody said getting rich was going to be peaceful and easy."

"Say no more."

"Kiss my daughter for me. And may Allah protect you both."

"One." I hung up the phone and looked up. Wifey was standing there staring at me. "Sup, baby girl? How you today?" I asked her.

"Better." She walked up and wrapped her arms around my waist and then angled her head for a kiss.

I leaned down and softly pressed my lips to hers. We hadn't been intimate since her Mom Duke got killed, so the feel of her swelled breast against my chest awakened my log.

"I need you, ma," I whispered to the side of her neck as I gripped her ass and pulled her closer. Her stomach had begun to poke out a bit, so I was careful not to squeeze her too tightly.

"Let's go back to bed, then," she said in a voice sweeter than a cherry swisher.

I took her hand and led her to the bedroom, where I waste very little time laying her down on the bed and enjoying every inch of her.

Her dark chocolate nipples melted on my tongue. Pregnancy had baby's body tight. The fifteen pounds she'd gain was proportioned out just right, so that now her petite frame held curves. I trailed kisses down her body, stopping at her little bump of a belly, affectionately kissing her naval.

"Sup, lil' souljah," I spoke to the life growing inside of her.

Kenisha rubbed my head and looked down at me with a smile on her face. I hadn't seen baby girl smile in weeks. It made a nigga feel good to bring a little happiness back into her light brown eyes.

I had promised to accept and raise the baby she was carrying as my own, and I knew that touched her heart, Ma's innocence brought out the mushy part of me, yo. *Real shit.*

Never in a million years would I have thought I would marry and love a female who was carrying another nigga'z seed. But shorty made me accept her situation with a big ass Kool-Aid smile on my face.

We had agreed to tell everyone that the baby was mine, and it helped that the baby's father was deceased. I still had questions about son, but I hadn't found the right time to ask them. And now definitely was not it.

Her hands urged me to go lower. I placed my nose on her pussy mound and inhaled her natural fragrance and then I tasted the effect it had on shorty. She was dripping like a faucet. I ran my tongue around her clit in circles, before pushing it deep inside of her. In no time at all, I had her clenching the sheet and pouring her honey into my mouth.

When I entered her, it was like paradise! The bun in her oven gave her pussy the feel of ecstasy. I found myself planning to keep her pregnant for years.

As soon as she has this baby, I'ma pop another one in her, I told myself. Pregnant pussy was the best shit since kilograms of coke.

A memory of Tamika tried to invade my thoughts but I rejected it and concentrated on Kenisha. Love was moaning softly and grinding her hips in rhythm of my strokes. Her pussy gripped and squished at the same time.

"Baby, you feel so good." I sucked in my breath and held it, to stop myself from screaming like a bitch.

"I wanna feel good to you ,boo," she panted heavily.

I sucked her titties and made slow, passionate love to her just like she preferred. She made a nigga want to please her without even trying. The difference in her and those rats I had fucked with in the past was like night and day. I didn't have to question her devotion. Therefore, when our bodies smacked against each other, and she cried "Nard, I love you." I took it to heart.

"I love you back, baby girl." I moaned as she came quietly and I growled like a beast, splashing my nut all inside of her delicate walls.

A minute later, I was snoring like a bear. Even in my sex-induced slumber, I could feel Kenisha moving around in bed. Suddenly I was shaken out of my sleep.

Paranoia caused me to shoot straight up.

"Fuck going on, yo!" I reached for my strap on the nightstand.

"I don't know but I would like an explanation." Kenisha's face was full of questions.

After coming fully awake and realizing that my enemies hadn't caught me sleeping, I sat up and hugged my wife. "Sup, yo!"

"Nard, who were you talking to earlier when I walked into the room?" asked Kenisha. She pushed herself out of my embrace and looked at me accusingly.

"Man Dog. Why?" The dishonesty came off of my tongue without a second thought.

"Nard, I'm your wife. Please don't lie to me."

"Hol' up, ma! What reason would I have to lie to you? I don't play those types of games." I frowned.

"So, you were talking to Man Dog, huh?" She placed a hand on her hip.

"Didn't I just say that?"

"Well, why is Daddy's number the last one on your call log? And why the fuck you been talking to him for hours every day?" She brought her free hand from behind her back and tossed my cell phone on the bed. "Nard, I want to know what the fuck you and Daddy have going on or I'm leaving."

CHAPTER
23
Eric

"I'm leaving! Y'all can't hold me here like a god damn hostage! I'm a grown ass bitch!" LaKeesha was going the fuck off again.

Rah just sat at the desk in his office room and let his sister spew. I admired his calm because I had seen his storm, and it wasn't nothin' nice.

"La, you can scream from here to Arabia, and I'm not letting you leave this house unless it's to board a flight to Atlanta where Big Ma's at."

"Rah, I keep telling ya ass I'm not moving to country ass Atlanta. No fuckin' way!" She clenched her hands down at her sides and screamed in frustration.

Fam didn't even react to her emotional outburst. His cool was somewhere between winters in Maine and life in the Artic.

"La, if you don't wanna go to the A choose some other destination—anywhere as long as it's not on the East Coast. Otherwise, you're not stepping foot out of this house," he said with the same finality his words exuded when he was directing our clique.

It made no sense for La to challenge him. She had been doing that for weeks, and Rah hadn't lightened his stance an inch.

"I'm staying right here in Newark!" She stomped her feet like a spoiled child.

"That's peace, lil' sis. Have it your way." He got up, came from behind his desk and kissed her on the cheek. "You don't seem to understand, I'm not tryimg control your life, I'm only trying protect it."

"I can protect myself!" she screamed at Rah's back as he walked out of his study.

He stopped in the doorway and shook his head.

"Eric, please try to talk some sense into her. Obviously, she thinks it's a game. Talk to her, explain to her how cruddy it is in The Bricks right now."

"I got you, yo," I said, although I knew that trying talk to La's hard headed ass was like whistling in the wind.

"Rah, I need to be with my kids," she tearfully tried a different approach. I chuckled under my breath because I knew what was coming.

"My nieces and my nephew are already down south with Big Ma. I had Eric and Shabazz drive them down last week." Rah walked out and closed the door behind him.

La turned her anger and frustration on me.

"You dirty ass bastard!" she hissed, but I wasn't the one for all that noise.

"Don't forget, I'm not your brother. Talk slick to me and I'ma go up top," I warned her.

"I wish the fuck you would put your hands on me again. My brother will fuck you up!"

I laughed. "That's some trife shit for you to say, yo. But you can't start no beef between me and Rah. That's my nigga. I love son like we came out of the same womb. What you need to do is stop acting like a gutta rat and do what your brother asked you to do. He has too much on his mind to have to deal with your childish ass too. Trust!"

I walked out the room and slammed the door behind me before La made me kick her ass for real. Niggaz was dying all around us and she was bumping her gums about nothin'!

She couldn't have been *that* worried about her children because until a week ago, they had been staying with a lady we all knew from Little Bricks. I happened to run into the woman at Paul Hot Dogs and she asked if I had seen Lakeesha.

"She left those children with me two months ago, and she hasn't been back. The least she could do is call and check on them."

I shook my head in disgust as I recalled that now. If La said another word about missing her kids I was gonna pull muthafuckin card.

***

Rah left the crib with Shabazz to go to Irvington to chop it up with a kid who supposedly copped his work from a relative of Zakee, one of Nard's mans. If son's info was correct, we were gonna put Zakee's dick in the dirt. It wouldn't be the same as crushing Nard, Man Dog or Big Nasty, their top goon. But smashing Zakee would put another chink in those pussies' armor.

An hour or so after Rah bounced, I was chillin' in his den playing games on the X-Box and thinking about CJ. I missed big bruh like mad.

One of the reasons I was fearless in the streets was because I didn't give a fuck about dying. Because wherever I took my last breath around this piece, I knew I was going to join my big brother. It didn't matter if that place was Thug's Paradise or in the pits of hell. I knew CJ would already have shit on lock when my spirit pulled up.

A sudden noise outside of the door caused my head to jerk up. And even though Rah had a top-flight security system, and Cujo's people kept a protective eye on the house, I rose up out of my seat with a banger in each hand, ready to smoke any beef that managed to slip past the security.

I sat back down and relaxed when I saw it was La. But my eyeballs bucked when she stepped into the room and dropped the towel that was wrapped around her body. Music played from the phone in her hand.

Her nipples were hard. All she wore was a pair of skimpy panties and some red fuck me pumps. Her lips were thickly glossed and her voice dripped with seduction.

"Eric, I'm a bad girl. Put me in my place, papi." She stopped in front of me and fondled her titties. There was no other sound in the house, other than the song playing from her phone and the heavy beating of my heart. Her barely covered pussy was an inch from my nose. The faint smell of her sexuality was fuckin' with both my heads. I begged fate to send Legend or someone on the team bursting through the door. But everyone was gone on a mission.

I swallowed hard as La rubbed my head and placed it up against her pussy.

"Fuck is you doing, yo?" I forced myself to say.

"I'ma give you what you've always wanted." She took one step back and gyrated her hips to the beat of the song.

"Nah, you got the game fucked up." I protested with a lack of conviction.

"No, boo, it's not like that. I've been wanting to give you this fat ass pussy for the longest." She propped one foot up on the couch and pulled her panties to the side.

Her shaved kat was as plump and pretty as a ripe cantaloupe. She used two fingers to open her juicy petals and I saw her clit ring. Straight the fuck up a nigga was stuck. Pussy came my way in abundance, but I had fantasized about La since I was old enough to get my first hard on.

She pirouetted around and around and then she stopped with her back to me. She grabbed her ankles and made one ass check bounce at a time and then both of them in harmony.

Looking back at me, she said, "Spank me, daddy. Put this bitch in place."

"La, stop talking like that." I reached down and adjusted my dick. It was threatening to burst through my zipper.

"Boy, don't play. *Tsk!* You know you wanna run your dick all the way up in this pussy. Mmm, come on, daddy, fuck me." She lowered herself onto my lap and bounced her luscious ass up and down.

"Reach around and touch my titties."

"Fuck no!" I clamped my hands behind my back.

"Scary ass nigga," she giggled as she leaned back and licked the side of my face.

"Ain't shit scary over here, yo." I bossed up. "I know your game. You're tryna get me to let you sneak off while Rah's gone."

'Nah, you're wrong. lil' daddy, I'm just tryna get fucked. A bitch need a nut. Let me cum on that dick."

"Nah, ma, it ain't happenin'! You can dead dat." I pushed her off of my lap, but that didn't stop her.

"It's cool, man. I know what you want. Chyna told me how you used to love to fuck her in the ass."

She was right. Chyna was this older broad who lived on the top floor of our building. She had turned me out to anal sex when I was only 14 years old. La wiggled out of her panties and slung them backward over her shoulders. They landed across my face. The intoxicating smell of her aroma was more powerful than gin with no chaser.

She bent all the way over, reached behind her and with both hands she spread her ass cheeks open wide. Her crinkled booty hole winked at me.

"Put your dick in this tight ass hole, daddy. Please! I ain't never been fucked in the ass before." I fought with myself to resist her, but I felt my resistance weakening. But just as I unbuttoned my jeans, my phone rang in my pocket. I couldn't ignore it because it might be Rah calling.

"You better not answer it," said La. I whipped out my phone anyways. It wasn't Rah calling, it was Young Stunna.

"Sup, son?" I answered.

"Yo, B! I think we lost another one. They got him coming out of Mama Kim's Deli. Snatched son up in broad daylight."

I lowered my head and let out a long sigh. The deaths of our comrades was never easy to accept.

"A'ight. Let me hit Rah up." I ended the call and stood on heavy legs.

La stopped the bullshit. She turned around and saw the worry in my eyes.

"Is everything okay?" she asked.

"No! That's what we keep trying to tell you. Nard and 'em ain't fuckin' playin', yo! Go put on some clothes, and get your mind right before you get us killed. We don't have time for your theatrics, La. Real shit."

After handing her back her panties, I pushed her ass out of the room and then called Rah.

"Sup, fam?" he answered immediately.

"Bruh," I let out a sigh. "They got Malice."

"Who got him?"

"Nard."

"Fuck! What they do? Shot him up?"

"Nah, son they *snatched him up*."

The line went silent. Rah knew first-hand what that meant. Our nigga was gonna suffer before they killed him.

CHAPTER
24
Nard

"**K**enisha, why you questioning me like you're the Jakes? Fa real, ma. What's the deal, yo?" I effected a baffled look.

"I overheard you on the phone talking about things I don't even want to repeat. Out of curiosity, I strolled through your phone while you were asleep. I saw that my father was the last person you talked to, so I'm going to ask you again, what's going on?" She got up and stepped into her sweats. I took that as a sign that she was leaving for real if I didn't confess.

Of course, I had no intention of doing that. I loved baby girl and being without her would've been a blow to the chest, but the truth was worse than a lie so I came back at her a different way.

I said, "First of all don't be going through my shit. We're not about to start that cornball shit, yo. Secondly, I was talking to your pops when Man Dog called. I clicked over to talk to him and your pops hung up. That's why it looks like your pops was the last person I talked to."

I saw her tossing my explanation around in her head. After a minute, the wrinkles in her forehead disappeared and she signaled her understanding by nodding her head, but she still looked at me weird.

"What's on your mind, baby?" I gently pulled her down on the bed.

"I just want to know what's going on around me. It seems like you're always on the phone behind closed doors whispering. I'm not allowed to go to Newark or to communicate with my Aunt Jada. That's not normal, Nard. How much longer will I have to live in seclusion?" she questioned me.

"Baby, I don't have you living in seclusion, nah mean? That's your pops call. Whatever he got going on with the Temple and those young renegade kids is serious. Neither one of us want you to be at risk. Just give it a little while longer and I'm sure things will be gravy."

"Fine, but I have to go to a prenatal appointment tomorrow," she reminded me.

"I'll go with you. Now wipe that lil' mug off of your face. I promise you things are going to be lovely." I gave her a kiss and then we went and took a long bath together.

After that, Kenisha fixed us something to eat. I was already getting dressed when I received a call from Big Nasty.

"Come to the house on Dayton, boss man. We got a package for you."

"That's what's up, yo." I hung up without asking what the package was because I could feel Kenisha hovering.

Dayton was the block I grew up on, and in that hood I was revered. So, I was mad relaxed as I drove down the street.

If Rah was bold enough to pull up and buss at me on this block, he'd never make it out alive.

I pulled up to the condemned joint where my mans was posted outside in a semi-circle smoking L's and talking mad loud. I hopped out and locked fist with Man Dog first.

"What's poppin', yo?"

"Thug life, nah mean?"

"All day, baby."

I hit Big Nasty, Quent and Zakee up with a pound.

"Why y'all niggaz cheesin' like y'all know some shit I don't know, yo?" I looked from one smirking face to the other.

"You're about to see," said Quent. But it was Man Dog who led the way inside of the house.

I stepped over soiled mattresses, broken bottles and splintered wood and even human feces as I followed him down to the dank basement. A fat rat scurried behind the water heater as we passed.

With us all on his heels, Man Dog walked over in a corner. I heard Lil' Nasty's familiar growl even before someone flicked a lighter illuminating the small area. I rubbed the killa pit's head. Since our last encounter, Lil' Nasty and I had made peace with each other. Being that both of us were real G's, we didn't let pussy come between us.

I squinted my eyes tryna see what it was they had piled up in the corner but the lighting was too faulty for me to make out anything more than a bundle of clothes and a pair of J's.

"Yo, somebody give me a flashlight," I said.

Zakee pulled out his phone, turned on the flashlight and handed it to me. I shined the light in the corner and that's when I realized what I thought was a pile of clothes was actually a nigga. He looked bloody and beaten, and I could see bite marks all in his face.

"Fuck is that?" I turned and looked at Man Dog.

"Malice. He's part of Rah's crew. He started out slinging stones for CJ on Avon Ave, and he put in work with that banger. Remember when they killed three of our men on Park Place at the Keys Club?" asked Man Dog.

"Yeah." I could never forget that. The homies that died that night were good cats.

"That was some of Malice's work. At least, that's what the talk on the streets was."

"Oh yeah? Well, I'ma give the streets some more shit to talk about." I looked from my brother to my goon.

"Big Nasty, make this kid talk, yo." I jabbed a finger at Malice.

Big Nasty stepped forward and commanded Lil' Nasty. "Attack!"

The vicious dog bit into the boy's shoulder and shook him like a rag. Malice's hand and feet were duct taped so all he could do was holla. After a couple minutes, I gave the signal and Big Nasty commanded Lil' Nasty to release his lock on Malice's shoulder.

I stood over him glaring down. His face was hideously swollen and he moaned like a lil' bitch.

"Ay, Black, we can make this a lot less painful. Tell me where Rah and Eric rest at. Just give me one of them and I'll show you mercy."

"Fuck you! You might kill me but Rah is gonna get at you, bitch!" he spat.

"Oh yeah? I'm a bitch huh?" I pulled my dick out and pissed in his face. He squeezed his swollen eyes further shut and tried to squirm away from the golden stream but my aim followed him.

I soaked his face with piss. "Who's the bitch now?"

"You're still a bitch!" he said, tryna remain gully. But I was determined to make him fold.

I snatched my strap off of my waist and shot him in the foot. "Son, we can do this shit all day."

"Let's do it, then!" He held firm.

Had Malice been on my team, I would've applauded his courage. But as it was, he was on the wrong side. So, I was gonna show him that his gangsta wasn't impenetrable.

"Yo, make this nigga talk yo," I said to Big Nasty. "Pull his pants down and flip him over on his stomach while I crush up these Viagra pills. Let's see how G'd up he is when Lil' Nasty fuck him in the asshole."

Hearing this, Malice started scooting back away from us in a frantic attempt to avoid what we planned to do to him. When Zakee caught up to him, he kicked out with both legs. "Get the fuck off of me!"

"Don't cry now, bitch ass nigga. We gave you a chance to talk but you wanted to play hard." Zakee bent down and yanked Malice's pants down around his ankles. "Nigga got an ass like a stripper," he cracked.

We all laughed.

"How long will it take them shits to work?" I asked Big Nasty. As I watched him crush three pills with the heel of his foot, reducing them to powder.

"Thirty minutes, maybe less." He scooped the powdery substance into the palm of his hand and fed it to his dog.

I leaned in and whispered something in Zakee's ear. Immediately he left to run the errand I had sent him on.

Big Nasty led Lil' Nasty over to Malice by the collar. He pressed the dog's face in Malice ass, and Lil' Nasty started slobbering and licking that nigga'z crack.

"Son, you're about to get violated," I taunted, as I saw Lil' Nasty's dick pop out.

Lil' Nasty climbed on top of him and started breathing hot funky breath on his back. He was just about to start humping when Malice lost his gangsta.

"Wait! I'll tell you what you wanna know."

I nodded at Big Nasty and he pulled the dog off of him. Lil' Nasty looked at me as if to say *Nigga this is the second time you blocked my nut.* I laughed so hard, I trickled piss on my own foot.

"Fuck!" I shook my dick and then put it back in my pants before Lil' Nasty mistook it for a Polish sausage.

When I told my niggaz how that dog looked at me, they couldn't do shit but laugh along with me.

"Lil' Nasty gay as fuck," quipped Man Dog.

Lil' Nasty looked at him and growled. Shit was bananas after that. It sounded like we were sitting around watching

Ricky Smiley Live. The only ones that didn't find shit comical was Lil' Nasty and Malice.

By the time Zakee returned, there was no more laughter in the basement. Shit had turned real. Malice didn't know where Rah or Eric rested their heads, but he told us where one of their top lieutenants lived. And he told us that Rah's sister, Lakeesha danced at Jersey Girl out in Elizabeth.

Satisfied that he didn't know anything else, I kept my promise and showed him a lil' mercy. Three shots straight through the heart quickly ended his suffering. Now there was only one thing left to do.

Zakee passed me the axe I had sent him to buy. Quent laid Malice's body just right. Everybody stepped back out of the way. I stepped forward and raised the axe high above my head.

With visions of the way they did my pops and 'em replaying in my head, I said, "Whatever you do to mine, I'ma send that shit back to you just as vile."

I brought the axe down with all my strength and my aim was perfect. Blood spattered and Malice's head rolled away from his body.

"Fuck y'all niggaz think you're fuckin with?" I huffed.

Man Dog stepped around me and kicked the head to Quent. Quent kicked it to Zakee and before long, those fools were playing soccer with the nigga'z head. I let the fun go on for a while before I brought it to an end.

"Fam, I'm starting to look at you cross-eyed," said Man Dog. "Every time a nigga try to have fun you fuck it up, yo." The slight grin on his face told me he was just clowning.

"The fun ain't over yet. I got something for their ass. This shit right here, yo," I paused. "will be talked about for years.

I wore a sly grin on my face as we prepared to mash out. In just a short while, I was gonna send shock waves all throughout the hood.

Twenty minutes later, we were strapped up and in our rides. We drove to The Bricks, where I knew Rah and 'em had trap houses. When we reached the corner of 11th and Clinton Ave, where they had a stronghold on the game, we all filed out of our cars.

We were masked up and packing more heat than an oven.

It was early evening on a Saturday, warm outside and busy with people moving about and that was perfect.

Big Nasty let Lil' Nasty out of the backseat of his car. When the dog jumped down with a human head clenched in his teeth and ran up and down the block, muhfuckas lost their minds. Women and children were running and screaming. Niggaz stood frozen in place. We stood in a full circle, with our choppas, AR-15's and Techs cocked and locked, waiting for a bitch nigga to buck up.

After we cleared the block, Big Nasty commanded Lil' Nasty to drop Malice's head at my feet.

With gloved hands, I bent down and picked it up. "Let Rah and Eric know," I boomed. "That when they fuck with me, I fuck with 'em!"

I let the severed head slip from my hands, and I puntedthat bitch, like a football, in front of their main building. Then we sent a rapid burst of gunshots through the windows before mashing out.

Two nights after that we caught Premo exactly where Malice told us he laid his head. But when we jumped out on him and started bussin' those hammers, Snoop appeared out of nowhere and clapped back.

"This what y'all pussies want! Huh?" *Boc! Boc! Boc! Boc!* "Now you muthafuckin got it!" *Boc! Boc!* His banger coughed at is loud and rapidly.

But he wasn't poppin' at no ho ass niggaz. We spun in his direction and lit the night up! A cacophony of gunfire crackled and roared at both of them. Premo wilted and I spinned his muhfuckin' top, but Snoop took down my nigga, Quent. He took two shots to the head and three to the chest and he was dead before his body hit the ground.

"Bitch, you're gonna die for that!" I barked as I ran toward Snoop, spittin' hot lead and murderous intent.

He was bussin back as he fled but his shots were aimless, and our return fire missed him, too. Somehow, he a managed to get away.

The blare of the jakes' sirens came loud and fast.

Big Nasty rushed up to me and pulled me back toward the car. "Boss man, we gotta push. That's them boys!"

My adrenaline was so amped I wanted to continue to give chase to Snoop. *Fuck the po's, they could feel my heat, too!*

Wisdom overruled cockiness, though, and I started running toward the car.

As I passed by Quent's lifeless body lying on the ground, with blood leaking out of his head, I promised myself that I would not stop gunning for Rah and nem until I wiped out every last one of them. They had cost me too much pain for this war to ever end in anything but a total annihilation of them or us.

We avoided the rush of police cars that swarmed down on the area, but in the days that followed, the heat from the jakes were so intense we had no choice but to shut down and lay low for a minute.

While I waited for things in Newark to cool down, I took Kenisha on a mini vacay to Disney World in Orlando, Florida.

But when I return I'ma come at y'all niggaz even harder than before.

Ca$h

CHAPTER
25
Rah

I hated the strong feeling of despair that washed over me every time we had to bury another fallen soldier. It wasn't simply a young life tragically lost it was also the decimation of families. Mothers would morn forever. Fathers would blame themselves for not being able to steer their sons away from the streets. Young sistahs would have to raise their children without a daddy. Homies would pour out liquor and reminisce of times that were gone forever.

I felt the same grief over the deaths of Malice and Premo as I had felt when we lost Da Quan.

Premo had been born to the streets, but he had four adorable children, all under the age of six years old. When I had to deliver the sad news to Premo's baby mamas, their screams jarred my soul, and their tears were like blood squeezed from my heart. They both blamed me for his death, and the truth of the matter was, they weren't wrong. All I could do was bow my head and offer them money. But how much money was worth a young man's life? I found myself asking my own conscience. *No amount*, the answer came back.

Malice's death was the toughest of all for me to talk about because it was so ghastly and because his body had yet to be found.

How do you hand a mother her son's severed head only and expect her to be able to sleep at night?

It was doubly hard to deal with when I met Malice's family for the first time. I was shocked to learn that he hadn't grown up in the hood. He came from a strong God fearing two-parent home out in Ivy Hill. His oldest brother was a fireman and his sister was a medical lab technician.

"We tried to keep him away from the streets, but he just wouldn't listen." His sister explained through sobs.

"How do you know him?" she asked.

I refused to lie to the poor girl.

"I was one of the people who kept your brother in the streets." I answered truthfully. "I'm sorry."

I expected her to attack me, to call me every vile name I deserved to be called. Instead, she hugged me.

"I'm going to pray for you, Raheem."

That rocked me harder than it would have had she tried to bash my head in. And later when I tried to give her older brother $50,000 as a token of sorrow, I was not surprised that he refused it. It was his statement that touched that part of me that lived underneath the person I had become.

"Our family have burial insurance. If you want to do something for my brother, give the money toward a kid's education."

"I will," I promised.

The next day, I made an anonymous donation of $50,000 that would provide $10,000 scholarships to five graduating seniors from Shabazz High School.

That didn't clear my conscience, though, because at the same time I was making the donation, Eric and the squad were combing the streets looking for anyone connected to Nard. Had they found a distant cousin, a friend of a friend of a friend—any fuckin' body that fit the bill on my orders, they would've left them dead in the streets.

On a subconscious level, I knew that my actions weren't in accord with my beliefs. But my animalistic hunger to avenge CJ was all that mattered to me.

I knew I needed to clear my mind, so I made a trip out to Montclair to visit the one person who could take my thoughts off of the streets and murder, if only temporarily.

Her face was flush with happiness and surprise when she opened her door and saw me standing there.

"Raheem! Oh, my God! I didn't think I would ever see you again." She threw her arms around me and pulled me in for a hug. In her excitement, she almost crushed the dozen roses I held in my hand.

I enjoyed the feel of her voluptuous body for a moment before holding her back at arm's length and looking her up and down.

"You look good, Queen. I see you've been in the gym."

"I have. Thank you." She ran her hands down her curves and smiled proudly. It looked like she had lost ten or fifteen pounds and had toned herself up. The last time we had seen each other Malika was beautiful and voluptuous. Now she was even more breathtaking.

I reached up and touched her hair. "Your locs?" They were gone.

"I just wanted a change. You like my short, sassy look?" she asked.

"Yes." Although I loved her locs.

"Oh, my God! Forgive me for being rude. Please come inside." Her smile was as wide as the universe.

I looked over my shoulder, back to the car, and gave a thumbs up, letting Legend and Young Stunna know that everything was peace. They would remain parked at the curb while I visited, even if I remained inside until daylight.

Legend still blamed himself for my kidnapping the night I took a drunk Kenisha home from the club and David X set me up.

"None of this shit could've happened if I had gone with you. CJ wouldn't even be dead." He had said on more than one occasion.

Of course, the blame wasn't on him. None of us could've known about Kenisha's dad's connection to Nard, but Legend refused to take a chance like that again.

Malika put the roses in a vase. After thanking me, her eyes focused on my cane.

"It's only temporary," I said.

"What happened? Were you in a car accident?"

We sat side by side on a futon.

"Nah, it's a long story."

"Well, I would like to hear it." She folded her legs underneath her and propped her hand under her chin, waiting for my reply.

I was not the type of man to lie to a woman and I definitely didn't want to tell the truth, so I smoothly changed subjects.

"It's nothin' really. I'll be off this cane in a few more weeks. But what's been up with you?"

"So, you're just going to ignore my question, sir? Don't you think that's kind of rude?" She lightly admonished. "But I get it," she went on, "obviously you don't wish to talk about it."

"I don't. If you don't mind?" I reached over and gently rubbed her hand.

"Cool." She didn't protest. "Well, I've been fine, missing you. Why did you stop calling?" She looked into my eyes.

I held her stare. "There's been a lot going on with me." I replied with vagueness.

"Please share."

"Nah, Queen. Let's not talk about me. I would much rather hear about you. I'm sure your life is a movie," I teased.

"I wish." She giggled, and that little burst of laughter lightened my soul. Before long we were holding hands as Malika told me what she had been up to the past months.

I noticed that she hadn't mentioned dating anyone, so I asked. "I'm sure you got right and tight for someone." I let my eyes roam up and down her new and improved figure. "So, who is he, and what does he do?"

"Raheem, there's no one. I thought the little extra weight was what drove you away, so that was my motivation."

"What? Queen, you gotta know I'm not that shallow. I was mad attracted to you," I spoke honestly.

"And now?"

I responded by leaning in and stealing a kiss. Her lips were so soft and welcoming. I stole another and another.

Pulling back for a second, I stroked her hair as I looked deeper into her eyes. "Did that answer your question or do you need me to answer it further?"

"Raheem, I see hunger in your eyes. Did you come here to seduce me?"

I thought I heard playfulness in her voice, but I didn't want to misread her. I didn't want Malika to think I would come at her like she was a basic female, and I just wanted to cut something with her. So, I explained, "Never that, Queen. I do desire your body, but it was your mind and your spirit that attracted me first." I leaned back to allow my desire to cool off a bit.

"I was half teasing, King." She smiled beautifully. "It's okay if you want to ravish me. I know it's more than carnal. I can tell by the way your eyes soften when you talk to me."

"Is that a fact?"

"Yes, King, it is. You can't hide what's in the heart."

"What about you? Can you hide what's in your heart?" I asked.

"No, I can't. And with you, I wouldn't want to." She leaned in and pressed her lips to mine.

As the kiss intensified, her arms went around my neck and my hands caressed her curves. I hadn't been with a woman in a minute, so my body reacted strongly. Especially, because Malika embodied everything that I found attractive about a woman.

The steel beam in my pants stood up like the statue atop The Empire State Building. It pressed against her thigh, causing her to take notice.

"Does this mean I really, really kiss good?" She brushed her hand lightly across my bulge..

"*That*, and a whole lot of other things. Let me whisper them to you."

"Umm." She licked her sexy lips in delight as I brought my kissers close to her ear.

"I've thought about you often, Queen. So many nights I needed to hold you in my arms. I needed to feel your essence close to me," I whispered while nibbling on her ear lobe.

"Why didn't you come for me?" She moaned softly.

"In my heart, I was on my way. Now I'm finally here, for real."

"Don't hurt me, Rah. Don't come back just to leave again."

"I won't." I sucked on her neck.

My promise seemed to unleash her passion.

When our lips locked again, and our tongues tangled, Malika's hands roamed my chest. Her touch was everything that I needed. I touched her back, the way she was caressing me. The heat between our bodies was uncontrollable. Clothes began to get unzipped and unbuttoned.

In the middle of our kissing and touching, my cell phone chirped. "Shit!" I cussed. With everything going on in the streets, I couldn't ignore the call. "Queen, I'ma have to answer that." I whispered.

"I understand," she replied on light breath.

I straightened myself and pulled my phone out of my jacket pocket. "Sup, fam?"

"Shawdy, you a'ight in there?" asked Legend.

"Yeah, son, I'm peace. If you want, y'all can leave and come back for me in a couple hours."

"Bruh bruh, stop playing. Ain't no way I'm leaving here until you're safely back in the car."

"Word. Get comfortable, then, 'cause it's gonna be a while."

"Not if you're about to hit. You know you're a minute man. Two or three pumps and it'll be over," he cracked

"Son, you're stupid as fuck!" I laughed.

"Fa real, though, shawdy. Step to the door so I can see you're good," said Legend.

"That's not necessary, dawg. I told you everything is peace." I assured. But my nigga wasn't satisfied with that.

"Fam, just relax my mind," he insisted.

I got up and walked to the door. I opened it and threw up the peace sign. Legend blinked the headlights on and off again, signaling back to me that he saw me.

When I shut the door, Malika was standing behind me. She wrapped her arms around my waist and buried her nose between my shoulder blades.

"What was all of that about?" she asked.

"I was just letting my driver know that I'm okay." It wasn't a lie but stretching the truth a little.

"*Mmm hmm.* Piss on my head and tell me it's raining." She turned and walked to the back of the apartment.

I stood there for a minute, kinda confused. Malika's response was unexpected, and it made her sound distrustful of me. I couldn't leave it at that so I followed her back to the bedroom, but I respectfully stopped at the door.

"Queen, do you take me to be a brother who's about games?" I watched her sit down on her bed and lean back against the head board.

"You can come in, Raheem. I don't bite, although I should."

"What you mean?" I walked in and sat down next to her.

"It doesn't matter, baby." She pulled her t-shirt over her head, tossed it on the floor and then unsnapped her bra. She dropped that on top of her t-shirt then wiggled out of her capris. There were no panties for her to remove. She was butt ass naked.

Under different circumstances, and had the mood been sensual as it was earlier, I would've savored the sight of her nakedness. But this right here wasn't sexy or romantic, and it threw me for a loop.

"Sup with dat?" My left eyebrow was raised in puzzlement.

"It's cool, Raheem, we don't have to open up to each other. If you prefer to just have sex we can do that. Go ahead and get undressed, it's been a long time since I've done this. I guess I'm overdue."

"Queen, I'm feeling a breeze coming off that invite." I folded my arms across my chest and tightened my jaw. "I mean, a minute ago you were the sweet, sensual sista I've known you to be. But right now you're somebody else. What's up with that? Why you flipping?"

"I'm not flipping, Raheem," she elongated my name in pronunciation. "Let's just fuck."

"What?" I chuckled. "You think I'm on some booty call shit? You think I would treat you like a gutta rat, baby girl? Is that how you think I am?" I couldn't believe what had come out of her mouth. "Queen, I got mad respect for you. Why would you come at me sideways?"

"Why are you lying to me and putting up a front like you're somebody you're not?" She stood up and put her t-shirt and capris back on.

I wasn't mad at that because her sudden shift in attitude had deadened the sexual energy we'd had a few minutes ago, anyway. I was peeved because she was implying that I was an imposter.

"Say what you're saying, yo, and quit beating around the bush." I was heated. In the blink of an eye, that hood shit rose to the surface. "You're talking mad greasy, ma. But you don't know what you're talking about. I am who I told you I am."

"Amongst other things."

"Other. Things. Like. What?" My question came out with a pause between each word, and it was hurled at her like a slap across the face.

Malika turned back to me. When she opened her mouth to speak, she choked up. She wiped at her eyes. "A few weeks ago, I became friends with a girl who grew up in Little Bricks. Somehow, she got on the topic that all men ain't shit and I defended that wasn't true. I was gushing to her about you, and telling her what a wonderful brother you are."

"Is that right?" I braced myself for the surprise I sensed hiding just beneath the surface.

"My friend knows you very well, Raheem. She told me about CJ, Tamika, Nard and everyone else. She described you to the T, right down to your raspy voice and your gentle ways. But underneath all of that, she said is a quiet killa."

"Oh yeah? What's your friend's name?" My mouth was tight.

"Her name isn't important. What's important is what she said. Tell me, was she lying?"

"Let people say whatever they wanna say. Judge me for yourself." It was truly how I felt because deep down I knew I was a good nigga. But Malika wouldn't leave it at that.

"My friend told me in spite of all the social consciousness you possess, your love for CJ will trump it all. Is that true, Raheem?"

I didn't respond.

"Nard killed Tamika, who CJ loved to no end. CJ declared war and you came back to Newark to help your brothers. Is that true, Raheem?"

I remained mute, but Malika went on.

"My friend said people started getting killed left and right on both sides but then somehow Nard caught you and CJ slipping. He killed CJ and left you for dead. Obviously, you didn't die but now you're out for blood."

"Your friend don't know what she's talking about?" I frowned because it felt like Malika was slick interrogating me.

"I follow the stories in the paper, Raheem. Young brothers and sisters are getting killed. Men and women—black men and women, never the less—are being mutilated and beheaded. When I read that shit it makes me sick to my stomach! I tell myself *No, it can't be my Raheem doing this. He wouldn't help commit genocide against his own race. Would he?*

She turned to face me, as tears ran down her face in rivers.

"Are you part of the problem, or are you part of the solution? Are you Raheem or Rah? Are you the gentle soul I thought I knew, or are you a beast who can murder another brotha and never shed a tear? Are you the business minded owner of night clubs in Atlanta, or are you the next drug lord of Newark? Who the fuck are you, Raheem?" Her voice bounced off of the walls, and her tears dripped from her chin onto the floor.

Her anger didn't hold up, though. In the time it took for me to exhale the breath I had sucked in and held while Malika was going off, she fell against my chest and wept.

I held her close to me and kissed the top of her head. Her tears soaked my shirt, and the strength in which she hugged me held the power of a thousand pairs of arms. Her weeping made me think. *Somebody is always crying or dying around me.*

Through her pained emotions, Malika begged me to reveal the whole truth about myself.

"Please, Raheem, tell me who you are. I need to know. I need to hear that you aren't a cold-hearted killer in disguise."

The painfully poetic and true words I had spoken on stage at the Café' in Greenwich Village, that night we were together, came to mind. I swallowed the lump in my throat and repeated them.

You might think you know me but you don't
And really you don't want to
I'm a complex man who knows how to love but I won't
Although I really want to
But see, I'm wrapped in eternal misery
Battling not to concede to fatal epiphanies
I don't ask for your tears or sympathy…

I continued on, line for line. My voice echoed my internal anguish, reflected the battle between right and wrong that was being waged in the vessels of my heart.

"I know right from wrong but my loyalty is my worst enemy." I released Malika from my embrace and started walking toward the front door as I continued to recite more.

"To stop me now it's gonna take ten of me!"

"Raheem!" she called out and ran behind me.

I stopped and spun around, penetrating her with a gaze that could've cut off her head had I been inclined to do so.

"Malika, I'm not on my deen! CJ was my A-1! My nigga had more love for me than you could fit in this whole muhfuckin' universe. He took his own life to save mine. But make no mistake, Nard killed him. And for that," I paused and pounded my fist in my hand, "that muthafucka is gonna die! And if it takes for me to kill a thousand people to get to him— well, that's what I'ma do." I turned back toward the door. "Judge me however you choose, Queen." I concluded in a humble tone.

As I reached for the door knob, Malika raced around me and blocked my exit.

"Please don't go, Raheem. Please, baby, let me be your peace tonight. We need each other."

***

When our bodies joined together it was like our souls became one. She had the softest place in the world, and it was exactly what I needed. Every moan that escaped her lips told me she needed me just as much as I needed her. Soft whimpers turned into *"I love you, Raheem. I've known it since the day we first met."*

I trusted her every word because her body confirmed her claim. She gave back what I gave to her, with so much passion.

She reached her peak before I reached mine, but I took her higher. The bottom of her feet found the top of my shoulders and her inner warmth was like an oven. She was tight. She was wet and slippery. She moved with untamed vigor.

Feeling myself about to reach the top of a mountain, I remembered that I hadn't strapped up.

"Queen, I need to pull out." I breathed more-so than I said.

"No, King, give it to me. Give me your essence," she strongly urged.

"But…"

"Raheem," she put a finger to my lips, hushing me. "We need to let it happen. More than you could ever know."

I had no clue what she meant but the roll of her hips and the softness of her valley demanded me to spill my seeds deep inside of her.

I closed my eyes and gritted my teeth and then I gave into her love.

Ca$h

CHAPTER
26
Nard

After a month of applying mad pressure on residents of The Bricks, with no results, the jakes finally eased up. We returned to the city and reclaimed our blocks. Any fool that resisted our return got dealt with. David X had blessed me with a new shipment of that white girl, and the best heroin to reach the city in years. Our stamps had the fiends clucking stupid hard for our packages.

Money was pouring in so fast, I needed several people to count it around the clock. We were still tryna get at Rah an 'em, and they were trying to clap at us, but with both crews being on point, the casualties became few and far between.

As summer kicked in, lil' shorties began to feel safe again to come outside and play. It seemed to be a cease fire referendum over The Bricks but I wasn't buying that shit, nah mean? I knew there could never be peace between the sides. And I didn't wish for it to be any other way.

"It's gonna come down to the last man standing." I predicted.

"Say dat," said Big Nasty

"Know dat," I replied, as I pulled away from our spot on Bergen. We had just put a new team in place there after our regular men got knocked. Shit like that had begun to happen on the regular.

Every week those boys were jumping out, running up in a different spot of mine and raiding it. I was beginning to suspect Eric and 'em of dropping dimes on us, because none of their buildings had been hit.

"The niggaz can't out gun us, so they're playing dirty, yo." I speculated.

"It wouldn't surprise me," said Big Nasty.

I shook my head and hit up David X and gave him the news, blow by blow.

"Other than the raid, how's everything going?" he asked.

"Lovely." I sparked a blunt.

"Any sighting of our friends?"

I knew who he was referring to Rah and Eric.

"Nah, they're not crazy nor brave."

"True indeed," he chuckled.

"How are things at home?"

"They couldn't be better. Kenisha's belly is way out there, but she's glowing."

"Good, Good. Bring her to see me this weekend. We'll have a fish fry. Inshah Allah."

"Sounds like a plan, by the way, I'll bring that guap with me, too."

I could tell he liked the sound of that. When it came to cheddar, his breathing quickened and his palms would be sweating mad hard. I loved those dead faces as much as the next man did, but David X's love for the almighty dollar was unparalleled. I still hadn't figured out how he managed to live such a double life without being exposed.

His super slick moves didn't bother me, though. As long as he continued to bless me with that work, he could quote the Holy Quran out one side of his mouth, and kilo prices out the other.

As soon as I hung up from David X and bent a corner, we ran dead smack into standstill traffic on Sunset, not far from one of our major money making spots where we still sold weight. We sat in traffic for ten minutes without moving forward an inch.

I looked over at Big Nasty. "I know business is booming but it can't have traffic backed up like this, yo."

"Nah, it's probably an accident up ahead." He assumed.

I drummed my fingers on the steering wheel and let the blunt burn in the corner of my mouth, while we waited for traffic to begin flowing again. But I had this nervous feeling in the pit of my stomach and I couldn't shake it.

"Bruh, I need you to take 5 of them joints and 10 pounds of loud to son and 'em out Sussex Ave." I instructed Man Dog.

"That spot is hot. Have someone else handle it, yo."

"Man Dog, this ain't even an argument. Make the drop. Why we gotta tongue wrestle about shit? Do I exchange words with you when it's time for you to get paid?"

"A'ight, you got that. But tell Slim to be out front waiting. I'ma pull up on him and pass him the bag through the window. I just don't feel comfortable going inside."

"Bruh, you're becoming paranoid, but if it will ease your mind, I'll hit Slim up and let him know how it's going down. What time you pulling up on him?"

"Between 5:30 and 6:00. And this is the last time I'm making this drop."

"Whatever, yo."

Recalling the conversation from earlier, I checked my Rolex. It read 6:17 p.m.. The uneasiness in my stomach turned into a hard knot.

"My G," I said to Big Nasty. "Slide behind the wheel. I'm gonna get out and see what's going on."

We were two blocks away from the spot. As I headed up Sussex Ave, people lined the streets, whispering back and forth and pointing up ahead. As I neared the building, I saw one of the Dodge Caravans we used to make deliveries sitting on the back of a flatbed tow truck. I visually counted at least six police cars parked at the corner.

"Fuck!" Shit wasn't looking good at all.

The picture grew uglier when I got closer and saw Man Dog in the back of one car and Lemora in the back of another. Their hands were cuffed behind their backs and they wore solemn looks on their faces.

I made eye contact with my brother. *"Don't worry, I got you,"* I mouthed.

I tried to force eye contact with Lemora but shorty had her head down. All I could do was hope she wouldn't fold under pressure, she knew enough to sink the whole ship.

I'ma have to bail her out of jail fast. And if her voice trembles when we talk, I'ma fold her up.

I wouldn't have to worry about Man Dog, he was official.

I looked up to see Cujo and a big black cop escorting Tone and Pappy out of the building in cuffs. Both kids had been down with me for more than three years. I wasn't worried about them folding either. And if they did, they couldn't tell much. Until his last breath, they had mostly dealt with Quent. They barely knew anything about me other than my name.

"Yo, boss! Yo, boss!"

I turned around to see Slim ducked off in the crowd. He gestured me over to an area a few feet away where we could talk in private.

"What the fuck happened, yo? Somebody must've talked." My voice was low and harried.

"I can't tell you that. I mean, as soon as they pulled up to the building, those boys came from everywhere! Your peeps didn't get a chance to do nothin'! He tried to pull off, but they had him boxed in. And they were waiting for him to make a country break. Muhfuckas had their hammers out, ready to let loose."

During the initial pandemonium, Slim just eased into the crowd that quickly formed outside.

"It was a good thing I did, too." He went on, "Because those jump out boys drove up a second later and ran up in the building. Damn! I almost got snatched up, too."

We both saw men with DEA emblazoned on the back of their jackets carrying bags out of the building.

"This is that Fed shit, yo. We better bounce." I said out of the corner of my mouth.

"I'm ghost, fam, I'll hit you on the hip," said Slim. He walked off and disappeared between some buildings.

Just as I was about to mash out. I looked up and saw Cujo staring at me with a sly grin on his face. I shot daggers at the cracker. It was mano a mano, as our eyes remained locked on each other.

I was grilling Cujo so hard, I didn't pay attention to his partna until that big black ass nigga was two strides away. He wasn't as big as Big Nasty, but that muhfucka was huge. I knew who he was because he fit the description of the new narc niggas had been talking about lately. He was thought to be on Cujo's team.

"Get down on the ground with your arms above your head!" he barked. He held up a police badge in one hand, and the other hand rested on his holstered gun.

I glanced to my left and then to my right, measuring my chances of escape. Before I could command my legs to move, he balled up his gloved hand and punched me dead in the jaw. A pain exploded in my head and buildings began to spin in circles. Then I felt the cold concrete against the side of my face.

"Clear the goddam area!" His authoritative voice boomed louder than a mega phone.

Feet shuffled, people cussed.

"Fuck the police! I hate all of you bitches!" A woman spat.

Big Boy turned me over onto my stomach, put his knee in my back and frisked me. I felt him remove my Glock off of my waist.

When he cuffed me and began reading my rights, the only thing on my mind was: *Is this gun clean?* I couldn't recall if I had murked anybody with it.

As I was snatched to my feet, I saw Big Nasty running toward us. He looked like a grizzly bear turned loose in the city.

"Take another step and I'll blow your ass away! Go 'head, try me, badass!" Cujo stood in a wide legged stance, gripping his weapon with both hands. He had the gun level with my goon's chest.

My whole face was swelling rapidly. One eye was already closed. I looked at Big Nasty out of the other one and shook my head *no*.

"Stand down," I shouted, spraying blood from my mouth. I could tell it took the restraint of God for Big Nasty not to go the fuck off. His chest heaved up and down and his nostrils flared like a bull.

"Flinch, muthafucka." Cujo tried to bait him. But Big Nasty didn't move. He understood that there would be other opportunities to get at Cujo. Right now, I needed him on the streets making moves for me.

CHAPTER
27
Kenisha

I knew something was wrong even before Daddy called to tell me Nard was in jail. I had been trying to reach bae for hours but his phone was off.

"Oh, my God, Daddy. Why is he in jail?" Tears fell from my eyes instantly

"He was charged with carrying a concealed weapon, resisting arrest and some other minor charges."

"Okay that's not too bad." I fanned myself and let out a huge sigh of relief, because I had feared the worse. Nard had never discussed his business with me, but I had seen enough to know what he did for a living.

"Princess, is there anything in the house that needs to be moved? Guns, money, anything like that?" asked Daddy.

"I don't know, Dad. Why would I have to move anything? Do you think the police might come by here to search the house? I mean, why would they do that?" I nervously fidgeted with my wedding ring.

"They probably won't, but we can't take that chance. I want you to search the house top to bottom. If you find any money, guns, drugs, scales, or a money-counting machine, I want you to get it away from there."

"And take it where?"

"Hold on, let me think. Shit! I'm out of town."

"Well, why can't I call Nard's brother to handle this?"

"Because he's in jail, too."

"Ugh!" I stood up and went into the guest room. We had just moved into the house a month ago, so the room was sparsely furnished but I had seen Nard lug duffel bags in there, in the middle of the night.

"Kenisha, are you still there?" Daddy's voice broke the silence.

"Yes," I replied, as I looked inside the closet and saw eight black duffel bags. With the phone held between my shoulder and the side of my face, I drug one of the bags out of the closet and looked inside of it. What I saw made me gasp.

"Kenisha, what's wrong?"

"Nothing. Hold on, Daddy?"

I sat the phone down on the floor and drug the other bags out as well. Behind them I found two tennis bags. I drug those out too. One by one, I opened each bag and looked inside. All of the eight duffel bags were filled to the top with neatly banded money. The two tennis bags contained different type of guns, small and large.

When I retrieved my phone, I was short of breath and shaking badly.

"Daddy, I just found bags and bags of money and a whole lot of guns. I'm scared." I started bawling.

"Kenisha, don't panic. I'll send someone over there. Better yet, call Jada and have her take everything to her place. And tell her to keep her damn mouth closed. If word gets out that she has all of that at her house, she won't be safe."

"Daddy, why can't I call one of Nard's boys?" That seemed like a better idea, but Daddy shot that down immediately.

"Because Nard doesn't have a bond yet. We're hoping they won't come up with more serious charges against him. But until we know for sure, and until his feet are back on the ground, we don't know when, or if, he's coming home. And, baby if he doesn't come home, friends can't be trusted with the amount of money you just described to me. Now call your aunt. Time is of the essence."

"Okay, Daddy, I will." I answered dutifully.

***

Jada hadn't ever been over to my house. In fact, she thought that after Mommy was killed, I moved in with Daddy. So, after following my direction, she came bursting through the door wide eyed and impressed.

"Bitch, you ballin'! This muthafucka is laced!" I followed behind her as she gave herself a tour of our 5 bedrooms 4 ½ bath home.

"You have more flat screen TV's up in here than Best Buy." She remarked as she went from room to room.

When she reached the kitchen, she marveled over the stainless steel appliances, the see-through refrigerator doors and the spacious island. Only then, did she seem to notice me.

"Oh, La! You're big as a house. But you look good, bitch!" She walked around me looking me over like I was up for auction.

"Look at you. That ass done got fat. Where your baby daddy at? I want to meet that nigga because homeboy been putting it down." She slapped my ass for emphasis.

"Let me find out you're gay." I laughed.

"*Umph! Umph! Umph!* Look at Miss Thang."

"Will you hush." I covered my mouth with my left hand to hide my smile.

"Hold up! This better not be what I think it is!" She pulled my hand down and studied my wedding ring.

"Kenisha Renee Garvin, I know your ass did not get married without inviting me to the wedding." I saw a look of genuine hurt flash in her eyes, and it made me feel bad.

"We didn't have a wedding, we just drove to Atlantic City and made it happen."

True to Jada's nature, she had a million and one question, but I held her off for the time being.

"Let's hurry up and move this stuff and then I'll tell you what I can." I promised.

"Okay, 'cause, bitch, I'm thirsty for that tea. I need to know how you went from crying over CJ to snagging a nigga who's got you living like a boss bitch. Damn." She shook her head from side to side. "I'ma have to switch up my game.

***

After the last bag was stacked in her attic and locked away, we were both hungry and exhausted. We ordered pizza and wings and we talked lightly about random things. When our food arrived, we tore into it like two fat women on escape from a Jenny Craig's asylum.

As I was about to bite into the last slice of pizza, my phone rang. It was Snoop calling and he had bae on three way. I got up and walked outside.

As soon as Nard started talking, I started crying.

"Ma, don't cry, this shit ain't nothin'! I'll be home before you know it." His voice was low and his words came out mumbled.

"Baby, I can hardly hear you. Are you okay?" Thunder roared and lightning cracked the ski, drowning out his response. A few seconds later, rain poured from the clouds forcing me back inside. "Nard, baby, I couldn't hear you, say that again." I raised my voice.

"I said these bitch muhfuckas fractured my jaw," he said.

"Oh, my God!" I cried. "Bae, who fractured your jaw?"

"One of the bitch muhfuckaz that arrested me. Anyways, stay away from The Bricks, niggas would love to pull up on you, on some grimy shit, while I'm locked up."

"Okay, Nard. But what's going on?" I was frightened to death.

"It's nothin' yo. Just stay away from Newark. I love you, ma. I gotta go now."

"I love you, too, baby."

When the call disconnected, I staggered over to the couch where Jada was sitting. I collapsed down and cried in her arms. She didn't say a word, she just held me until my tear ducts were completely empty and my tears dried on my face.

"Here. Drink this." She handed me a bottle of water. I took a few sips and then sat it down on the table.

"Thanks."

Jada could be all types of extra but as my mom's youngest sister, she had always been like a big sister to me.

"So, that was hubby, huh?" She treaded lightly.

"Yeah."

"I heard you call him Nard. Is that his name?" I didn't respond.

"I guess that means *yes*." She surmised and since she already knew, I nodded confirmation.

"Okay, and when we were moving those duffel bags, one of them came open and I saw that it was loaded with Benjamin's. So, putting 2 and 2 together to come up with 4, Nard is getting to the money, big time. Isn't he?"

"I don't know, Jada. And please don't start pressing me because I don't ask my husband about his business." I tried my best to shut her down, but the bitch was like a dog with a bone.

"Kenisha, you're so fuckin' gullible. You make me want to throw up!"

"Good, Jada! Because you make my ass itch!" I fired back. "Why do you have to pry?"

"Boo, I'm not prying. I'm trying to see if my suspicions are correct. Because if they are, you're about to have a serious decision to make."

"Jada, what on Earth are you talking about?" She could be so damn dramatic.

"Does Nard have a brother named Man Dog? And is Man Dog's bitch named Lemora?"

I nodded my head *yes* to both questions.

"Do you have a picture of Nard?" she asked.

"Of course." I picked up my cell phone and handed it to her. A picture of Nard was my screen saver.

Jada took one look at it and handed my phone back to me. Her mouth said nothing but her eyes said a lot.

"What?" I asked.

"Girl, you don't even want to know." She shook her head from side to side.

My heart started pounding. I really didn't want to know because I feared she was gonna tell me that Nard was fucking around with some bitch he knew. If that was so, my heart would shatter into a million tiny pieces.

Despite my fears, I had to know.

"Jada, if you know something about Nard, please spit it out."

"Are you sure you want to know?" she asked.

"Yes." I held my breath.

She looked at me and didn't blink. Then, she leaned over and jabbed her finger against the screen of my phone right at Nard's face.

"Your bae is the nigga who killed CJ."

"Oh, God! No!" I gasped.

My baby kicked and my food rushed up. I jumped up and raced to the bathroom, spewing streams of vomit along the way.

CHAPTER
28
Rah

Cujo was doing everything he could to bring down Nard's entire operation. Every other day, it seemed, he was organizing a raid of one of their spots or knocking off a delivery of theirs. Soon the losses they were suffering would have a major effect on their pockets, and that would force Nard into a corner.

I understood the strategy, but I didn't approve of those tactics. Fuck I care about Nard's pockets leaking or his workers getting cased up, nah mean? *Fuck that!* I wanted to bury those muhfuckaz. Until I folded that young nigga up, my soul couldn't rest, and neither could my nigga'z

As I stood in the mirror strapping up, I touched my fist to my chest and reiterated my vow to CJ.

"Fam, I promise you on the lives of my G-ma, my sister and my unborn children, I'ma lay son on his ass."

Earlier Cujo had called to tell me about the raid of Nard on Sussex Ave.

"We hit his ass hard. We have his brother and his girl in custody on major drug charges. Even though they may eventually bond out, they'll end up doing 15-20 years fed time. So, they're essentially out of the way. And we have Nard in custody on a weapon's charge. We can plant drugs on him, too." He informed me.

"Fuck that! I'm not down with that type of shit. This thing between me and Nard gotta be settled in the streets. I really don't give a fuck about the rest of his crew. But Nard, Man Dog and Big Nasty are gonna die by my hands. I don't want them taken out of the game no other fuckin' way! So, kill that noise you're talking, because a bitch ass muthafucka serving

twenty years, or even life in the pen, ain't justice for what they did. Hell no, fuck that!" I went off.

Cujo tried to get me to look at the bigger picture, which was as long as we came out on top, the means by which we accomplished it was secondary. In some other time, I may have agreed with him. But not in this one.

"Understand me, and it will prevent us from bumpin' heads in the future," I said in a tone as easy as Sunday morning. "I don't care about the money or the power. None of that shit means anything to me. I'm doing what I'm doing for CJ. Vengeance is the only thing that motivates me."

"Okay, but let's get this over with in a hurry," he said.

"Cool. Here's how we can kill two birds at once. You have Nard and Man Dog in custody, right?"

"Yes."

"A'ight, all you have to do is lock me and Legend up on some bogus charges and put us in the holding tank with those pussies. Make it possible for me and my man to carry knives inside of the jail, and we'll do both of them in the holding tank. End of Story." I laid my plot out on the table.

"Hmm, let me make a few calls and get back to you. Stay close to your phone.

"Don't worry, I'm not moving a muscle until I hear back from you."

A while later, Cujo called back to inform me that getting to Man Dog was impossible. For reasons unknown, he was already in federal protective custody.

"But I can get one of you in the holding tank with Nard. Which one of you will be it?" he asked.

"Me," I said without a second thought.

I turned away from the mirror and walked out into the living room. Eric sat on the sofa next to La. Legend was posted up by the door picking at his fingernails with the very tip of his machete.

"Why is everyone wearing a sad face?" I asked, taking in their collective visage.

No one answered me. I had told all three of them what was about to go down. La already had tears in her eyes. I walked over to her and pulled her to her feet, and into a hug. My injuries had healed completely, so the strength in which she held on to me didn't cause me any pain.

"Bruh bruh, make sure you come back."

"You can bank on it."

She had already tried to talk me out of going but that was like talking to the wall. She stood on her tippy toes and placed a kiss on my cheek.

"Please be careful and make sure you stab his hatin' ass once for me. Punk muthafucka could never be the boss CJ was," she correctly stated.

"I got you, sis." Lately the rift between us had begun to dissolve, and the love and respect for each other that Big Ma instilled in us had risen to the surface.

Once La stepped out of my embrace, Eric stood up. We locked hands and bumped chests. "Do the muhfucka to that nigga, yo."

"Yo, B, you already know. Just watch the news."

We bumped fists and I headed toward the door.

Legend was planted firmly in front of the door, looking like he had no intentions on moving to let me by.

"Sup, Dirty?" I tried to soften him up with some of his ATL flow.

"Shawty, let me handle this. The team need you too bad for you to take this risk. Real talk, my G, you don't have to get blood on your hands. Let me handle it, my nigga. This is what I do." Legend pled.

I shook my head *no*.

"Bruh, you know this shit is personal. Don't even sweat it. This shit is gonna be like taking candy from a baby. Niggaz like Nard ain't shit without that toolie in their hand. But you know it takes a different breed of killa to push that knife. Just be easy, gangsta, your boy got this."

"You sho?"

"Is a pig's pussy pork?"

"24/7, 365."

We both smiled.

"Don't let this baby face fool you." I joked, stroking my hairless chin.

"Neva dat. Gon' do what G's do. I salute." He made the gesture with his hand.

"Salute." I gestured back.

***

Cujo and Tim were parked outside when I stepped out of the door. I climbed in the backseat of a non-descript vehicle, and I was surprised to find a frail looking white chic sitting in the backseat.

Few words were spoken, and I didn't know why she was there until we reached the precinct. As soon as we drove into the lot and parked, the necessity of her presence came to light. In less than 30 minutes, she had done wonders with make-up and a wig. And when Cujo escorted me into the building in cuffs, I looked like a 45-year-old Rasta.

***

The deputy smoothly tucked the knife in my waistband as he escorted me to the holding pen at the end of the corridor.

"Yo, shotta, what they got you for?" someone yelled from a pen as we passed by.

I kept my head down, ignoring everything and everybody. The only thing on my mind was a bitch nigga'z murder.

Cujo already had it set up so I could escape after I killed Nard. I haven't been fingerprinted or processed, the disguise was for the cameras. So, there would be no trace of me ever being arrested after I slumped Nard and got in the wind.

I didn't know how many favors had been promised or how much fetti had changed hands to make this happen and it didn't even matter, nah mean? I just wanted to feel Nard's life leave his body when I shoved the knife in his gut. Legend had told me to shove it right under his rib cage.

The anticipation of this kill had my adrenaline pumping stupid hard. My legs moved so fast that the deputy could hardly keep up.

"Slow down." He whispered out of the corner of his mouth.

I willed my legs to cooperate with my mind, and we proceeded at a moderate pace. The last twenty feet felt like a five-mile hike. Then, we were standing in front of the holding pen where Nard sat alone.

Ca$h

CHAPTER
29
Rah

He was laid back on the steel bench, with his hands behind his head, staring up at the ceiling. When the iron door slid open he sat up.

Before I stepped into the pen, the deputy repeated instructions on what I was to do after I killed Nard.

"Do not leave the knife behind," the young brother of about 22 or 23 years of age said.

I responded with a head nod. The door slid closed behind me but I was aware that it wasn't locked. Nard sat up and placed his feet on the floor. I sat down on the bench opposite of him and turned so he would only get the side view of me. The scraggly beard that had been pasted on my face was knotted up and my eyebrows were thick and bushy.

Twenty minutes passed without either of us uttering a word. I sat calmly but the fever in my blood was boiling.

Out of the corner of my eye, I saw him sizing me up. Not for beef, but to determine if I was on a level worthy of his conversation.

Having done a bid, I knew that four walls and prolonged silence was a difficult thing for most men to endure. The walls could close in on you fast, especially when you had a lot going on, on the streets. So, it didn't come as a surprise when Nard initiated a conversation.

"Yo, Dread, where you from, yo?"

"Brooklyn." I kept my head down.

"Oh, yeah? How did you get locked up in Jersey?"

"I was looking for a pussy who killed mi bruddah." I tried to effect a Jamaican accent. My attempt was horrible, but Nard seemed not to notice.

"Did you find him?" he asked as he stood up and went to take a piss.

"I think so!" The hate I held in my heart against him coated my words. I could barely contain myself. My jaw twitched and my nails dug deeply into the palm of my hands as I clenched my fist tightly.

I was sitting only a few feet away from the muthafucka who had cut out my heart. I was anxious to rip his insides out and spill 'em in the floor, but this nigga deserved to die slow and painful.

I heard a stream of urine hit the water, Nard flushed twice and then walked back over to the bench and sat down.

"You think you found him?" He half laughed.

"Fuck you find so funny?" I spat in my own voice, but he didn't catch it.

"Fuck you talking to?" He spat back.

I sprung up. "I'm talking to you, bitch!"

Nard pounced to his feet, too. "Rasta man, you must wanna die up in here. Do you know who the fuck I am, yo?" He widened his stance, prepared for combat.

"Yeah, I know who you are. But do you know who the fuck I be, nigga?" With one hand, I whipped out my knife. With the other, I wiped the make-up off of my face.

Recognition flashed in Nard's eyes, and he smiled. "You must've forgot what I did to your punk ass the last time we were face to face."

"You didn't do shit, bitch, I'm still breathing."

"Yeah, but your boy not." He chuckled.

"Soft ass, nigga, you didn't take him out. You feared CJ's gangsta. You used me as a shield because you knew he would've crushed you."

"What he crushing now?" Nard taunted.

"He's about to crush you from his grave."

"Not if he sent you to do it."

His cockiness was about to speed up his time of death.

"Hoe ass nigga, you should've known I was coming." I stepped to him, gripping the six-inch knife securely.

"What, you think I'm gonna bitch up because you got a knife? I'll take that shit from you." He stepped toward me with no fear. But that only got him ate the fuck up.

I closed the distance between us, and slashed him across the forearm as he brought both arms up to protect his face. "You're not hard, nigga!" I slashed him again.

Blood ran down his bare arm and dripped to the floor. Nard ignored the wound. He fired a punch at me with his uninjured hand. It connected with my brow.

"Bring that shit on, nigga! You're fuckin with a beast!" He circled around me trying to gain an advantage from the back, but I was just as swift as he was on my feet.

I moved in a circle with him, step for step. "You're not no beast. You're a reckless little peon. A CJ wannabe!"

The insult caused his mouth to turn down, and he lunged at me carelessly. "What the fuck did you say?"

The answer he got was sharp and cold, and delivered with evil intent. I plunged the blade in his gut and twisted it. "Never fuck with a boss. My nigga reached out and touched you from the grave."

I yanked the knife out of his body and plunged it in again. He folded over and clutched his stomach with both hands, wincing. But he didn't go down.

"That's all you got, fuck boy?" He grimaced.

"Nah, nigga, I'm just getting started!"

Blood gushed from his wound when I pulled the knife out this time. He slid down the wall at the back of the pen, holding his belly, trying desperately to keep his insides from falling out.

"You're still a bitch." He gargled blood from his mouth as he looked up at me.

"Yeah, I'm a bitch—*a bitch killer!*" I stabbed him again.

This time, he let out a small cry. I stood over him, looking down with no mercy. I thought about pulling out my dick and pissing on that bitch, or biting him in the face like they had made the dog do to me. But I was a gangsta, not a goon. In my mind, there was a difference.

I grabbed a handful of Nard's collar and jerked his face up to mine.

"You rock with David X, huh? Since you his bitch, I'ma sign his name across your face so he can recognize you when he joins you in hell."

"Fuck you!" His voice was weak but his courage remained strong.

It didn't matter, though. His fate was sealed. It had been sealed from the moment he took the beef with CJ to another level.

"Nah, blood, *fuck you!*"

I drew my blade back and slashed him across the face viciously twice, leaving a deep X running from his forehead to the bottom, of both jaws.

"Die bitch!" I stabbed him one last time and then I was out.

***

When I got home, La rushed into my arms the second I stepped through the door. I was still wearing the wig and the bloody clothes. Cujo had wanted to get rid of them for me, but I felt more comfortable taking care of that myself.

"Eww!" My sister shrieked when she felt the sticky blood on my black shirt.

"Go change out of what you're wearing, shower and then put these clothes in a plastic bag so we can get rid of them," I said and she immediately went to do as I instructed.

"Did everything go right?" asked Legend.

"Like a piece of cake, yo."

"Say no more."

"Say less." I bumped fist with him.

I didn't see Eric initially but I ran into him coming out of the bathroom as I went to my room to change clothes and shower.

"How you?" he asked, stopping in front of me looking in my eyes."

I smiled. "I'm good, fam."

"Is that nigga dead?" he asked.

"Deader than a door knob."

He followed me to my room as I gave him a blow by blow account of the killing.

"Damn! I wish I could've smashed that pussy with you. But you handled your B.I.," said Eric.

"True indeed." It felt good to avenge my brother.

"I know CJ was looking down at that shit." His eyes teared up just for a second and then he regained his composure. "Rah, I got mad respect for you, man. Most niggaz talk that shit about riding for their homie but as soon as they toss dirt on his casket, they forget about him."

"It's never that with me. CJ was my fam."

"Respect. And one love." He held out his fist.

I bumped it with mine. "One love."

After I showered and changed into a new 'fit, I sat down with my peeps and we ate some nachos that La hooked up. We sat around reminiscing about CJ laughing and cutting up.

Until the stories made us all realize how much we missed our nigga. I almost broke down at one point.

Although I had crushed Nard, the pain of losing my dawg wasn't any less than it had been before I took that nigga'z life.

"I need to clear my head," I said abruptly.

I got up from the table and grabbed my keys. Legend got up too. "Not tonight, fam."

"It's all good. I'm on point." I grabbed my banger off of the counter and put it on my waist. Pointing to the plastic trash bag on the floor, which contained me and La's blood stained clothes, I told him to take them and burn them.

"I'm on it," he said.

"Fam, where you headed?" asked Eric.

"By Malika's."

"A'ight. Be safe."

I was relieved not to have to argue with Eric or Legend about traveling dolo. I figured with Nard no longer breathing, they felt more at ease with me riding alone. Besides, I had my strap on my waist with 17 hollow points in the clip.

***

I let myself in with the key Malika gave me a couple weeks ago. It was close to midnight when I arrived and she was sound asleep. She stirred awake when I undressed and slid under the sheets, spooning our bodies together.

"I didn't expect you tonight," she said in a hoarse tone.

"Does that mean you got a nigga hiding in the closet?"

"Raheem, don't play." She reached back and punched me on the shoulder.

"I thought you like it when I play." I whispered softly in her ear as I rubbed her pussy.

She moaned and reached back and stroked my dick.

"I do like it when you play like this." She guided me inside of her.

By now, we had been intimate more times than I could count on both hands, so our bump and grind was harmonious.

Malika climaxed before me, as usual, but I wasn't far behind.

I think we told each other good night before we closed our eyes and fell asleep, but I couldn't quite recall.

A couple of hours later, I was in the land of peace when my phone started vibrating all over the table by the bed. I had forgot to call Legend and I assumed he was now calling to check on me.

I reached over and grabbed my cell phone. Clearing my throat, I answered, "What's good, son?"

"We got trouble. Major trouble!" I heard mad alarm in his voice. But it wasn't Legend.

I slid out of bed and went into the bathroom. Speaking barely above a whisper, I asked, "What kind of trouble are you talking about? Did one of our people get knocked?"

"No, it's worse than that. He didn't die. He's fucked up bad, but he ain't dead," said Cujo. "And we couldn't finish him off. The guard that found him in the cell isn't on our payroll."

"A'ight. Don't panic, we'll get another chance."

"You better hope so." Cujo hung up the phone.

Ca$h

CHAPTER
30
Kenisha

I was still in a state of shock over what Jada had told me about Nard supposedly killing CJ when I received a call telling me that there had been an attempt on Nard's life at the Prince County Jail. He had been brutally stabbed, and they weren't sure if he would survive.

I felt my entire world caving in as I sat in the passenger seat crying as Jada sped to the Emergency Room. By the time we got there, Nard was already undergoing emergency surgery, and I was told due to the enormous blood loss he had suffered, he would need several blood transfusions, as well.

"I need to know if my husband is going to make it!" I grabbed the doctor by her shoulders and shook her.

"Ma'am!" She stepped back with her mouth hanging open in shock. "We'll do everything we can to save him. The rest will be left to God."

A sharp pain sliced through my stomach. A pain unlike any I'd ever experienced. I fell to the floor, holding my belly with both hands.

"My baby!" I cried.

As other medical personal rushed over to attend to me, I felt a gush of blood run down my thighs.

"Hurry!" she's hemorrhaging!" barked the doctor.

Another intense pain shot through my belly and all I could do was scream and cry out. I feared God was taking my baby as a payment for the sins of his father and the sins of the man I had chosen to marry.

Maybe in his omniscience, he knew the hell it would be if Nard ever found out CJ was the father of my child.

Jada's friends told her the hate between Nard and CJ had caused so many deaths. *Was my baby going to be another one?* I wondered.

Would God allow me to carry a child for 6 1/2 months, and then take it from me?

Apparently, He would, I feared.

But why? My baby is innocent, Lord!

Fear made me call on the person He had already taken from me. "Mommy, I need you right now!" I cried as the pain caused my head to whip side to side

"Call her mother!" someone shouted.

"Her mother passed away. I'll call her dad." I heard Jada say.

"Auntie! Please don't leave me! I need you! My baby is dying!" I sobbed.

***

A Week Later

"Look at God!" Happy tears ran down Jada's face as she used her phone to take a picture of me holding my premature baby boy.

"Allah is truly the most magnificent," smiled the proud G-pop.

My son was so tiny and adorable. By turning one week old today, he had already proven that he was a super strong boy and he was getting stronger by the day.

As soon as Daddy stepped out of my hospital room, Jada leaned over the bed rail and whispered, "Girl, that baby looks like CJ spat him out his mouth. Look at him! Bitch, you better get ready to lie your ass off."

Holding Ca'Ron Jalen Gideons in my arms and smiling down at my blessings, I replied to Jada without looking up.

"I'm not going to lie to Nard. I'm going to tell him about CJ. Why would that destroy what we have? That was before we even met."

"Stop acting like a blond! If you tell Nard that shit, he's gonna leave your dumb ass. Niggaz like him already don't wanna raise the next nigga'z seed."

"Nard isn't like that." I defended him.

"Bitch, are you not hearing me. Nard hated CJ. Nard killed CJ." She counted on her fingers. "Trust, he will leave you before he'll raise his enemy's son. Shit, he might even kill your stupid ass when you tell him you fucked the nigga he hated more than anyone else in the world."

"Shhh!" I was glad I had a private room because Jada had gotten loud. Her fussing caused Ca'Ron to cry.

I cooed to him and rocked him in my arms until he quieted down. Then, Daddy returned, so my conversation with Jada discontinued for the time being, but I was thinking about everything she had said. She was right, I would be risking a lot by telling Nard who my baby's daddy was, but I just didn't want to be deceitful.

Nard was already dealing with so much, he deserved honesty from his wife.

"Daddy take me to see my husband, please."

Nard was only a few floors down from me. He was still in police custody in the hospital but today his wife and stepson would get to visit him for the first time.

Jada lowered her brows at me as Daddy helped me into the wheelchair by the bed.

"Don't be no damn fool," she mouthed.

I looked at Ca'Ron and tickled his little stomach, blocking my aunt completely out.

"Well, stinky poo, it's time to go meet Dada." I cooed.

Ca$h

CHAPTER
31
Nard

Kenisha broke down sobbing when she saw my face. It had required 62 stitches to close the X mark that nigga cut into my face. My head felt like it was the size of a basketball, and my body felt even worse. But I was alive, and I was getting well, plotting the most savage retaliation ever seen.

Through my swollen eyes, I saw the outline of the baby. David X had told me Kenisha had given birth to him prematurely, and that her and lil' man were doing just fine. Seeing them confirmed it.

Smiling hurt, but I had endured much worse. So, I tolerated the brief discomfort and flashed lil' mama a smile.

"Don't be crying, ma. What don't kill me makes me stronger."

"Oh, my God, bae!" she wept.

David X rubbed her back. After a few minutes, she stopped crying.

Sweetheart, I'm going to give you and your husband some privacy," said her father.

"Okay, Daddy. Thank you."

A few seconds later, I heard the door shut softly.

"Sup, ma? A nigga looking bad right now. It's all gravy, though."

"Nard, who did this to you?" She stood up, looking down at me, with the baby in her arms.

I shook my head from side to side. "Not right now, baby, the walls have ears."

It was true. Two deputies were posted outside of my room. I pulled the sheets from over my legs and showed her the ankle monitor and how the other leg was cuffed to the bed.

Kenisha nodded her head, letting me know she comprehended what I was saying.

I inclined the bed so that I was sitting up and then I held my arms out.

"Let me hold this lil' dude. I need to see what he's built like," I joked.

"He's built like a baby," she laughed.

"Yeah, but in a week or two I'ma have him hard body, yo. C'mere lil' man." I stretched out my arms to receive him.

He was quiet as a mouse. But the minute I took him from Kenisha, that lil' nigga raised hell. He was crying and wailing at the top of his lungs. Nothing I whispered or did could calm him down. Finally, I had to give him back to Kenisha. She bounced him in her arms a few times and he shushed.

We waited a few minutes and then she handed him back to me. Again, lil' man started crying. I passed him back to her.

"Man, I must look like a muhfuckin' monster. Shorty scared to even let me hold him." I felt ugly as shit and, because my jaw was fractured, my words came out garbled and like a whisper.

"No bae, he just has to get used to you," said Kenisha. She leaned down and kissed my lips tryna let me know I wasn't ugly in her eyes.

I appreciated the love but I could feel how fucked up my face was. Rah was gonna die real pay with his life for what he had done to me.

Kenisha wiped a tear from my face that I hadn't realized I shed until it reached my chin.

"Ah!" I jumped. The slightest touch hurt like hell.

"I'm sorry." She apologized.

"You good, baby. Anyways, I'll be back shining in no time. That bitch nigga can't stop me." I had enough dough to hire the world's best plastic surgeon.

Kenisha didn't comment other than to tell me that she loved me no matter what. Her sweetness, her love and devotion was unchanged by my scars or my situation.

"That's why I wifed you," I told her. "Now, we just need lil' man over there to stop crying when I hold him."

"He will. Won't you, Ca'Ron?" She rubbed noses with the baby.

A frown came on my face. Although, due to the bandaged and swelling, I don't think Kenisha saw my expression change.

"Run that back one time. Did you just call him Cam'ron?" I asked through clenched teeth. "I know muhfuckin' well you didn't name him that!" Anger shot out of my mouth on its own.

"No, I said Ca'Ron. C-A- apostrophe- R-O-N," I clarified.

"Man, I was about to lose it." I exhaled.

"Why? I'm confused. Why would you be so upset had I named him Cam'ron?" she asked.

"Because that's that rap nigga'z name. I never liked that bitch nigga'z style." I lied. "Anyway, Ca'Ron is good. What's his middle name?"

"Jalen. His name is Ca'Ron Jalen…"

"Ca'Ron Jalen?" The irony of those initials, CJ, threw me for a loop. I dropped my head and sighed. A sharp pain shot though my fractured jaw. I bit down hard to drive the pain away.

"His full name is Ca'Ron Jalen Gideons," announced Kenisha. The pride in her voice when she said our last name erased the bitter taste that came in my mouth over lil' man's first and middle initials.

As much as I hated CJ, even in death, I wasn't gonna allow myself to be petty over some initials. And in a twisted way, the coincidence was funny. But I loved Kenisha and I had promised to accept her child as my own.

I'm not about to let some punk ass initials vex me.

I had other shit to deal with. Fuck the hate I still carried for CJ. As strong as it remained, it was only a speck on an elephant's ass compared to the hate I now harbored for Rah.

My wife misread the crease in my forehead.

"Baby, if you don't like the name we can change it."

"No, I'm not tripping." I pulled her closer to me and gave her a kiss on the cheek.

She smiled and then we changed subjects. I listened as she spoke excitedly about finishing the nursery that she had begun decorating for the baby a few weeks ago.

Occasionally, my mind drifted to Rah. He had tried to take me out but he had failed. But every day when I looked in the mirror and saw how bad he slashed up my face, the thirst to kill him became obsessive.

Right now, though, I didn't want to make Kenisha feel like I wasn't just as excited as she was about decorating the nursery for Ca'Ron. So, I blocked Rah out of mind and gave my girl my full attention until it was time for her to leave.

I even kissed lil' man before they left.

CHAPTER
32
Eric

Summer had died out and fall was in full effect. I could tell it was gonna be a cold winter because it was cold as fuck in ATL, and it was only the end of October.

Back home it was rainy and in the low 50's, but by all accounts, the dreary weather wasn't stopping our team from eating. I couldn't wait to get back to The Bricks. I missed my dawgs, and I missed the excitement of bussin' moves. The game had me hooked. But I had been sitting at Rah's elbow watching and learning how to be more than a D-boy. I was learning how to be a boss.

Rah was much different than CJ. They both said what they meant and meant what they said, but Rah rarely raised his voice. And he was a good listener. Above all else, he wasn't a stunna.

I had decided to adopt part of his way of doing things and incorporate that with what I learned from CJ. Having learned from one of the best, there would be no way of stopping me when Rah turned the throne back over to me. In the meantime, I held my position as second-in-command.

For the past three months, there hadn't been any major gunplay. Nard had gotten out of the hospital and bonded out of jail on the gun charge Cujo cased him up with. It was being said in the streets that he was somewhere recovering from the thrashing Rah put on that ass, and he wasn't making no noise. They still had a few spots open, though, but no friction to be had,

"Turn the heat up some, it's cold as hell in this car," complained La.

"You know your ass can hop on a flight." I turned the heat up to 75 degrees and jumped on the highway.

We had spent two weeks in the A. La had made her third trip there to spend time with her kids and Big Ma. I had taken her because she was afraid to fly.

Somehow, over the past six months, she had convinced Rah to let her stay in Newark, at least until our problems were solved permanently, and he moved back down south himself.

Rah agreed to that, but La couldn't just run around the city as if everything was gucci. Basically, she was on house arrest and she was not allowed to communicate with any of her friends. And whenever she went anywhere, one of us accompanied her for protection.

This was my first trip with her to the A. Rah had drove her down once and Legend had brought her the other time. I hadn't been crazy about chauffeuring her ass all the way to The Dirty, but I gave in to her pleading because she had been on her best behavior.

Just keepin' it real, the getaway turned out to be mad fun and relaxing. We took her kids to Chuck-E-Cheese, shopping and a whole lot of other places. When she was chillin' with Big Ma and the kids, I was making contacts in the A, lining up future business.

I also got to meet Tanisha, who was DaQuan's wife and his seeds. Son had gotten killed by Nard and 'em a little over a year ago.

Ma was living good because Rah made sure of that. He sent her no less than ten stacks a month, but she was still tore up over DaQuan's death.

I was thinking about fam, and how he popped those hammers for us when La started screaming for me to pull over to the shoulder of the highway.

"Hurry up. I'm sick!" she cried.

"Yo, you better not throw up in my shit!" I had just gotten my truck washed and detailed this morning. I quickly maneuvered over to the shoulder of the interstate.

As soon as I stopped, she bolted from the car and ran off a few feet, coughing and retching.

"You good now?" I asked when she climbed back in my whip.

"No, not really." She laid her head against the headrest and closed her eyes.

"You pregnant, yo?" I asked as I pulled off.
"Funny!" She smacked her lips. "How am I supposed to be pregnant when I haven't had any dick since dinosaurs walked the earth."

"You stupid, ma." I laughed.

"And I'm a whole lot of other things."

I pretended not to catch the sexual hint dripping off of her reply. La was sexy and all that, but she was too hard headed and too goddam dramatic for my taste. I had witnessed up close with CJ how a female like that could cause a nigga mad stress.

To block out any other sexual shit in La's mind I blasted the sound system and blazed up a stick of sour.

Three hours into our drive back Up Top, La started complaining that her stomach and head was hurting. She wanted to stop and get a motel room for a few hours, so she could lay down and stretch out. I sighed in frustration, pulled off at the next exit, went and bought her ass some Advil and reclined her seat all the way back for her.

"That's as good as it's gonna get." I slammed her door and went and hopped back behind the wheel.

We got back on the interstate but minutes later, La was moaning and crying like she was about to die.

I felt myself becoming aggravated. *This is why I should've never drove her down here!*

Agitated, I drove on until I saw an exit with motels.

I got off the highway, once again, and copped us a room with double beds. Inside the room, I tossed the room card on the table and flopped down on the bed, mad stressed because I was ready to get back to The Bricks.

La looked at me with drooping eyes.

"I'm sorry, I got sick, man! It's not like I did it on purpose." She sounded like she was on the verge of tears.

Usually, she was talking shit and being overly combative, so I cut her some slack.

"It's all good. We can rest for a few hours." I sat down on the bed and started twisting one up.

"Thank you. But you're still mean for no reason," she said.

"Whateva, yo."

"Ugh! I can't stand your ass!" She tossed her coat in my face and headed for the bathroom.

"Don't forget to brush and rinse," I called behind her. "Real talk, your shit is humming!"

"Fuck you!" She threw up her middle finger and slammed the door behind her.

CHAPTER
33
Lakeesha

As soon as the bathroom door shut, I grabbed my stomach with both hands and started cracking up inside. It took all the strength in my body not to let my laughs slip out.

Nigga think he's all that like a bitch can't trick him. Humph! I fooled that ass good.

Wasn't a darn thing wrong with me besides being horny as fuck. I knew if I didn't get me some dick now, it was a wrap once we got back to Newark. Because Rah be all up a bitch ass. I understood why he monitored my every movement, but understanding it did nothing to put out the fire between my thighs. Man, a bitch needed to get fucked badder than a bald-headed ho needed a wig.

I stripped out of my clothes and took a quick shower. After applying some body lotion and getting my pussy wet by thinking about how close I had come to fucking Eric that once, I opened the door and stepped into the room wearing nothing but a scandalous smile. When he saw these 38 D's and this bare pussy headed in his direction, his scary ass jumped up so fast, he stumbled over his own feet.

"Don't try me, yo," he said, mugging me like I had kicked in the door to rob him.

"No, baby boy, don't you try *me*. I'm about to smash that." I declared. "And I'm dead ass, yo." I stepped up in his chest and made that muthafucka kiss me.

I reached for his zipper but he shoved me away.

"Fuck outta here!"

"Dude, I'm not taking *no* for an answer. You know you want this pussy. Quit acting hard and put something hard in a bitch." I made seductive eyes at him and stroked my pearl.

When I re-closed the distance between us, he had the nerve to mush my face.

"La, back the fuck up, yo! Don't get fucked up."

"I'm tryin' to get fucked up, down, from the back, in the mouth. Any way you want it, daddy. Feel how wet this pussy is." I grabbed his wrist and forced his hand between my legs. "Bitch, got that wet-wet, don't I?"

"It doesn't matter." He snatched his hand away and turned his back to me. But I had seen the desire in his mean eyes. Looking at all of my treasures was too much for him to stand.

I wrapped my hands around his waist and pressed my titties against his back and then I whispered, "Daddy, please fuck me—just this once."

"No!" He flung me off of him.

Some other bitch might've given up, but not me. I was Lakeesha. My pussy was so good it could make cotton rock up. There was no way in hell Eric was going to turn me down again. But I was through begging his ass.

"Nigga, you must think I'm playing with your ass." I balled my fist up.

"We're either gonna fuck or fight." I waited on his response but when he said nothing, I went in on that ass.

Whap!

I punched his short ass in the nose.

"Oww! That shit hurt!" He grabbed his nose.

"Good! Now you know a bitch ain't playing with you."

Before he knew what had hit him, I two-pieced that ass again.

Whack! Whack!

"Call me La Money Mayweather, nigga." My titties jiggled up and down as I bounced on my toes. I aimed a punch at his throat but he swatted it away.

"Fuck is your problem?" he scowled.

222

"I don't have a problem, lil' daddy," I answered sassily, feeling myself. "Like I said, we're gonna fuck or fight."

I faked a punch to his face. When he threw his arms up to block it, I scooped him off of his feet and we crashed to the floor, with me on top. He easily flipped me over but I hung onto the front of his shirt when he tried to get up. He snatched away and his shirt ripped right down the middle.

Huffing angrily, Eric looked down at me. "You tore my shit."

"Tough luck. Use that muthafucka for a do-rag." I pounced back up on my feet, ready for more.

He saw the look in my eyes. And I saw the look in his. He wanted a bitch, even if he didn't know it himself. But he was still acting hard.

"A'ight, I'm tired of playing with your silly ass. Put your hands on me again and I promise you, I'ma split your shit wide open," threatened Eric.

"Nigga, that's what I want you to do. Split this pussy open."

"You know what the fuck I'm saying."

"We fuckin' or not?" I asked with my hands on my hips.

"No! Fuck no!" he spat.

"A'ight." I charged that ass again.

This time we landed on the bed. We wrestled from the head board to the foot of the bed and back. When he gained the advantage, I bit his ass.

"Ahhhh!" he yelped and I unclenched my teeth.

"We gonna fuck? 'Cause I fight dirty, don't I?" I was breathing hard, but so was he.

"A'ight! A'ight!" He huffed, and then he stood up and unfastened his pants. "This what you want?" His fat, black, beautiful dick was standing up like a flag pole.

"Yes, daddy," I purred. "Are you going to give it to me?"

"Face down, ass up. And your shit better be good," he said.
I assumed the position, confident in these sugar walls.

***

I watched Eric sleep with a goofy grin on his face. We had gone three rounds and that muthafucka hadn't won a single one. I fucked and sucked him so good, he had sung love songs in his sleep. And when he woke up, it was almost check out time.

"Pussy platinum, ain't it, daddy?" I teased him when his eyes fluttered open.

"It will do."

"Ha! Tell me it's not the best you've ever had?" I challenged as I lit one of the blunts I had rolled while he was asleep.

"It's the best," he admitted with a crooked smile.

He sat up and I straddled his lap and blew him a gun.

He returned the favor and then we fucked again. My pussy was sore but he made it hurt good. I was on birth control so he didn't have to pull out. I rode that fat ass dick until he shot a whole army of his little soldiers in my cocoon.

A little before noon we checked out of the room. A bitch legs felt wobbly as shit as we walked to the car.

"Grown man shit!" Eric bragged when he noticed me staggering like a drunk.

"Yeah, I can't even front, you did that shit." I was all teeth.

My body felt so good when I climbed inside of Eric's truck and settled into the soft leather seat. All of my sexual frustration was gone. I was singing along with every song that came on the radio.

I wasn't the only one in a good mood. The mean ass nigga in the driver's seat had lost his perpetual scowl, and he kept glancing over at me grinning and licking his lips. This sweet cookie had made him shelve that mean shit.

By the time, we made it back to Newark, Eric had promised me the sun, the moon, the starts and the rainbows. He just asked me to go back to school and to hold him down without any drama.

"I knew I was gonna get you one day." I teased him as we pulled into Rah's driveway.

"You don't have me yet. Get that GED, then we'll talk," he stressed.

"I will," I promised.

We were both smiling when Rah opened the door and let us in, but the sullen expression on his face wiped the smile off of ours.

"What's up?" asked Eric.

"They killed Legend, my nigga," said Rah with heavy heart.

Ca$h

CHAPTER
34
Rah

"**H**e had gone out with a shorty he met at the club in Atlanta, years ago. She just happened to hit him up and let him know she was back in the BK visiting her peoples. We thought everything would be okay since they would be in Brooklyn. But Nard somehow must've got a dime on them," I explained to Eric, sitting at the bar in the basement.

"The bitch must've set him up," he said.

"Nah, son, they murked her, too."

"Fuck!" He tossed back a shot of Henny.

I was drinking mine straight out of the neck and taking it straight to the head. I turned the bottle up and took a swig. The liquid burned my throat but it soothed my mind a bit.

I had watched Legend get tortured by those niggaz, on live video, until I couldn't watch anymore. Those images were burned in my mind, as was every other detail, large and small.

After not hearing from him all the next day, after he went out, I called his phone.

Nard had answered, "I wondered how long it would take for you to call. What you thought? That shit you did had me shook? What you did to me was play-play compared to what I'ma do to your boy!" He hung up Legend's phone.

When he called back, him and his crew were on video, the same way they had called CJ when they held me captive, except now they were masked up. Nard was holding Legend's machete in front of the camera.

"Don't ever bring no bama niggas to the Bricks to help you look for me'!" he spat. I knew it was Nard from the sound of his voice.

He turned the camera on Legend. My nigga was laying on the floor with his head bust open and one eye hanging out of the socket.

"Fuck these bitch ass niggaz, Rah, it's one love, shawdy," he moaned. "To the grave!"

Big Nasty kicked him in the face.

"Shut up, bitch!" he growled. Then he stuck his head close to the camera.

"Yo, Rah, remember this? Attack!" he barked.

I heard Lil' Nasty growl before he came into the picture frame. He locked his powerful jaws around Legend's neck and dragged him across the floor.

Eric tossed back his fifth shot as I continued to describe the shit they did to Legend.

"They beat son so bad, he couldn't move a limb. Then, they stripped off his clothes and laid him on his stomach. His hands and feet were duct-taped so he couldn't stop them from doing what they were doing. But he fought them the best he could " I said, sadly.

"Why did they strip him?" asked Eric.

I sighed heavily. "You remember gay ass Charlie who lived on the 5th floor of our building?"

"Yeah." Eric nodded his head.

"They brought him in the room and that faggot ass muhfucka smiled in the camera and blew me a kiss. Fam, I tried to jump through my phone!" Tears ran down my face, I hurled the bottle of Henny against the wall and it shattered.

"They didn't have to do that foul shit to him! I couldn't watch it, fam. I dropped the phone and cried," I recounted.

"They let Charlie…" Eric's words trailed off. I nodded my head.

"When I picked my phone up, Charlie was pulling up his pants." No more needed to be said. Charlie was a nasty, homo nigga from Lil' City, who we both knew well. He had spent most of his life in and out of prison. Until I saw him on cameras, the last I heard he was doing time up in Rahway.

"Rah, we gotta kill that sissy!" spat Eric.

"I wish we could, but Nard already did that. Before he hung up the phone I watched him shoot him in the back of the head."

"Fuck!" Eric steamed.

After another shot of Henny, he asked about Legend's body. There was no need for him to even ask if my dude was still alive.

"They drug it outside and set it on fire. But they threw his charred head in the front yard of our spot on Avon Ave," I said, dropping my head and resting it on the counter of the bar.

Ca$h

CHAPTER
35
Nard

***B**am!*

Just like that, the tables had turned. For almost six months in a row we were taking L's and every move Rah's squad made had been a winning one for them. Now the dark clouds had shifted over to their side.

The look on that nigga'z face when I let Charlie fuck his boy was priceless. He had himself to blame for that. He should've made sure he handled his business when those dirty ass cops on his payroll helped him slide up in the holding tank. But he didn't, and now I was on some savage shit.

For months, I just sat back biding my time, healing up, plotting and waiting for Man Dog to get a bond so we would be at full strength when we struck back. It was hard being patient because every time I looked in the mirror, and saw what Rah did to my face, I was tempted to get on some reckless shit.

But David X kept preaching, *"Just have patience. Sooner or later the worm will come out of the ground."*

It finally did! That country nigga wasn't the big worm, but losing him fucked Rah up. I saw the pain in his face. Straight up, that shit go my dick hard. That bitch ass nigga'z tears worked like Viagra. Now, we were sitting back waiting for them to react in a way that would expose their whereabouts.

While we waited, I was spending time with my wife. We were going out to dinner and to the movies, looking for summer homes over in the West Indies and enjoying quiet nights together. I was putting in mad work trying to plant my own seed in her.

I loved Ca'Ron, he was crawling around now, but lil' man was wishy-washy with me. Sometimes he fucked with me but most times he didn't. When I held him he would be cool for a minute and then he would just start screaming and crying. I chalked it up to him being a mama's boy. But the way he acted made me want my own seed. I was sure my own mini-me wouldn't cry when I held him, like Ca'Ron was doing now.

"Here, baby. Come put him to bed. I think he's sleepy." I held him up for his mama.

Kenisha took him from my arms and laid him across her shoulder, rubbing his back. In no time at all, he was asleep. While she carried him to the nursery, I hit my brother up. Him and Lemora had met with the lawyers earlier.

I asked, "What that Jew boy talking about?"

"He's saying I'll probably have to do 15 years, maybe 10 if I'm lucky," said Man Dog.

"What about Lemora?"

"The same thing unless I take the charges." He let out a long, hard sigh.

"Bruh, I'ma fire his ass and find a lawyer who can pull a few strings. I'm not paying him $150,000 to get y'all 10 or 15 years. Fuck that!" I shook my head.

"Man, you already know Cujo is behind that shit. But, yo, don't your plug got some people who can shake something?" I heard desperation in his voice.

"Nah, man, he's saying his peeps are close to cutting him off because of all the killings. Shit, yo, he's slick been banned from all of the Temples on the East Coast. They're just keeping it on the DL."

"Fuck, yo! I tried to tell you I didn't feel good about that move that day. I wish you would listen to me sometime, instead of thinking you know everything," said Man Dog."

"That's my bad, yo. But bitching about it won't change nothin'. I'ma toss 300 bands in that Jew boy's lap and see if he can't get that offer cut in half. You can do a nickel standing on your head, that ain't shit," I guessed.

"Yeah, see what you can make happen."

"You know I'ma do whatever. And if any amount of guap will keep you out here, I'ma spend it," I promised.

"A'ight. One."

"One."

Kenisha walked back into the room a few seconds after I hung up. I pulled her down on my lap and tongued her. My stiffness pressed against her leg, which was proof that I couldn't get enough of her. We had been going hard all weekend.

I slid my hands under her nightie and cupped her breast. Before I could get started, she said, "Wait, Nard, we need to talk."

"Now?" I asked.

"Yes, if you don't mind."

"Of course not." I made it a point to always be sensitive to her needs.

She climbed off of my lap, sat down beside me and covered her face with both hands. She took a deep breath and let it out in one big woosh.

"Okay, I think I'm ready," she said.

And maybe she was ready, but I didn't think I was because the tear trickling down her face warned me that what she was about to say was graveyard serious.

Ca$h

CHAPTER
36
Kenisha

My hands shook like an old spiritual woman stealing out of the collection plate at church. Jada's warning kept ringing in my ear but I had to do the right thing. And if my marriage was what I believed it was, Nard and I would be fine. I could not hide the truth from him another minute because with each passing day, Ca'Ron's features were starting to almost be identical to his father's.

I swallowed the lump in my throat and lifted my eyes so that they looked directly into Nard's. He was sitting there somewhat impatiently, bouncing his leg up and down. I cleared my throat and placed a hand on his knee to stop him from bouncing his leg. It was making me more nervous than I already felt.

"What's up?" He broke the silence.

"Baby, do you love me?" My voice was just a squeak. "I mean, really, truly love me?"

"What kinda question is that, ma? You know I love you."

"I do know that. But is your love unconditional? Is there anything that would make you leave me?" I delved.

"Cheating." He cocked his head to the side and fixed me with a look of uncertainty. "Kenisha, don't tell me you fucked another nigga. Because we can't get past that."

"No, my love, I would never do a thing like that," I made clear, and his shoulders relaxed.

"We good, then." He leaned in and kissed my lips, causing my heart to flutter.

"Nard, do you love Ca'Ron?"

"Of course," he chuckled. "Even though his lil' ass don't fuck with me half the time. He still my dude. I don't know why you asked me that. Ma, I love everything that's a part of you." He took my hand and held it against his chest. "You feel my heartbeat?"

"Yes." I nodded.

"It would stop if you and lil' man wasn't in my life."

"Aww, baby, that's one of the sweetest things you have ever said to me. My heart beats for you, too," I said with my deepest sincerity.

I loved him with all of me. I didn't know the beast he supposedly was in the streets. All I knew was the loving, gentle, faithful man he was to me. In spite of Jada's warning, I just couldn't see anything disrupting his love for me.

I took another deep breath and then I jumped off of that cliff, confident that my husband wouldn't let me crash on the ground.

"Nard, I want to tell you about Ca'Ron's father." I swallowed to control my nervousness, then I continued. "He was a big-time drug dealer from Newark. I apologize for telling you before that he was from South Philly. It's one of those little white lies that came back to haunt me. Again, I'm sorry."

"Apology accepted. But you just said he was from The Bricks. What's his name? If he's from around my way, I gotta know him."

I spat it right out.

"His name was Cam'ron, on the streets he was known as CJ."

As soon as those words left my mouth and hit Nard's ears, I knew I should've listened to Jada. Nard's eyes turned fire red, and his face contorted into something indescribable.

"Did you just say CJ! Is that who Ca'Ron's daddy is?" The heat coming off of his brow scorched my forehead.

I couldn't have answered if my reply would've brought mommy back, I just dropped my head and started crying.

"Hol' the fuck up!" Nard jumped up and stormed off into the nursery.

Fearing in his anger, he might hurt my baby, I raced behind him. "Nard, please don't!" I grabbed the back of his shirt.

He swatted my hands off of him and kept going, taking long strides. When I caught back up with him, he was standing over Ca'Ron's bed, staring down into my son's face.

"Ain't this a bitch? How the fuck did I miss that?" he muttered. "He looks just like that nigga, no wonder he doesn't fuck with me."

"Nard, he's just a baby. He doesn't even know what happened between you and CJ."

"Do *you* know?" He turned to look at me.

I answered by nodding *yes.*

"How?"

"Jada," I replied truthfully.

"Tell that bitch to stay outta mine." He pointed his finger in my face.

The threatening gesture and the harsh tone he used was upsetting. Until now, he had never raised his voice at me. Tears spilled from the corners of my eyes as I watched him walk across the room.

Bam!

He punched a hole in the wall.

"That nigga just won't let me live! This is some straight bullshit, yo. It could've been anybody—anybody but that pussy nigga. Man, I would've rather Ca'Ron's daddy been my own goddam brother than CJ!"

"But it was before our time, baby!"

"It don't matter!"

"It only happened once, Nard please don't let that break up our happy home." I pleaded as I walked up behind him and hugged his waist. "He's dead, baby. You won. Ca'Ron doesn't ever have to know anything about CJ. You're his father in my eyes."

"No the fuck I'm not!" He spun around and looked at me with distaste written on his face. "You don't understand how much I hate that nigga. I'm not playing daddy to his seed. No fuckin' way! It's not happening!"

"Nard, please don't say that. Ca'Ron is innocent," I cried.

"Man, you just don't understand, I wish you hadn't told me, now I'm seeing images of that nigga fuckin' you. I gotta get the fuck out of here, yo!" He pushed past me and walked out of the room.

A short while later, I heard the front door slam. My shoulders rocked as sobs came from the depths of my heart. I picked Ca'Ron up out of bed and sat down on the floor, crying.

"CJ, I hate you!" I screamed

Even from the grave he was fucking up my world.

CHAPTER
37
Rah

I flew back to Atlanta with the only remains that were found of Legend. He had been raised in the foster care system, so he had no real family to speak of. But dozens of people who had met him when he was the deejay at my nightclub joined me to send him off with a nice service.

I mourned in my heart, but I couldn't allow Legend's gruesome death to paralyze me with grief. The beef with Nard had gone on way too long. It was time to crush him, once and for all.

The day after the funeral, I was back in Newark telling Cujo those exact words.

"I couldn't agree more, and I have some good news for you," he smiled like a shark.

I wasn't disillusioned, I knew he would bite my head off to save his own. But I wasn't planning to give him the chance.

"What's the good news?" I looked up from my plate.

Me, Cujo and Solaski were seated in the same restaurant outside of Freehold, where I had gone with CJ once.

Solaski responded to my question. "There's a major drug investigation underway against David X. However, it's not being conducted by my people. The investigation is headed by ATF. I figured we let them take the good minister down. With his supplier gone, Nard's power becomes even less. And a weakened animal is easier to trap and kill," he explained in a hushed tone.

I sat my fork down on my plate. "I thought I told you once before that I don't want to see none of them in prison. I wanna put them in the dirt—point blank period!"

"Raheem, someone has to take the fall for all of the killings that have happened. If you kill all of them, the only ones left to take the fall is—guess who?"

"Ding. Ding. Ding." Cujo jumped back in, pointing his fork at me.

"Imagine that, yo." I said.

"Exactly," echoed Solaski.

"So, you have to decide who gets to die in prison, David X or Nard?"

The choice tasted bitter in my own mouth, because I owed both of them some white chalk and a black bag. But if I had to let one live, the choice was easy.

I told Solaski and Cujo, "Ain't no way in Allah's universe I'll let Nard live."

"Okay," said Solaski, "now there's one other thing to discuss. You're also under federal investigation."

"Me?" I touched my finger to my chest.

"Yes," Solaski confirmed that I had heard him correctly.

"I just found out about it because it didn't originate here in Newark. The investigation originated in Atlanta. It's being directed by an agent by the name of Selena Bradford." He opened up a folder and slid several photos across the table.

"This is Selena. Do you recognize her?"

I didn't answer. The blood in my veins was too hot for me to speak. *That bitch!* I said to myself as I bolted up from the table, rushed out to my car and peeled off with my tires smoking.

An hour later, I arrived at my destination, angry as fuck.

I let myself in with the key she had given me. The house was quiet but I knew she was home. I could smell her stench in the air.

She came out of the kitchen, smiling like everything was peace. But the corners of her mouth quickly turned down when she saw the look on my face and the strap in my hand.

"Raheem, darling, what's wrong?" she rushed up to me.

"Nothin', everything is good, Selena," I said as I stepped back and aimed the banger at her head.

"You found out?" She dropped her head.

"That's not all I found out."

"There's nothing else. When I started working for the Bureau, I wanted to rid the streets of crack dealers who preyed on our people. I thought I would start out by bringing down black kingpins because they were directly destroying the inner city." She fidgeted with her hands.

I watched her closely. One false move and I was gonna cook her cabbage. She went on talking but all I could hear was the moans in my ear, the whispered terms of endearment and false claims of love.

"You're the worst kind of snake," I cut her off. "You slither into a nigga'z heart using your smile and your body to gain his trust. Then, you betray your own kind to the white man. You're no better than a crack king, Selena, you destroy black families, too." I threw the hammer back on my fo-five and lowered it to her treacherous heart.

"But I didn't betray you, Raheem. I couldn't. My job was to bring you down. That's what was on my mind when we met on the plane. But once I started to get to know you, I fell in love with you and I betrayed my oath. The first night I slept with you, I did it so that none of the information gathered could be used against you. The investigation is dead, baby. Dead!" she said.

"I don't believe shit that comes out of your deceitful mouth, Agent Bradford," I spat.

"I'm no longer with the Drug Enforcement Agency. I resigned last month and every piece of evidence I collected against you has been destroyed."

"Good. But you still gonna die!" I gritted.

"Raheem, wait!" She threw her hands up. "Baby, if you kill me, you'll kill your child. I'm pregnant with your baby!"

"What?" I relaxed my trigger finger just a little.

"I'm carrying your child. Baby, please don't do this."

Her tears were real but I couldn't trust her.

"I don't believe your conniving ass. Prove it or get yourself right with God."

"I can prove it, baby. Please, follow me."

I held the gun in the back of her head and marched her into her office. There, she showed me a copy of her resignation letter and proof of her pregnancy.

If it was a hoax, she was putting on an Academy Award winning performance.

"I don't trust you, Selena." My eyes were cold.

"Raheem, all you have to do, King, is put your head on my stomach and listen to the tiny heartbeat," she said.

Cautiously, I leaned down, placed my ear against her stomach and listened. After a minute or so, I rose up and starred her in the face. I shoved my gun in my waistband and without saying another word to Selena Bradford—a woman I didn't even know—I turned and walked out.

CHAPTER
38
Nard

The revelation that Ca'Ron was CJ's son fucked me up. My head was in such a bad space, I hadn't been home for weeks. Kenisha was blowing my phone up every day but I wouldn't answer. If I talked to her now, in the frame of mind I was in, I most definitely would've said some shit that I could never take back. I didn't want to do that because I knew our love was genuine, but she had dropped a bomb on me.

I would've rather she told me she had HIV. I didn't know what I was gonna do yet, and the half dozen empty bottles of Ciroc that were scattered around the suite I had rented at the time did not help provide the answer. The only thing I was absolutely sure of was I wasn't raising that nigga'z son. I refused to spend another night under the same room with that baby. So, the decision was really on Kenisha. She could smother that lil' muhfucka, give his ass shaking baby syndrome or give him up. It had to be one or the other because she couldn't have us both.

It was bad enough I had to get over the fact that CJ was Kenisha's first. It felt like he was mocking me from his grave.

Nigga, you got my sloppy seconds. Next time you eat her pussy tell me how my dick taste.

"This is some bullshit!" I slapped the half empty bottle of Ciroc off of the table. At the same time, my phone rang. It wasn't Kenisha's ringtone playing so I answered it.

"Yeah, what's up?" I disguised my pain. I hadn't told anyone anything. All my crew knew was that I was staying at a hotel, alone, getting my mind right.

"Nard, I need to see you. It's urgent," said Lemora.

"A'ight. You know where I'm at."

"I'll be there in 30," she said.

A half hour later, Lemora was sitting in my suite.

"What's the emergency?" I asked.

"I need you to listen to something." She pulled her phone out of her Michael Kors bag and sat it on the table in front of us. After a few seconds of silence, a recorded conversation began playing.

Man Dog: Baby, I'ma do it.

Lemora: You're going to do what? I hope it's not what you mentioned the other day.

Man Dog: That's exactly what it is.

Lemora: But why? Nard is your flesh and blood. If you cooperate against him, this whole thing of ours will go down. Besides that's just not real man shit, papi.

Man Dog: Fuck all that! It's self-preservation. If he hadn't forced me to make that drop, we wouldn't be facing time in the pen. Anyway, I still haven't forgotten that he shot me.

Lemora: I understand that, papi. But don't snitch on him.

Man Dog: Bitch, whose side you on?

A long pause could be heard.

Lemora: Yours

Man Dog: Rock with me, then. I'm gonna have my lawyer work out a deal where both of us will walk if I give them my brother.

"Turn it off!" I didn't need to hear no more. *That rat bastard!* I leaned over and hugged Lemora. "That's some real shit you just did, ma."

"I love your brother but I lost all respect for him when he told me what he planned to do. No matter what has happened between you two, snitchin' should never be an option. That's bitch-type shit," she said.

"Facts!" I shook my head in disgust. "I need that recording, so when I confront that nigga, he won't be able to deny it."

"Okay. Hold up, I'll send a copy to your phone."

"Say dat!"

"Know dat!"

I stood up and went to the closet to get a backpack full of money I had collected from Zakee yesterday. I returned and gave the backpack to Lemora.

"What's this?" She looked at me curiously.

"It's 115 thou'."

"No! I'm not letting you pay me for being a real bitch," she said, tossing the loot back at me.

"Nah, baby girl, I wouldn't disrespect your gangsta. But dig, yo. Once I deal with my brother, you'll be the only one left to take the rap on those trafficking charges. That money is for you to get ghost with. Go to the islands or to the West Coast and start all over."

"Your mom is in Colorado, right?"

"Yeah." We had moved her there six months ago. "Don't go there, though. You gotta disappear, ma. Wait until tomorrow and then take whatever money Man Dog has stashed and go fall off the map, yo."

"Okay, I'm going to miss y'all niggaz." A few tears trickled down her face.

"We'll miss you, too."

We hugged for a long time

When we broke the embrace, Lemora looked up at me and said, "Nard, please don't relax your guard. I hate Rah and 'em with a passion but I gotta give respect where respect is due. That nigga's gangsta is real."

"Fuck that clown and his punk ass gangsta! But I won't sleep on him," I promised.

"Okay, I love you, man."

"Love you, too."

We hugged again and then she was gone.

Later that day

We were at the spot where I divided up the product to my team. Only Big Nasty, Zakee, Man Dog and myself were present. The latest package from David X was much less than our usual supply, but we would have to make it do what it do.

I had already given Zakee instructions on how the work was to be dispersed. Now, we all were just sitting around choppin' it up. I did little talking, but my mind was in a whole notha place.

Earlier, I had issued my stipulations to Kenisha. She hadn't taken it well, of course. So, that was heavily on my mind.

I sighed and pushed those thoughts aside as I prepared myself to handle the business before me. I didn't look forward to it but it had to be done. Betrayal was an unpardonable violation.

I looked up to see Man Dog straddling a chair backwards and texting on his phone.

"Man, Lemora won't hit me back. I'm getting worried. I hope those niggaz haven't snatched her up."

"Nah, fam, she's good. She's probably emptying out your safe right now," I said in a nonchalant tone.

"Say what?" He arched an eyebrow.

To my left, Zakee was staring at me with a puzzled look on his face. Next to me, Big Nasty, who I had already prepped, stood up and casually strode behind my brother.

"I told her she could have your bank, nigga. Because you don't deserve it." I bristled.

"Fuck is you saying?" Man Dog snapped, but I could see in his eyes he knew what this was about.

He tried to ease his hand to his waist. But Big Nasty pulled out and put a burner to the back of his dome piece.

"I wish you would, yo!" he growled.

Man Dog let his hand fall to his side.

"Lil' bruh, what's up?" He acted confused.

"You tell me." I stood up, pulled my phone out and went to the recorded conversation Lemora sent to my phone. With tears running down my face, I pressed *play*, turned the volume up and sat the phone on the table in front of us.

When the recording started playing, my brother tried to remain stoic but the beads of sweat that formed on his brow cracked his facade.

I looked down at him. "Man, I'm your flesh and blood. Listen at how you planned to do me." My voice broke and my heart ached.

Man Dog said nothing.

I ran my hand down my face and tried to wash away the tears as his plan to betray me hit me with full force.

Why? Why would he sell his soul like that? I asked myself as the recording played on.

Nothing in this world would've made me do no sucka shit like that to him. We had bumped heads but we were still family, and I loved him just as much as I had loved him before that shit happened.

Minutes later, when the full conversation ended, I looked at him with wet, sad eyes. "Bruh, why you do it like that? Nigga, we came out of the same womb. No beef between us should ever be that serious. You broke my heart, man. I swear to God you did." Tears poured from my eyes like water from a faucet.

"Yo, that's not my voice! That bitch is lying!" Man Dog tried denying.

"Bruh, first you plan to betray me. Then, when I find out about it, you'll sit here and lie in my face." I shook my head in pity.

"Nigga, I'm not lying," he maintained with a straight face. And that shit enraged me.

"Muthafucka, don't you dare lie to me!" I whipped out my chrome and pointed it in his face. "That's you, nigga. Now, be 21 about it! Admit it's your voice or I'ma do you right here, right now!"

I could tell he was contemplating my ultimatum by the way his eyes shifted from side to side, weighing my threat.

"A'ight, it was me," he confessed. Then, he started crying. "You changed, man. You let the money and the power change you."

"How?" I snapped. "Nigga, when I ate, you ate! We're all livin' good 'round this bitch. Fuck is you saying?"

He wiped his face with his hand. "I can't explain it, bruh, but you are different. You was ordering me around like I was one of these niggaz." He pointed to Zakee and then to Big Nasty. "But I helped you put this shit together!"

"And I rewarded you!" I barked back. "Nigga, you're my blood. What's mine is yours and vice versa!"

"Is that why you shot me?" The question came out of left field.

"I shot yo ass because you tested my authority. Fuck you wanted me to do, let you walk all over me?" I stood up breathing fire. "It can't ever be but one head. Facts, nigga!"

Big Nasty and Zakee were nodding in agreement.

Having lost that point, Man Dog said, "That don't even matter, bruh. This shit started going downhill when you killed that bitch. You put all of us at war over a ho. That was some sucka shit. Count how many people died because you couldn't accept that Tamika wanted CJ over you. That shit is not gangsta."

"You have the right to feel what you feel, but that don't justify you turning rat. If you didn't like how I get down, you should've walked away from this shit, not bite the hand that feed you! That's not gangsta!"

"Yo, Nard, fuck talking to this clown. Let me fold his ass up and let's be done with it," Zakee cut in. "Brother or not, a snitch gotta die."

Still posted up behind Man Dog, with his banger still pressed to the back of my brother's head, Big Nasty nodded in agreement.

I knew the code of the streets, *snitches die or they'll testify*. But Man Dog wasn't no random nigga, he was my brother and I loved him.

"Nard, I'm sorry." He looked up at me with eyes that begged for forgiveness. "I love you, man. I was angry, and that made me talk foolish. I never would've gone through with it."

I didn't buy that shit. If a muthafucka would contemplate snitchin', they'd do it. Because a thought like that never crossed a real nigga'z mind. Not ever!

Knowing that, I couldn't give Man Dog a pass. He deserved what any other potential rat deserved.

The expression that came over my face must've forewarned him of his fate. "Lil' bruh, I swear I wasn't gonna go through with it," he repeated tearfully.

"Yes, you would've. You was gonna sell your soul, against your own flesh and blood. And that makes you the worst kind of nigga!"

I clicked one in the chamber and creased my brow. My jaw became set and my eyes were like red hot coals.

Fear gripped Man Dog, and it turned him into a bitch. He fell to his knees, grabbed my pants leg and cried, "Don't do it, man. I'm your brother!"

"Nigga, you ain't shit to me! Get up! Die on your feet like a muthafuckin' man!"

"Nooo! Please!" He sobbed pitifully.

I couldn't spare him if Jesus and all of His Disciples descended from the clouds and begged me to show mercy. Not only was he a rat, he was a bitch in disguise.

"No mercy, rat muthafucka!"

Boc! Boc!

Man Dog's head splashed open and he toppled over on his side.

Boc! Boc! Boc!

Three slugs to the heart knocked him onto his back.

He was stretched out with his arms and legs akimbo. Blood surrounded his body. I looked down at him. His eye were staring up at me in death, like he couldn't believe I had killed him.

My face was wet with tears. But I felt no regret. Like Zakee had said, *brother or not, snitches had to die.*

CHAPTER
39
Rah

I could see Nard's end coming, and soon. The domino effect had him by the throat. His shit was as precarious as a house of cards. If the wind blew in the wrong direction, what remained of his little piss ant operation was gonna cave in.

Two weeks ago, Man Dog's body had been found on the side of the road. Nobody on my team had killed him. All types of rumors as to who murked him floated around on the ghetto wire. I couldn't decipher fact from fiction, but it didn't matter. As long as he was dead.

They put a kid named Chip, from around our way, in Man Dog's place. He started making drops and doing pick-ups at the few remaining spots they had. But he barely lasted week. Snoop, Shabazz and Eric caught him at the wrong place, at the wrong time, and they swiss cheesed that ass.

Last night, those fed boys hit David X at a house he had in Philly. Caught him with 100 bricks, 25 kilos of heroin, 2 million dead faces and a shit load of weaponry. The story was on every news station, including CNN. They were playing up his position in the Nation of Islam real big, making the Muslim community look bad.

I still wasn't at peace with not getting a chance to serve street justice on him, but I suspected karma would get him before he ever made it to trial. Those brothers in Philly, where David X was locked up, was serious about their faith. They wouldn't let him get away with bringing shame to the Islamic community.

I turned the channel from the news to ESPN.

"Man, I wish I could've twisted his cap. But it's all good. Sometimes you gotta put your personal feelings aside and do what's best for the team. Never forget that," I jeweled Eric, who was seated in the recliner adjacent to me in my study.

"Copy," he said.

I looked at him and thought, *He's gonna be a good leader, because he's a sponge.*

Just then, La knocked on the door.

"Come in," I said.

She came in pushing a dumb waiter. Then, she served us lobster, crab legs and corn on the cob. When she was finished fixing our platters, she kissed Eric before excusing herself from the room.

I looked at him and smiled.

After their trip to Atlanta, they came back with a closeness to each other that wasn't there when they left. When they were in my presence at the same time, I would catch them stealing looks at each other.

Being far from dumb, I suspected something happened between them during their trip, but I didn't question either of them. I wanted to see if they would tell me themselves, especially Eric. If he didn't, it would weaken my perception of him because real niggaz didn't hide shit like that from the ones they were supposed to be loyal to.

Normally, ya mans' sister was considered off limits. But if you did cross that line, you had to be 100 about it.

Step to me like the young boss I think you are, and tell me the deally. yo, I thought every time Eric and La would find an excuse to leave the house together.

I knew they were fuckin' because my sister glowed every time Eric came over. He had always liked La, so it wasn't a big surprise. As long as he didn't treat my peeps foul, I would okay the relationship.

But don't try to hide it!

That's the shot that got Manny killed by Tony, in the movie *Scarface*.

Just when the taste in my mouth was close to turning sour, Eric asked if we could talk.

Him and La had just came back from the store. The three of us was seated in the living room.

"Yeah, what's on your mind, soldier?" Before he could reply, I looked at La, who had taken a seat across from me. "Lakeesha, step out of the room. We're about to talk business."

She stood up to leave but Eric placed a hand on her arm, stopping her. "No, baby, stay here."

She sat back down and stared at the floor.

Eric looked up at me. "This isn't about business, family. Me and La have something to tell you. I've been trying to find the right time to talk to you about it, but real talk, I've been nervous as hell."

"Nervous?" I squinted my eyes. That contradicted his gangsta.

"Yeah, fam. Nervous." He nodded his head. "Because I don't know how you're gonna feel about what we're about to tell you."

I chuckled. "Son, I already know. The shit is mad obvious. Y'all walking around making goo goo eyes at each other, or either y'all trying not to look at each other at all when I'm in the room."

"Damn! I thought we were being smooth." He chuckled tensely. "Anyway, bruh, I love your sister, man. Always have." He pulled La onto his lap and wrapped his arms around her lovingly. "I'm asking your blessings to be with her."

"Please, Rah!" La clasped her hands together in a gesture of prayer.

I stared at them both but I didn't respond for a full minute or more. My silence caused them to fidget. When I finally spoke, my voice conveyed my seriousness.

"Eric, your first love is the game. You and I both know that," I said.

"True indeed," he admitted. "But it won't force me to neglect or mistreat what I have at home."

"But can you assure me that you won't let any harm come her way?"

"Nah, Rah. You know how this shit goes. There's no promises in it, yo." He lifted La off of his lap, stood up and began pacing the floor, swinging his arms out animatedly. "Anybody connected to us can be harmed by what we do. That's just the nature of the game, baby. But you know I'll lay my life on the line for mines! I can promise you that!"

"I respect that, yo." I looked from him to my sister. "La, are you good with playing second to the streets? Can you live with knowing you might end up being a young ass widow? Or you might end up having to make weekends trips to visit him in prison for the rest of his life, one day. Are you about that life, lil' sis?"

"I'm about it for him. Hell yeah," she said unequivocally.

"And what if some niggaz run up in your crib with you and the kids there?"

"I'ma blow their asses right back out the door. Eric has already started teaching me how to pop those hammers. And the same blood that flows through your veins flows through mine, Rah. I'm not no punk broad. We got this, man. Just give us your blessing. Please!"

This time her eyes weren't staring at the floor. She looked at me with supreme confidence in their relationship and her ability to be a gangsta'z wife.

There was only one more answer I needed.

Turning my head from La back to Eric, I asked him, "Are you sure you're ready to settle down? Because you know I couldn't sit back and watch you play my sister."

"Rah, relax. She's in good hands now. I'm not those other niggaz." He looked at Lakeesha with pure love in his eyes. The way I had looked at Sparkle, and the way CJ used to look at Tamika.

I knew that their relationship wouldn't be perfect, none were. But I felt confident that Eric would love my sister with all of him.

I stood up and walked over to them. "I give you my blessings," I said.

They both smiled and then we shared a group hug.

"This is so lame!" cracked La.

We all started laughing.

In the weeks that followed, La seemed happier than I had ever seen her.

"You're good for her. I can already see the transformation," I said.

"Yeah, fam, that's my boo," he smiled back.

"I know," I chuckled. Their blooming love was one of the good things to come out of this bloody prolonged war.

***

Allah had to be heaping blessings on me, clearing the path for me to return to my deen. Because days later, I sat parked in a van with Cujo and Tim. Tim had his binoculars on the front door a few houses down from where we sat.

Cujo checked his watch.

"He should be coming out to walk his dog shortly," he said. They had been watching Big Nasty's crib for weeks, and they had his schedule down pat. "Let's get in place."

"Remember, take him alive," I reminded my cohorts. "The dog too."

"We'll do our best," said Cujo.

Tim passed me his binoculars and then jumped out of the car and got in position. Cujo was right behind him.

I slid the side door open and watched things unfold through the high-tech lenses of the night binoculars.

Moments later, Big Nasty came out of the house with Lil' Nasty on a dog leash. They moved down the driveway to the sidewalk, where Tim stepped out of the darkness. He raised his arm and shot Lil' Nasty with the tranquilizer gun. The dosage in the dart must not have been strong enough because the killa pit bull lunged up in the air and locked his teeth into Tim's forearm.

"Ahhh!" he screamed as he frantically tried to shake the dog off of his arm.

Big Nasty reached out to grab Tim, but Cujo emerged from the shadows just in time to thwart him. But when he ran up on Big Nasty, the behemoth goon clocked him so hard, I heard that shit from where I sat in the truck.

To his credit, Cujo didn't go down. He stumbled back and righted himself.

"Bring that shit!" he snarled.

Big Nasty didn't hesitate, he brought it. He hit Cujo with a haymaker that came way from East Rutherford.

"Do you know who the fuck I am, cracker!" Big Nasty belted. "I'm Stanley muthafuckin' Green. The baddest man The Bricks has ever seen!"

He grabbed Cujo by the collar, pulled him close and then bit him in the face.

"Ahh shit!" Cujo screamed. But Big Nasty had fucked up by getting to close up on him.

Sparks flew from his chest when Cujo hit him with the taser.

Bzzz! Bzzz! Bzzz!

He kept tasing him until Big Nasty fell to the ground, flopping like a fish.

A few feet away, Lil' Nasty was trying take a bite out of crime. He hung on to Tim's forearm, growling, but I could hear his growl weakening. Tim slung his arm left to right, back and forth, trying desperately to shake the crazy dog off of him, but Lil' Nasty wouldn't release his lock until Cujo came over and zapped him with the taser.

The dog's body jerked, he released his jaw lock and fell to the ground wailing. Seconds later, the tranquilizer must've kicked in, or else the dog was dead. He laid on his side still as a log.

I tossed the night binoculars on the back seat and climbed up front behind the wheel and drove the van up closer. They cuffed and shackled Big Nasty, put a muzzle over his dog's mouth and then loaded both of them into the back of the van.

"*Whew!* I'm getting too old for this," groaned Cujo, wiping sweat from his forehead as he locked the rear door.

I looked at Tim's arm, it was bloodied but not mangled. He seemed to be in a little pain but the bites weren't fatal.

The blare of police sirens wailed nearby. In the flash of a few seconds, three patrol cars surrounded us. Six officers from NPD hopped out their cars with their guns drawn.

It was tense for a minute but several of the cops recognized their brethren and before long, the situation was under control. Cujo was able to convince them that he and Tim were making an arrest. To authenticate it, he pretended to arrest me, too.

Inside the van, it reeked of sweat, shit and piss. Apparently Big Nasty and the dog had lost their bowels when they got tased.

"Roll down the windows," I said.

"Why? It's nothing but a little boo boo," cracked Tim. Then him and Cujo laughed their asses off.

"Ain't shit funny, yo."

"Tim, do you hear that killer back there whining about a little poop?"

"Yep, ain't that some shit."

They roared with laughter as Cujo pulled off.

CHAPTER
40
Nard

I hadn't heard from my goon, Big Nasty, all day. As evening approached, I began to worry. The squad was already down to me, Big Nasty and Zakee, who was in the suite with me, and a handful of foot soldiers. I could not afford to lose Big Nasty not when I was only a step away from getting a new plug. As long as we had the yack, we could always rebuild.

"Zakee, try his number again." As the demand left my mouth, my phone rang in my hand. I looked at the screen and saw Big Nasty's number pop up. "Never mind, this him calling now," I said.

I was so relieved to get a call back from Big Nasty, I didn't pay attention that the call was FaceTime until I accepted it.

"Peace, fam," said the hooded man whose face was on my screen. His scratchy voice sent a chill up my spine because I knew who the voice belonged to. And since he was calling from Big Nasty's phone, I knew what that meant.

I dropped my head and let out a long sigh. This nigga was winning at every fuckin' turn. I knew he wasn't a better man than me, he was just playing with a stacked deck.

"The shit hurts, don't it?" Rah taunted me.

'What you want, yo?" I asked.

"A life for a life. Your life for your man's, the same offer you gave CJ." He put the camera on Big Nasty. He was on his knees with his hands cuffed behind his back and leg shackles around his ankles. His face was hideously swollen.

Rah moved the camera off of my goon and put it on Lil' Nasty. He was chained to a pole and muzzled.

"Now the tables are reversed," he gloated.

"Bitch nigga, I'ma snatch that bass out of your voice when I find you. Turn you into a straight pussy!"

"You're just talking. If you really wanna see me, make me know it," he shot back.

"Your day is coming!"

"My day can be today. Are you a bitch or a man? CJ proved how real he was. It's your turn now. What you gonna do? Meet me in the same place you told CJ to meet you. Be there in three hours or it's a wrap for your mans. We're about to see what kind of balls you got."

The screen went black.

Zakee, who had been watching over my shoulder, asked, "Nard, what's the move?"

I responded without a second thought. "I'ma stay G'd up, blood."

CHAPTER
41
Rah

My gunners were posted up all around the condemned building. The weather was frigid. We all rocked heavy, winter fatigues, which was Eric's idea. He wanted to commemorate the way CJ had them all fall up in the club the night of Nard's birthday party, when CJ came to reclaim Tamika.

I approved the outfits we were wearing because I wanted to remind Nard that CJ lived on, through every single one of us, especially through me.

We waited and waited and waited. Hours past the deadline, Nard still hadn't shown up. I hit his number from Big Nasty's phone.

"Yeah," he answered dryly.

"I know you were a bitch. You gonna turn your back on your mans? That's how you rock?" I baited.

"Fuck you, Rah. We'll meet again." He hung up the phone.

I turned to Big Nasty, who was sitting on the ground cuffed and shackled, "You see the difference in him and CJ?"

"Suck my dick and choke to death on it!" he spat.

He was talking greasy and maybe he truly didn't fear death, but looking down in his face, I could tell that it hurt him that Nard hadn't shown up. His voice was strong but his eyes were watery.

"Nah, fam. Ain't no homo shit over here." I jabbed my finger in my chest. "But that's probably how you and your bitch ass boss man rocked. And now, that nigga won't even lay his life down for you, after you went all out for him." I shook my head disgustedly.

"It don't matter. I came in this world by myself and I'm prepared to leave the same way. But I'ma die like a G. I'm not about to beg like a bitch." His tone told me he had accepted his fate.

"I feel you, big homie. But watch what that brave shit get you."

***

We were back at the warehouse. My crew stood around waiting to see what level of savageness I would reach in exterminating Big Nasty and Lil' Nasty. Both of them had brutally tortured and killed men we loved. In addition, they had tortured me. Now it was time for them to reap what they had sewn.

Big Nasty was strapped and chained to two work benches we had lined up to accommodate his mammoth size. His arms were stretched out, and both palms had been nailed to wooden blocks, as if he was laying on a cross. A thick leather strap was tied around his mouth holding his head firmly in place.

Several feet away, Lil' Nasty remained muzzled. The dog was chained to a pole with a thick short chain that restricted his movement. He was growling viciously, slobbering out the side of his mouth and bucking widely to free himself.

"Down, boy, you're not going anywhere." I raised an aluminum baseball bat high above my head. "Remember me?"

He lunged up at me but the short chain snatched him right back down on his hind feet, almost strangling him.

I swung the baseball bat like I was in the World Series.
Thonk!

It made contact with his head, knocking him on his back.
Erk! Erk! Erk! He wailed.

"You not so vicious now, huh? Remember when you bit me in my face?"
Thonk! Thonk!

262

I beat him in the chest.

"You're just a viscious animal, I'm the beast up in this bitch!" I swung the bat with all of my might.

Thwack! Thwack! Thwack! Thwack!

Blood and dog hair was everywhere. I looked down at Lil' Nasty, sweating and breathing hard. He was broken up and bloodied, barely moving. The image of him dragging Legend across the floor replayed in my mind, and a fresh bolt of anger rose up in my chest. I dropped the bloody bat and whipped out my piece.

Boc! Boc! Boc! Boc! Boc!

I fired bullet after bullet into that dog until my clip was empty.

Click! Click!

All that was left of Lil' Nasty was a puddle of blood and a pile of hair and bones.

I wiped blood off of my face with the sleeve of my shirt and then I let my banger clang to the floor as I slowly turned around and stepped over to where the dog's master laid.

Tears ran from the corners of Big Nasty's swollen eyes. He was muttering something around the leather gag in his mouth, but I had no interest in what he had to say. My voice was the only one that mattered.

"It's time to pay the piper, big boy." I nodded my head at Eric and then I resumed talking to Big Nasty.

"I'm what you call a quiet storm. Somebody should've warned you that size ain't shit when you fuck with me. The worst mistake you ever made was teaming up with a nigga who don't have the same loyalty to you as you had to him. Take that thought to the grave with you."

I was done talking. I stepped aside and let Eric display his gangster. "He's all yours, fam. Show this nigga how CJ's lil' brother gets down."

Eric stepped around me and held up a heavy-duty chainsaw. He forced eye contact with Big Nasty. "You helped kill my brother." His voice revealed the pain that still resided in his heart. In the next instance, it conveyed his anger. "Now, it's your time to pay for that. One limb at a time, starting with your arms."

Eric powered the chainsaw on. The motor roared loudly. The metal teeth gnashed, making an ominous sound. For the first time since we snatched him up, Big Nasty showed a sign of fear. I walked over to him and removed the gag from over his mouth. I needed to hear his screams when Eric started sawing off his limbs. I wanted his yowls to reach the sky and echo off of the walls of Thug Paradise, so CJ could rejoice.

I stepped out of the way. Turning back to Eric, I shouted over the loud gnawing. "Cut off the foot first, I want this big muhfucka to suffer and die slow."

Eric lowered the saw onto his ankle and Big Nasty screamed. His foot fell off and plopped down to the floor with the sit shoe still on.

"Now, the other one!" said Eric, mercilessly.

Big Nasty screamed as Eric slowly sawed off his other foot. Blood splashed all over his face, but my lil' nigga was unaffected by the gore. This was revenge for CJ.

Sweat poured down Big Nasty's forehead, and he began going in and out of consciousness.

Eric drew a hand back and slapped him. "Wake up! Look in my face as I take your life!"

Big Nasty stared up at him, not in submission, but in what I took as defiance. He wanted us to know that he could not be broken.

I respected that, but it didn't earn him any mercy from my protégé.

Eric powered the bloody chainsaw back on and then he went to work on Big Nasty's legs, one at a time.

This time, when Big Nasty passed out from the pain, Eric didn't stop to slap him back awake. Meticulously, and with no compassion, he butchered that big muthafucka up.

When it was over, the area looked like a slaughter house.

"Another one bites the dust," he announced with blood dripping from the chainsaw.

"Just one more to go," I added.

We both were fiendin' for that kill.

Ca$h

CHAPTER
42
Nard

When another video call came in, I knew it was Rah, calling again from Big Nasty's phone. I thought about not answering it, but against all hope, I prayed he was calling back to invite me to where they were. This time, I was going.

Fuck those niggaz! I don't give a fuck if they have the advantage or not, we're going to try to save our comrade. It's do or die season!

Big Nasty had been loyal. Leaving him to die just didn't sit right with me. I knew that even after I showed up, Rah wasn't going to release him, but he would have to kill me, too. And I would go out clapping hard at those muthafuckaz.

"Yeah, bitch ass nigga, what do you want?" I answered the call. "I'm ready to see you. Stay right there!"

"Too late. You should've found your little ass nuts when I first hit you up. Now, your top goon is lying on the floor in little pieces. Burn *this* image in your memory."

Rah moved the camera lens around the room. Eric stood next to a metal work bench, holding a chainsaw. Body parts and blood was strewn everywhere. I saw my nigga'z severed head laying on the floor next to a severed arm.

"You bitch muthafucka!" I gulped.

"Nah, we some *baaddd* muhfuckaz! Respect my gangsta!" exclaimed Rah.

Eric looked into the camera and smiled. "You're next," he taunted and then he picked Big Nasty's head up and slammed it back down on the floor.

I dropped my head and fought hard not to let that shit make me holla. Zakee, who was looking over my shoulder, turned and walked away. He went over and sat down on the bed with his face down in his hands.

I looked back in the camera and spoke to Rah and Eric real clearly, and without any compromise in my tone.

"I'm gonna stand over of your graves, yo. If it's the last thing I ever do!"

I disconnected the call, walked over and put a consoling hand on Zakee's shoulder. "They haven't won, my nigga. It's war to the last of me."

***

I left the suite alone and went for a drive to clear my head. As I drove aimlessly, the faces of each and every one of my mans who had lost their lives, in the war between our team and CJ's, appeared in my mental.

I silently apologized to all of them for pulling them into what was more personal than business. But my niggaz' voices were as one.

We lived and balled as a team, and that's how we die. You didn't fail us, boss. We rode with you for the love. Fuck everything else. Now, go out and smash those bitch made muthafuckaz!

It was as if we were all in one room, seated around a table like old times, and I could hear each of my fallen soldier voices distinctly.

Their love and loyalty broke a thug down. Before I knew it, tears were falling from my eyes, elevating the level of hate I had for the other side. They had taken the lives of good men, niggaz who had nothing but love and respect for me.

I didn't regret this war. I hadn't started it. I had been minding my own, traveling in my own lane, when CJ pulled up and tried to disrespect a young G. Him and that bitch had murdered my one and only seed. Rah and nem was an extension of CJ, and they had killed my pops and some of my crew. Now, I despised him as much as I had despised his boy. And I wouldn't rest peacefully until he took his last breath.

Without even planning to go there, I ended up at home where Kenisha was. Shit was fucked between us, for obvious reasons. Not only did she have a huge decision to make giving up her and that nigga'z baby, she was also stressing about her pops. I wanted to be her comfort, to show her that a love like mine was her bridge over troubled waters. But I couldn't do that as long as CJ's child was a part of our lives.

For a long time, I sat in my car, in the driveway, with my head resting against the steering wheel, pondering some other solution to our problem. But in my heart of hearts, I knew there were none. It was either me or the baby. Kenisha had to choose. If she couldn't, I would choose for her.

I looked up to see her peeking out of the blinds. Feeling like the weight of the world was on my shoulders, I got out of the car and went inside to find out if her love for me was in tune with the vows we had taken. As my wife, she had vowed to place me above anything and anyone. *Anyone.*

I knew the moment of truth was on the other side of the front door. So, as I placed my key in the lock and turned the knob, I was prepared for the worst.

I love her, but I'm not accepting Ca'Ron. No way, no how!

Just saying that baby's name in my mind, knowing who his daddy was, put a foul taste in my mouth.

I turned my head and spat on the ground before stepping inside.

Kenisha had taken a seat in a chair in the living room when she saw me. She held the baby in her lap, bouncing him on her knee.

"Hey, hubby," she looked up and spoke.

"Sup." I walked right past her and into the bedroom.

I was in there, staring at the walls, when she came into the room. She wasn't carrying the baby, so I assumed she had rocked him asleep and put him in the nursery.

She walked up and stopped a foot away from me, as if she was afraid to come closer.

Looking into her beautiful face, I felt my heart pound with love for her. "Baby girl, come here." I held my arms open to her, and she stepped into them.

"I missed you." She started crying.

"I missed you, too." I kissed away her tears.

Kenisha hugged me tightly, and in a timid voice, she asked, "Nard, what are we going to do. I don't want to give my baby up." She began sobbing.

I rubbed her back. "I understand. You don't have to give him up. I'll walk away. Give me up."

"No! I can't live without you. Mama's dead. Daddy is locked up. I need you, baby, and I love you." She held me like a person drowning would hold onto a rope.

"I'll still take care of you," I promised her. "That's my responsibility and I'm a man of honor."

"Baby, it's not about money or security. I need my husband. You're my life, my happiness." Her eyes brimmed with fresh tears. "My skies were dark gray until you came into my life and loved me like I deserved to be loved."

"You did the same for me, and I thank you for that, ma." I kissed the top of her head. "I was straight thuggin', not giving a fuck, until you came into my life. But baby, the shit between me and CJ and them runs deep." I pleaded for her to understand, but she couldn't.

"I know it does, Nard. I can see it in your eyes when you talk about it. But Ca'Ron is innocent," she argued.

"He's still that nigga'z seed." I let her go and I walked to the other side of the bedroom. I looked in the dresser mirror at my reflection. The stress showed on my face.

I let out a sigh before turning back to face my wife. "Baby, what you're not comprehending is how deep my hate for that nigga is, even though he's dead. His mans, Rah, is still out here killing everything that's moving. Today they killed Big Nasty. And let me tell you how dirty they did my nigga."

I walked back over to her and gave her the grisly details. By the time I finished describing what they did to my mans, I was crying and Kenisha had darted to the bathroom to throw up.

When she returned, I was packing my clothes. As I packed, I recounted every single murder both sides had committed against each other.

By the time I finished telling those stories, I had packed most of my clothes. "So, you see, this shit runs deeper than words can express. Every time I look at lil' dude now, I see his daddy. I love you, baby, but I can't accept CJ's child."

I picked up two bags and headed out of the bedroom. It took several trips to load all of my things in the car. All the while, Kenisha and I said nothing else to each other. She sat on the bed, weeping into her hands.

Her crying squeezed blood from my heart, but I remained resolute in my decision. Carrying the last bag over my shoulder, I stopped in front of her and gave her my keys to the house.

"I'm sorry, ma! I'll make sure you're okay, financially. You won't have to worry about that. Take care. I love you."

I cried inside as I headed for the door. Baby girl was my all, but I had to do what I had to do. I would've been a lesser man had I remained with her and ended up abusing an innocent child.

When I reached the door, I heard Kenisha call my name. "Nard!"

I turned around. "Yeah, what's up?"

"I love you! You're my husband. I'll give Ca'Ron up for adoption." Her voice was tinged with tears.

"Nah, ma. You'll end up hating me," I said.

"No, I could never do that," she pledged as she rushed up to and hugged me. "Just promise me you'll never stop loving me."

"I won't, baby." I dropped my bag, and my gangsta for a moment, and me and my wife hugged each other and cried together.

CHAPTER
43
Kenisha
A month later

I stood in the cemetery looking at his headstone. It was huge, and it stood out from the rest just as he had made it a point of emphasis for him to stand out in a crowd when he was alive.

The cold wind whipped around my face, but it could not dry the bitter, angry tears that wet my cheeks. The tears poured in abundance, fueled by my loathing of his black ass.

"CJ, I hate you! I hope your soul is burning in hell!"

Because of Cam'ron Jefferies, I had lost so much, beginning with my innocence. And from the grave he had continued to torment me.

Nard had told me everything, starting with Tamika. Because of CJ and that ratchet bitch, my mother was dead and my husband had lost everyone he loved except me and his mom.

I now knew the connection between Nard and Daddy, and though it broke my heart to learn that my father was involved with drug dealing and murder, it did not diminish my love for him. Family was family.

CJ and his boy, Rah, had destroyed my family. For that, I hated them both. I prayed that Raheem would die in the streets like CJ.

With my arms folded across my chest and a look of pure hate on my face, I said, "You got what you deserved, you black bastard! I'm glad you're dead. I hate you."

I blamed CJ, not Nard, for me having to give up my baby.

"I had your son, the one you wouldn't have claimed. I named him Ca'Ron Jalen Gideons. Last week, because of all the shit you did, I had to put him up for adoption. It tore my

heart out to do that, but I would've lost my husband had I not."
I inhaled and then exhaled. "Yes, I'm married. To Nard,
matter of fact. Your strongest enemy. I hope that tortures your
soul. And I love him to the death of me. He's everything you
were not! He's kind, gentle, loving and faithful. Your ass was
a hoe! I gave myself to you, conceived your child and you spat
me out on the ground with no remorse. For that, I pray that
you're rotting in Hell! You and Rah didn't break my man.
He's still standing. Let your boy know it's not over. Nard will
bounce back."

I wiped my tears with my gloved hand and sniffled up the
snot that ran from my nose and then I continued.

"You haven't won shit, CJ! Muthafucka, you're dead!
That's exactly what you deserved, bitch!" I hawked a glob of
spit on his grave.

"I wish I could dig your ass up and spit in your face, but
you're not worth my time."

Out of breath, I turned to leave. The person standing
behind me caused me to jump out of my skin.

"Raheem!" I gasped.

CHAPTER
44
Rah

I could literally see the pee run down Kenisha's leg and stain her jeans when she turned around and saw me standing behind her. She had been zoned out, spewing mad insults at my nigga, when I walked up. The shit that came out of her mouth enraged me, but now I knew what she had meant that night.

I hadn't driven a mile when I had to pull over and helped Kenisha out of the car so she wouldn't throw up all over my seats.

"Shorty, this isn't a good look, you can't let a man get you all twisted like this," I told her as I helped her back inside of the car and strapped on her seat belt.

"I can't help it," she cried.

"Yes, you can."

"No, I can't," she slurred.

"It's more than you think." she broke out in sobs.

"So, you were pregnant with CJ's son when he died, and you gave the baby up for that nigga, huh?" My words were laced with acid.

"I had to. He was going to leave me and he's all I have," she said.

"So, he forced you to put my brother's son up for adoption?"

"Yes." I could tell she was lying.

"Did he force you to spit on my nigga'z grave?"

"Uh…"

Whap!

Before I knew it, I had slapped her to the ground.

"Get up and go clean that shit off of his grave, and you better find it!" I snatched my heat off of my waist and pointed it down at her.

Kenisha got on her hands and knees, and she crawled over to the spot where she had spat. Crying she used two hands to shovel up a pile of snow.

"I ought to make you eat that shit." I snarled.

"Please, Raheem, I'm sorry." Her eyes begged for mercy that her ass wasn't going to get. Not from me!

"No, you're not! You meant every word I heard come out of your mouth. You're not muthafuckin' sorry!" I blasted.

Kenisha let the snow slip through her finger tips as she folded her hands in prayer, begging me not to kill her. She tried to kiss my feet but I quickly stepped back. I didn't want her lying lips to desecrate my boot.

I looked down at her with flared nostrils. "I used to think a lot of you, but you're just like your fake ass daddy."

"No, Raheem, I'm not fake. Your boy made me this way. He dogged me, and you know it. I gave CJ something special and he treated it like it wasn't shit." The bitterness in her voice was thick.

"And you think that justifies giving his seed away? A child you carried in your womb. I don't respect that shit." I grabbed her by the hair. "Get up!" I shoved the gun in her mouth, chipping a tooth in the process.

"I had no other choice," she cried harder.

I wasn't the same Raheem who took her home from the club that night. So, her tears didn't mean shit to me.

"Save that shit!" I spat. "You're gonna walk with me to my car and if one string of hair on your head blows the wrong way, I'ma crush you. Do you understand?"

"Yes," she muttered fearfully.

"Start muthafuckin' steppin'!"

I spun her around, threw my arm around her shoulder pretending to be the consoling boyfriend, in case some nosey person was watching. My banger was in the opposite hand tucked inside of my coat.

I could barely contain myself as I led her to the parking lot. It was bad enough she had married that chump Nard. That alone could've gotten her wig split. But the shit she said about CJ, spittin' on my nigga'z grave—none of that was excusable.

CJ didn't make you the way you are. Can't nobody bring nothin' out of you that wasn't inside of you to begin with. All my dude did was peel back the outer layer and expose what was underneath.

"Good afternoon," an elderly black woman spoke as she passed by.

"Same to you." I eased my gun out a little in case Kenisha tried to attract her attention. I was gonna turn the white snow on the ground red.

When we reached the lot, Snoop saw us approaching and he slid from behind the wheel of his truck. He had driven me to the cemetery but he hadn't accompanied me to the gravesite. He walked toward us, and we met in front of a vacant car.

"Look who I found," I said.

"That's the lil' honey CJ fucked with. David X's daughter, isn't she?"

"None other."

"She was at CJ's grave?"

"Yep."

"Is she friend of foe?"

"Foe," I said emphatically. "She wasn't here to mourn son, she came to spit on his grave."

"The fuck?" He drew his fist back to punch shorty in the mouth.

"No, not here," I stopped him. I then looked at Kenisha. "Where's your car?"

She pointed to a Lexus about 30 feet away. Nard had her riding good but her little joy ride was about to come to a horrific end. I made her disengage the alarm and give me the car keys. Me and Snoop marched her to her car and put her in the trunk.

"Let's take her to the spot. I need to devise a plan for us to get Nard. I'm going to drive her car, you follow me." I whispered so Kenisha couldn't hear.

We took her to the warehouse, where I instilled the fear of God in her. Shortly after I took the noose from around her neck and lowered her from the steel beam where we had threatened to hang her, she gave us the info we wanted.

By now Eric and Shabazz had joined us.

With Kenisha directing the way, we headed out to snag an elusive bitch nigga.

CHAPTER
45
Nard

"Blood, we had a helluva run but's it's over now. The plug is gone, Big Nasty is dead—everybody but you and me. We can't fight those niggaz by ourselves, they're too deep. And with the police in their pockets, they're strapped. Sometimes you just gotta tip your hat to your enemy and let it go," advised Zakee.

We were standing in his back yard with our heads ducked against the cold.

"I guess you're right, my dude." I didn't tongue wrestle with him. But the shit that was coming out of his mouth wasn't what I wanted to hear. I expected him to be like. *Fam, we don't need nobody but you and me. Let's ride on those niggaz, and those dirty ass cops on their team, too!*

But Zakee wanted to throw in the towel, just walk away and surrender victory to those muthafuckaz after all the shit we had been through.

I wasn't feeling that fuckery. *My niggaz didn't lose their lives just for us to fold.*

Zakee must've read the expression on my face. "What's on your mind? You're not thinking about staying here and going after them by yourself, are you?" He shook his head, disapprovingly. "I hope not, man, that's suicide."

"Shut the fuck up, yo!" I didn't wanna hear another word he had to say. "Nigga, you talking like those bitch muthafuckaz walk on water! Rah and Eric bleed just like the next nigga!" My body shook with rage.

"It ain't about that, yo." Zakee tried to defend his position. "I know they can be put in the dirt just like we can, but our team is weak right now, Nard. All of our best men are dead.

At least, let's fall back and regroup before we go after them again."

"Never! And I can't believe you're saying no bitch shit like that to me. What? You pussy now?" I whipped out my banger and pointed at his chest. "What happened to your heart, blood?"

I suspected him of losing his gangsta after witnessing what they did to Big Nasty, but damn!

"Haven't shit happened to this!" He tapped his fist against the left side of his chest. "But I'm not in no hurry to die! They got us down bad, don't you see that?"

"I don't see shit but murder, nigga." I stepped up in his grill and put that steel to his dome. "I don't need your pussy ass to ride with me! Fuck you! I'll ride alone!"

Boom!

My fo-fo sounded like a cannon.

I watched his body fall to the ground, blood leaking out of his head. But I felt no pity.

"Me, surrender? Bitch, you must've forgot who I am!" I breathed fire over his slain body.

I aimed the gun down at him.

Boom! Boom!

"Next time you'll watch what the fuck come outta your mouth!" I stepped over him and jogged to my ride, which was parked in his driveway.

As soon as I climbed up in my truck and drove off, Kenisha called. I took a few seconds to allow my breathing to slow down before answering.

On the fourth ring, I picked up.

"Sup, ma?" I could hear my voice echoing. "Why you got me on speaker?"

"I'm not feeling well."

"Oh, well, lay down and get some rest. You're probably stressed out."

Shorty had been through hell. Her pops was locked up, she had lost her Ma Duke and she had to choose between me and her son. I hadn't been sure what her choice would be but baby girl proved her undying love when she chose me.

"Bae, what time will you be home?" she asked.

"I'll be there in a couple of hours. Do you need me to bring anything?"

"Just bring yourself," she said as sweet as always. But I could tell her spirits were low because she didn't sound like her usual self.

"A'ight, ma, I'll see you in a few. Love you."

"Love you, too."

I hung up the phone feeling a little worried about my girl. As for Zakee, I didn't give a fuck about killing that nigga. I was better off with him dead than alive. Because when the chips are done, real niggaz stand strong. Only hoes lift up their skirts and show their pussy like Zakee had done.

I didn't need a dickless muthafucka on my team.

Ca$h

CHAPTER
46
Rah

"**A**ww, ain't that sweet," I mocked her when she hung up from Nard.

We were inside their house in Harlem. Me and Eric stood watching over Kenisha, who was sitting on her bed weeping. We had collected all the guns Nard had stashed around the house and put them in one of the empty moving boxes they had.

Most of their personal things were packed away. Shorty admitted that they were planning to leave town soon.

I had told her, *"You can't save Nard's life. We're gonna kill him, whether you help lure him to us or not. But you can save your own life. And once this is over you can go get you son back. I'll provide for him because that's my nigga'z seed."*

Kenisha agreed to help lure Nard home, although I could tell that she really loved him and she was heartbroken about being forced to make that call.

She had been crying for hours. But most people would do what she was doing when real killaz had that hammer to their heads. I hadn't wilted under the threat of death when Nard had me in this exact fucked up predicament and wanted me to lure CJ into a trap. But I was cut from a different cloth than most. With me, it was *death before dishonor*.

I walked over to the window and parted the blinds. It was early evening and the sun had just begun to fade behind the clouds. The street was quiet, absent of pedestrians. I saw Snoop, Shabazz and a dozen of our young goons parked up and down the block. They were on the lookout for Nard's truck. But the plan was to let him come inside so we could grab him without the threat of being seen by neighbors.

I called Snoop on his cell phone and gave him an update.

"Let the others know," I said.

When I hung up, I ordered Eric to duct-tape Kenisha. We didn't need her jumping around screaming when her man came in the door and we threw down on him.

"Now, we wait." I sat down at the foot of the bed and replayed my life in my mind, going way back to when I was a little snot nosed boy, ripping and running with CJ and gettin' my ass tore up by Big Ma.

I chuckled at the memories. The years moved on until I reached high school. I saw Sparkle's face as clear as if she was standing in front of me.

I stumbled on this photograph/It kinda made me laugh/It took me way back/Back down memory lane...

I wiped at my eyes as I recalled her dedicating that song to me at the talent show, and winning the First-Place prize. It seemed like such a long time ago. Almost a different lifetime. Before we all became grown-ups and life got serious.

I recalled the first-time CJ told me about Cujo and 'em. I remembered his excitement when he made his first mil'. *Man, you was supposed to live to grow old and gray. Tamika, too.*

"Bruh, this shit hurts," I said all of a sudden, as I stood to my feet.

"What hurts, yo?" asked Eric.

"I was thinking about CJ again. Fuck, man! Fuck!" I pounded my fist in my hand.

"Bruh, is still with us, my G." Eric, came up to me and threw an arm around my shoulders.

Tears poured down my face.

"Let it out, yo. You remember what CJ used to say?" he asked.

I nodded yeah and then in unison we said, "Thugs Cry."

My nigga was probably looking down on us right now, cracking the fuck up. Probably saying some shit like, "Look at your emotional ass! Nigga, I'm good. I'm up here lamping, in Thug Paradise, with Tamika and mad muthafuckaz from The Bricks. Just handle ya business, yo. Shit is gravy where I rest."

A smile came over my face. I dried my tears and turned my thoughts to his son, Little CJ. I couldn't wait for the day I could see him, pick his lil' ass up, sit him on my knee and tell him how strong and brave his daddy was.

I bet lil' dude looks just like my dawg.

And this bougie rat gave him to the system! Chose a nigga over CJ's seed!

The anger in me was so intense, I almost went over to where Kenisha was tied up and stomped her head in the floor. But it felt like Big Ma was watching and wagging a disapproving finger at me.

That gave shorty a pass.

To help restrain the beast in me, I went in the bathroom and washed my face with cold water. When I returned to the bedroom, my phone started ringing in my pocket.

"Sup?" I pulled it out and answered.

"Nard just pulled up!" said Snoop, sounding excited.

"One." I was all business and deadly purpose.

I snatched my toolie from my waist and told Eric the deal. Together, we hurried to the front door.

My heart pumped hot and fast. I could almost taste murder on my tongue. Eric stood on one side of the door, gripping his heat with both hands. I stood on the other side breathing lightly, coiled like a Cobra ready to snare its prey.

As soon as Nard stepped through the door, I yoked that nigga up from behind, almost crushing his wind pipe with my forearm. I kicked the door shut with the back of my heel and Eric stuck his banger to Nard's forehead.

"Welcome home, blood. Glad you could join us." Eric taunted.

"Fuck y'all maggot muthafuckaz doing in my goddam house!" He wrestled to break free from my lock.

"We came for your life!" I strengthened my hold.

Nard knew what time it was. We were there to kill him, nothin' less. With nothin' to lose, he bucked like a wild bull.

"You not getting shit!" He used legs to push back and rammed me into the wall.

I felt him trying to reach for his waist.

"Get his strap!" I barked to Eric as I held on and tightened my grip.

Nard fought to grab his gun but Eric beat him to it. My own tool slipped from my hand and hit the floor as I choked that muhfucka 'til he started slobbering out of the mouth.

By now Snoop, Shabazz and a few others were in the house. Quickly, they helped us slam Nard to the floor and pin him down.

I stepped on his head, applying all of my weight, while Shabazz duct-taped him. With him securely restrained, we stood him up in his feet. Once again, we were toe to toe.

I saw the jagged X mark I had cut into his face as I stepped all the way up in his grill. "You don't have to look for me no more, I found *you*. This time, you won't live to tell about it."

Nard didn't blink or shudder. He stuck out his chest and his lips peeled back, exposing his clenched teeth. "Am I supposed to be scared? Nigga, fuck you! You're still a bitch! Your whole squad pussy."

Eric moved me aside and slapped him across the face with his steel.

Whap!

"I'ma make you respect this shit!" he gritted.

Whap! Whap!

Nard stumbled back from the second and third blows, but Snoop held him up. Blood leaked from his brow and his mouth.

"That's all you got, little fuck boi! You soft just like your brother!" Nard laughed, mocking Eric's gangster and insulting CJ's street legacy.

It took every ounce of strength in my body to hold Eric back and stop him from killing that nigga, right then and there. But I had to stop him. I had a special type of death planned for Nard, one that niggaz in The Bricks would never forget.

"Don't kill him yet, yo! Just hold up, I got something for that ass." I coaxed Eric out of gorilla mode.

He eyed Nard with fury and hatred that emanated through his pores. "I'm the one you should've killed first! Now, my face is gonna be the last thing you see. I promise you that!"

"Like I said, nigga, you're soft just like your punk ass brother." Nard continued to disrespect. But we would get the last laugh.

I bent down and retrieved my gun off of the floor. Rising up, and turning to Shabazz, I said, "Go in the back and get his bitch."

Ca$h

CHAPTER
47
Nard

When those niggaz dragged Kenisha into the living room by her hair, bound and gagged, and with tears running down my face, I felt the strength of Hercules enter my body.

"Ahhhh! Y'all are gonna die for that!" My voice shook the whole room. There wasn't a bitch nigga alive I would let harm my woman without me going ham.

My wrists and ankles might've been duct taped, but they couldn't put restraints on my heart. Fuck if I was gonna let them come up on my shit and do my girl dirty.

Y'all hoes gon' have to kill me first!

I head butted Rah in the mouth, drawing blood. When he staggered back, I lowered my shoulder and drove it into Eric's chest, knocking his frail ass back.

"Y'all pussies not built to fuck with a nigga like me!" I disrespected all of them.

Had my hands and feet been free, I would've took those chumps guns and wet every single one of them up for fuckin' with my baby.

Rah licked the blood off of his lip and then he punched me in the jaw, knocking me down. He stood over me glaring down like he had done something big.

I looked up at him and challenged his manhood. "Free my hands and feet and then me and you can go one on one, man to man."

It surprised me when he smiled, and then looked at Snoop and said, "Cut his bitch ass a loose. I'ma show him I'll whoop his ass. Then, I'ma kill him.

***

Rah

Nard must've thought I was hiding behind the strap in my hand. Like, without a gun my gangsta was suspect.

Oh yeah?

I could hardly wait for Snoop to cut the tape off of that bitch nigga'z hands and feet. We had already snatched up the weapons he had stashed around the house, and if he tried anything, my mans would light his ass up.

Eric tried to talk me out of shooting Nard an old school head up brawl. He wanted to kill the nigga and be out.

"Nah, he think he want this, so I'ma give it to him. I'ma send him to his grave with a freshly kicked ass." My confidence in my hands was like none other.

While Snoop unbounded Nard, I moved the furniture around to make room. After pushing a chair all the way against a wall, out of our way, I gave my ratchet to Eric.

"Hold this, fam, while I beat this nigga like the bitch that he is."

"I'm about to show you who's the bitch," he retorted.

Eric pointed both ratchets at him. "Nigga, shut up before I slump your ass!" He was itching to 187 Nard.

"Stand down, lil' bruh. I got this pseudo thug!" I said as I got into my fighting stance, hands up, chin down, feet spread and on my toes.

My peeps formed a circle around us and me and Nard went at it. I had grown up boxing, so he really didn't stand a chance. He charged at me swinging wildly, throwing wide haymakers that I deftly sidestepped and then I unleashed a flurry of precisely aimed counter punches that snapped his head back and wobbled his knees.

"You fight like a broad, yo," I taunted as I circled him.

Wham!

He landed a lucky punch high on my forehead. I shook that shit off with ease, and caught him with a vicious blow to the kidney. He winced and backed up a bit, bumping into Shabazz.

"Fuck off me!" Shabazz shoved him dead smack into a powerful overhead right that I threw with vengeance.

This nigga had killed my Ace.

I could hear CJ's voice in my mind. *Knock him the fuck out, Rah! Don't play with his ass!*

Nard was still woozy from the last punch that rocked him, so the next two connected with his chin without a defense.

He staggered back and fell on his ass. Half sitting, he tried to shake the cobwebs out of his head.

"Get up, nigga! Fight back!" I spat.

"Bitch, I'ma do that!" His mouth was much slicker than his hands.

I waited for him to climb back to his feet before I squared up with him again. When he put his guards up, I feigned a left jab to his midsection, causing him to drop his left arm to block it. That's when I blasted a straight right hand that snapped his head back, once again.

My mans was hooting and hollering.

"Drop that chump, Rah!" cheered Snoop.

"Put his ass to sleep!" said Eric.

I could see in Nard's eyes, he realized that my hands were superior to his. I was kicking his ass, man to man, like he asked for, in front of his woman. Had her mouth not been gagged, I'm sure she would've been screaming and bawling.

I danced on my toes as I peppered Nard's face with lightning quick combinations that had his shit rocking like a bobble head.

The nigga knew he had no win, not with the hands. So, he ducked low and rushed me like a linebacker. I stepped back and shot a powerful uppercut straight to his chin.

Whack!

The punch landed with such violent force, I felt its power all the way from my fist to my shoulder. And I knew Nard was out as soon as his face smacked the floor.

I stood looking down at him.

"This that real G shit!"

I was still hyped several minutes after knocking Nard out, and I was a little bit out of breath. I stood there awhile longer, until I caught my second wind and then I converted back into boss mode.

I told my mans to roll Nard up in the large rug that was underneath our feet and carry him out to his truck.

"Load some of these boxes in the truck, too. Just to play it off, in case a neighbor is watching. You already know where to take him. I'll be behind y'all." I headed for the door.

Eric grabbed my elbow. "Rah, what about Kenisha?"

The question wasn't unexpected. I had pondered her fate for hours. If there had been a way to let shorty live without jeopardizing us all, in spite of the foul shit she said and did, I probably would've let her walk away unharmed. But I couldn't chance it. Her loyalty to Nard had made her give up her own son. There was no doubt in my mind, she would run straight to the police if we let her go.

"E, do what has to be done but first wake that bitch ass nigga up and make him watch. And don't shoot her in the head, yo. I don't want her to die ugly."

"Say no more," he said.

As I stepped out of the house and before closing the door, I heard the loud, unmistakable sound of gunshots.

292

Boc! Boc! Boc!

"Kenisha!" The sound of Nard's broken voice crying out miserably was sweet music to my ears.

And though the kill was necessary, I didn't want shorty to go out like that.

I felt a little sadness come over me. This thug shit was hard on a brotha'z heart. But Kenisha had made her bed.

As I headed to my whip, I stopped momentarily and looked up at the sky.

"Fam, it's almost over," I said to my A1 from Day 1.

And I could feel CJ smiling down at me.

Ca$h

CHAPTER
48
Rah

A couple of hours later, we pulled up in The Bricks in a four-car caravan. It was early evening and the sun was still up strong The rest of our crew, over 50 members, strong lined the street awaiting our arrival. Hordes of regular hood dudes and chicks stood outside in the cold, aware that something was about to go down.

I pulled to the curb, in front of our main building in the Spis. A street soldier came up to the car and opened my door for me.

"Salute, youngin'." I climbed out and touched fists with him.

"Salute, OG Rah." He nodded respectfully.

I didn't consider myself to be an original gangsta, but apparently, he did. The work I put in since CJ's death was well known amongst the squad. I was street certified, and they respected that.

Eric, Snoop and Shabazz had climbed out of their vehicles. They met me at the front of my whip.

"Y'all ready to do this, yo?" I asked.

"I've been ready!" said Eric.

"Me too," added Snoop.

"I'm ready to rock." Shabazz rubbed his hands together, displaying his anxiousness.

"Let's do it, then." I led the way to the truck where Nard laid, bounded, on the back seat.

Together, we lifted him out and dropped his punk ass on the hard, cold ground. The crowd inched closer to see his identity.

A collective gasp could be heard when they realized who it was. Nard was well known in The Bricks, and there wasn't a soul around that hadn't heard about the deadly war we had waged against each other.

For months and months, the outcome was up in the air, as each side struck brutally hard. But today, the onlookers would witness the war come to an end, in a fashion that would go down in hood lore.

I instructed my mans to stand Nard up and cut the tape from his wrists. "Leave his feet tied so this bitch can't run."

"Run? Nigga, I'ma go out like a man, the same muthafuckin' way I lived!" Nard declared as they stood him up and freed his hands.

"We'll see." I turned my back to him and faced our soldiers. To them I said, "This nigga right here killed CJ. And he murked other mans of ours. Today we're going to serve street justice for our brothers, and send a message to any other muthafucka that think he wanna fuck with us!"

"Hell yeah!" shouted the youngin' who had opened my car door for me.

"Rah! Let me do that nigga!" Another one of our soldiers shouted from the back and then a chorus of voices joined in. Everybody wanted to put a bullet in Nard's head.

I pushed both palms to the ground, making the gesture for them to quiet down. Immediately, my soldiers went silent.

I glanced up the block just in case the rollers happened to be cruising by. On the way over, I had hit Cujo up and told him to secure the area. He promised to do so, but I was just taking extra precaution.

Far as my eyes could see, everything was gucci. I slowly turned back to Nard.

"It's the end, yo. You know that, don't you?" I held his stare.

"Do what you do!" He bit down on his bottom lip.

I didn't bother responding. Instead, I took my banger off of my waist and removed the clip. Eric held his Glock to Nard's head, daring him to move a muscle, as I emptied the clip of every bullet except one.

I slammed the clip back in place and click-clacked the single bullet into the chamber.

Handing the gun to Nard, I said, "One bullet. One shot. Put it in your mouth and squeeze the trigger. Show me you're a boss."

"Die like my brother did," said Eric. "Or you can make me twist your muthafuckin' cap!" He pressed his tool harder against the side of Nard's dome.

Nard looked at me curiously. I guess he couldn't believe I had given him a loaded gun.

"Kill yourself, nigga! If you don't, we're gonna pump a thousand holes in you," I threatened.

His face frowned up. "Nigga, didn't I tell you I'ma die like a man?" He lifted the gun and brought it up to his mouth.

My eyes remained trained on him. I wanted to see him squeeze the trigger and knock the sauce out of his own head.

The tip of the gun rested at the opening of his mouth. His eyes sparked pure hatred for all of us. The vein on the side of his head jumped like a live wire.

The cold wind howled around us but I was immune to its bite. I could almost *see* the words as they left my lips.

"Squeeze the trigger or get squeezed on!"

Nard took a deep breath. Now that the moment of truth had him by the throat, his gangsta seemed to be on pause.

"You could never be CJ's equal," I sneered.

"Nah, 'cause I'm better!"

In one quick motion, he lowered the gun from his mouth and pointed it at my face. As if things were moving in slow motion, I saw him squeezing the trigger.

Boom!

The shot echoed up and down the street.

Time froze.

The back of Nard's head flew out the front, and his whole forehead disintegrated, spraying on my coat in a splack of gooey red. His body lurched forward and he smacked the ground face first.

Eric's tool was smoking. He aimed it down at Nard's twitching body and fired twice more.

Boc! Boc!

Snoop and Shabazz joined in on the kill. Their gats popped off simultaneously. With each slug that ripped into Nard's body, it jumped and wiggled.

When their guns quieted, the spare one I snatched from the small of my back roared.

"This is for CJ!"

Boc! Boc! Boc! Boc!

I didn't let up on the trigger until my gun went *Click! Click! Click!*

Out of ammunition, I spat on Nard's bullet riddled body. "You wasn't no boss!" I drew my foot back and kicked his bloody head.

Eric did the same.

Youngin walked up, whipped out and pumped more hot lead into Nard's corpse. The others followed suit, one by one they came up and blasted the body.

When the last soldier tucked his banger back on his waist, I took one final glance down at Nard. A puddle of blood surrounded his body. He lay sprawled this way and that way, tattered with to pieces.

I casted my eyes to the sky and smiled up at my fam. "It's over, baby boy! Now, you can rest in peace. I love you, nigga!"

Tears ran down my face and into my mouth. But, this time they didn't taste salty. We had avenged our beloved brother. Nothing in this world tasted sweeter than that.

My Jihad was finally over.

Ca$h

CHAPTER
49
Rah
A week later

Now that we had wiped out Nard and his entire team, The Bricks would return to peace and order. The lasting message we had sent to all of those that might have entertained the thought of testing us was that we weren't to be fucked with. We killed brazenly, out in the open, and in broad daylight. And no heat from the po's ever came our way. Niggaz could either respect our power or get crushed by it.

However, murder wasn't the motive. Money and respect was what our clique was about. And as long as fools didn't bring drama our way, they wouldn't get murked in the streets like Nard.

I had made our objectives and our rules blatantly clear to the entire team before I stepped down from the throne and passed the crown back to Eric, its rightful heir. Lil' bruh was well equipped to handle any and everything that came with the position, and the crew would respect his leadership. And if any problem got too big for him to handle, I was only a phone call and a flight away.

I reiterated those words to him now as we stood in the living room of his condo.

"I have the same loyalty to you that I had for CJ," I vowed.

"You know I know, my G." He locked fists with me and pulled me into a long G-hug.

"The Bricks are yours now, make your brother proud," I said.

"I'm gonna make you proud, too." Eric spoke with confidence that belied his age. At 19 years old, his prowess in the game was remarkable.

"I'm already proud of you." Stepping out of the brotherly embrace, our fists remained gripped together.

Eric looked at me with true love and respect in his eyes. "To hear you say that means everything to me. If I can learn to be half of the gangsta and gentlemen you are, I'll be winning hands down. Real spit, Rah, I respect how you get down."

"And, I respect your get down, too. Now, let go of my hand, yo." I cracked a smile.

"You stupid, fam." Eric laughed and released my hand.

"All jokes aside." My voice turned serious. "I love you, lil' bruh. Keep your head up and your eyes open at all times, even when you sleep. And make sure you take good care of Lakeesha. You know that's my heart."

"No doubt, B. You know I learned from the best, CJ and you. As for La, she's my heart, too. As soon as she get that GED and enroll herself in college, I'ma wife her. Change her last name and all of that, nah mean?"

We both looked over at my sister, who was sitting not far away from us on the couch. She pretended to be engrossed in something on her phone, but the wide smile on her face betrayed her.

"Stop fronting, yo. I see you over there cheesing mad hard," Eric teased her.

She stuck her middle finger up in the air and stuck her tongue out at him. "I can smile if I want to." She grabbed the pillow behind her and flung it in our direction.

"See, how bold you get with your brother is around," said Eric.

We all shared a brief laugh before I decided it was time to bounce.

"Nah, I'm out." I walked over to my sister and pulled her up into a hug. "You got yourself a young King. Be a true queen to him." I whispered to the side of her face.

"I will. And thank you for not giving up on me." Tears pushed from the corner of her eyes.

"Never ever that." I dried her eyes with the pads of my thumbs.

I didn't want to prolong our goodbye, or else La was going to start bawling. Between the all of us, we had shed enough tears to overflow Newark Bay.

"Girl, give your brother a little of that sugah and stop all of that crying," I talked to her like she was still in diapers.

She knew I was just trying to lighten the mood before we hugged and said goodbye. Her smile brightened my face. She puckered up he lips and gave me a kiss on the cheek.

"We'll be coming down to Atlanta in a few weeks to get the kids. So, I'll see you soon," she said.

That was another thing I respected about Eric, he demanded that La get her children from Big Ma and raise them herself.

"A'ight, sis, I'll see you soon." I hugged her tightly, then I was out.

Ca$h

CHAPTER
50
Rah

My heart felt light, but I still had something important to wrap up before going back to the *A*.

I listened to Sparkle's last cd *A Long Way Home* as I drove to Montclair. Her soulful voice had the effect of a massage and deep meditation wrapped in one. I didn't think about the troubles we encountered once she attained fame, or her tragic ending. I thought about the beautiful moment we had shared and how I hadn't allowed myself to love since her death.

I missed having a queen to laugh with and to build with. Someone whom I could share my dreams and inner most feelings with. A woman who would trust me with her heart and secrets. I hadn't been whole since I lost Kayundra.

For what is a king without a queen? I asked myself.

"Only half of the mighty man he could be," I said aloud. "Go get your rib."

I hadn't talked to Malika in months. I didn't know if she had terminated her pregnancy or moved away. But I was determined to find her. Pride had cost me my first love. I would not let it cost me Malika.

If she could love me, in spite of all the killings she knew I had committed, regardless of the cause, I could love her back. It didn't matter that it all began with her planning to build a criminal case against me, that part of our lives was over.

The 25-minute drive to Malika's house gave me enough time to clear my thoughts of all things except us. I smiled when I saw her car parked in the yard.

At least she hasn't moved.

I felt a little nervous as I got out of my car and walked to her door, carrying 100 long stem roses. One for each year I would love her if she would take me back.

When I reached the front door, I rang the bell and waited.

A short while later, she opened the door.

"Raheem." My name sounded bland coming off of her tongue, like I had left a permanent bad taste in her mouth.

I could understand that, if it was the case. Our last encounter hadn't been anything for her to cherish. I just hoped she would allow me to fix things between us.

I swallowed the lump that unexpectedly formed in my throat.

"Malika," I said cautiously, "how have you been, Queen?" She was not Selena to me.

"I've been making it, or should I say we've been making it?" She rubbed her enormous belly.

By my calculations, she would've been 5 or 6 months into her pregnancy but she looked ready to pop at any moment.

"May I step inside? It's kinda cold out here," I feigned a shiver.

"Yes, of course." She stepped aside and closed the door behind us.

I handed her the roses.

"Oh, wow! Thank you." She raised them up to her nose.

"You like?"

"Yes. But why so many?"

"I'll explain in a few," I said.

"Okay, have a seat while I go put these away." Malika headed off.

I removed my coat and re-tucked my gun. I hung my coat on the coat rack by the door and then sat down and waited for her to return.

While I waited, I told myself that her keeping the baby was a sign that we could work things out, but I was anxious to hear her say so.

A few moments later, she came back into the room nibbling on a banana with mayonnaise on it.

"That's just nasty, yo." I frowned.

"Nope, it's delicious," she giggled, as she took the last bite of the fruit while walking over to where I sat.

"Whatever, man." I stood up shook my head. "Anyways, am I too late?" I took her hands in mine and stared up into her eyes.

"Too late for what?"

"For us to be together." I rubbed her arm affectionately.

"Well, that depends, Raheem." She pulled her hands back and sat down on the couch, turning her head away from me.

I moved in closer to her, placing a finger under her chin and turning her head so she could look into my eyes.

"Queen, you don't even have to say it. I know I reacted wrong, and I apologize for that. Will you forgive me?" My heart ached while I waited for her response.

"Are you truly sorry?" She lifted her pretty browns up.

"Truly, baby," I conveyed from my heart.

Slowly her eyes brightened and a smile spread across her face. "In that case, no, you're not too late."

I smiled with relief. "Man, I thought I had lost you."

"Baby, I was hurt, but I would've waited forever," she said.

"Forever?" I gave it a doubtful look.

"Yes, Raheem, forever *and a day*. But I knew I wouldn't have to. I knew you would come back because I know the man that you are. I told your babies, '*Daddy will be back*.'"

"Wait! Did you say babies, as in plural?" I lifted an eyebrow.

"Yes, I did." She did a little happy dance in her seat.

"As in twins?" I held up two fingers.

"Nope." Malika held up three.

"Wait! You're having triplets?" My mouth hit the floor.

"*We're* having triplets, don't forget you went half on these little suckaz."

I let out a breath filled with excitement. "Man, Queen, that's beautiful." I smiled proudly and shook my head in disbelief.

"Two more and we'll have a baseball team," she joked.

"Un uh. We only need one more. There's already a fourth one," I announced.

"And who is that?" She squinted her eyes at me.

I knew what she was thinking. "Nah, Queen, it's nothin' like that," I chuckled. "The fourth one is Little CJ. My man got a seed and we're gonna adopt him."

"Huh? CJ has a baby. By who?" She looked puzzled.

"Baby, you're not gonna believe this," I said, and I began telling her parts of the story.

I told her the baby's full name and all other pertinent information I was able to get from Kenisha.

"Raheem, is Kenisha still alive?"

"Nah." I confessed. "We had to do her too."

With a look of strategy, she said, "Then we need to wait a few months before I do an inquiry. We wouldn't want to draw suspicion on ourselves."

"Cool, but I absolutely gotta have him."

"And we will, baby. If we have to, we'll turn Hell and Earth over to adopt him." Her enthusiasm matched mine.

"That's how it's going down."

"Exactly," she reaffirmed.

With those things out of the way, I wrapped her in my arms and delivered the final surprise. "Queen, it's time to put

Dirty Jersey behind me. Start packing, we're going back to ATL. It's time for me to get back on my deen"

"Seriously?" Her mouth dropped open and her eyes widened. "Yes! Baby, when you're rocking that kufi, you're a sight to behold."

"Keep talking like that and we're going to have quadruplets." I looked at her with hunger in my eyes.

"I'm not scared." Her look mirrored mine.

"I tell you what…"

"What do you tell me, baby daddy?" she giddily cut me off.

"Meet me in the bedroom. That's where it's going down."

"You don't have to threaten me with a good time." Malika took off before I did.

As I followed behind her, I felt a sense of happiness and peace come over me.

I had been through hell, but Allah had delivered me from the burning fires. And although I had destroyed families, He had blessed me with one of my own.

After all I'd done, I didn't deserve her or them. Perhaps He understood I caused much mayhem, not because of greed, power or jealously, but because of love, love for my brother, CJ.

But whatever the reason my heart was able to thump with new purpose, I knew He was truly The Most Magnificent.

I smiled at my blessings, closed the bedroom door behind me and I began to undress.

"Baby, I'll be right back. I have to pee," said Malika. She walked off to the adjoining bathroom and I laid across the bed, anxiously awaiting her.

Ten minutes later, she still hadn't returned. I was about to call out and ask if she was okay when she finally stepped into the room.

"I'm sorry, I feel very sick all of a sudden. Can you just hold me for a while?" she asked.

"Of course, Queen." She laid down beside me and I held her until we both drifted off to sleep.

Sometime later, a thunderous boom startled me awake. The bedroom door came flying open, crashing against the wall and six men rushed inside, pointing guns at me.

Instinctively, I sprung up off of the bed looking for my banger, but it wasn't on the floor beside my clothes where I had left it when I undressed.

"DEA! Don't you dare fuckin' move!" barked a tall white man.

Out the corner of my eye, I saw Malika on the other side of the bed holding my heat. They didn't light her as up so I knew what time it was.

The look on her face, and the calmness in her eyes, told me that she was still one of them.

"You lowdown, dirty bitch!" I spat. She had dropped a dime on me when she went to the bathroom.

Her fellow agents rushed over and slung me to the floor. As the cuffed my hands behind my back, I turned my head and looked up at the most cold-hearted woman I'd ever known.

"This is how you do the father of your children?" I gritted.

"Raheem, you're not the father of my child. I wouldn't bring another *you* in this world! You're a murderer and a drug dealer. I despise you, and everything you stand for. Your entire crew is being arrested as we speak. Eric, Snoop and dozens of others. Cujo, Agent Solaski and all of the dirty cops on your payroll. All of you are going down! With your ilk off of the streets, Newark will be a safer place for everyone."

I couldn't believe what was coming out of her mouth. I thought she had truly loved me. Her betrayal cut deeper than all other wounds I had suffered in my life. And her cold-heartedness was exclamated by what she said next.

"You're under arrest for murder and operating a continuing criminal enterprise. You have the right to remain silent. Anything you say can, and will, be used against you in a court of law. You have the right to an attorney ..."

As she went on reading me my Miranda Rights, a tear slid down my cheek for the heartache my arrest would cause Big Ma. Everything else I could handle with no regrets.

My brother had given his life for me. Now, I had done the same for him.

The End

Stay Connected with Us!

Text **LOCKDOWN** to 22828 to stay up-to-date with new releases, sneak peaks, contests and more...

Thank you!

Coming Soon from Lock Down Publications/Ca$h Presents

BOW DOWN TO MY GANGSTA

By **Ca$h & Jamaica**

TORN BETWEEN TWO

By **Coffee**

BLOOD OF A BOSS **IV**

By **Askari**

BRIDE OF A HUSTLA **III**

THE FETTI GIRLS

By **Destiny Skai**

WHEN A GOOD GIRL GOES BAD **II**

By **Adrienne**

LOVE & CHASIN' PAPER **II**

By **Qay Crockett**

THE HEART OF A GANGSTA **II**

By **Jerry Jackson**

TO DIE IN VAIN **II**

By **ASAD**

LOYAL TO THE GAME

By **TJ & Jelissa**

A DOPEBOY'S PRAYER **II**

By **Eddie "Wolf" Lee**

A HUSTLER'S DECEIT **II**

THE BOSS MAN'S DAUGHTERS **III**

BAE BELONGS TO ME **II**

By **Aryanna**

A KINGPIN'S AMBITON

By **Ambitious**

<u>Available Now</u>

(CLICK TO PURCHASE)

RESTRAINING ORDER **I & II**

By **CA$H & Coffee**

LOVE KNOWS NO BOUNDARIES **I II & III**

By **Coffee**

LAY IT DOWN **I & II**

LAST OF A DYING BREED

By **Jamaica**

PUSH IT TO THE LIMIT

By **Bre' Hayes**

BLOOD OF A BOSS **I II & III**

By **Askari**

THE STREETS BLEED MURDER **I, II & III**

THE HEART OF A GANGSTA

By **Jerry Jackson**

CUM FOR ME

CUM FOR ME 2

CUM FOR ME 3

An **LDP Erotica Collaboration**

BRIDE OF A HUSTLA **I & II**

By **Destiny Skai**

WHEN A GOOD GIRL GOES BAD

By **Adrienne**

A GANGSTER'S REVENGE **I II III & IV**

THE BOSS MAN'S DAUGHTERS

THE BOSS MAN'S DAUGHTERS II

A SAVAGE LOVE **I & II**

BAE BELONGS TO ME

By **Aryanna**

A DOPEBOY'S PRAYER

By **Eddie "Wolf" Lee**

WHAT ABOUT US **I & II**

NEVER LOVE AGAIN

THUG ADDICTION

Ca$h

By **Kim Kaye**
THE KING CARTEL **I, II & III**
By **Frank Gresham**
THESE NIGGAS AIN'T LOYAL **I, II & III**
By **Nikki Tee**
GANGSTA SHYT **I II &III**
By **CATO**
THE ULTIMATE BETRAYAL
By **Phoenix**
DON'T FU#K WITH MY HEART **I & II**
By **Linnea**
BOSS'N UP **I & II**
By **Royal Nicole**
I LOVE YOU TO DEATH
By Destiny J
I RIDE FOR MY HITTA
I STILL RIDE FOR MY HITTA
By **Misty Holt**
LOVE & CHASIN' PAPER
By **Qay Crockett**
TO DIE IN VAIN
By **ASAD**

316

BOOKS BY LDP'S CEO, CA$H
(CLICK TO PURCHASE)

TRUST IN NO MAN

TRUST IN NO MAN 2

TRUST IN NO MAN 3

BONDED BY BLOOD

SHORTY GOT A THUG

THUGS CRY

THUGS CRY 2

TRUST NO BITCH

TRUST NO BITCH 2

TRUST NO BITCH 3

TIL MY CASKET DROPS

RESTRAINING ORDER

RESTRAINING ORDER 2

IN LOVE WITH A CONVICT

Coming Soon

BONDED BY BLOOD 2

BOW DOWN TO MY GANGSTA

Ca$h

Made in the USA
Middletown, DE
12 February 2023

24725872R00179